Poisoned pen

We don't want lesbians here. Homosexuals are against God's law and are filthy.

I'm sure it will come as a surprise to you to know that your wife is having an affair with Dr Barnes.

The letters contained all the malice of a venomous village bigot. But did they, as they multiplied, contain grains of truth?

The tiny community of Shelbourne was torn apart – and finally devastated – when suspicion and mistrust escalated into murder.

Anthea Cohen, creator of the Nurse Carmichael series of 'Angel' crime novels, offers a riveting new departure for her many fans and for those new readers who relish clever plotting and vivid characterisation.

Previous books by Anthea Cohen,
featuring Agnes Carmichael

Angel without mercy (1982)
Angel of vengeance (1982)
Angel of death (1983)
Fallen angel (1984)
Guardian angel (1985)
Hell's angel (1986)
Ministering angel (1987)
Destroying angel (1988)
Angel dust (1989)
Recording angel (1991)
Angel in action (1992)
Angel in love (1993)
Angel in autumn (1995)

POISONED PEN

Anthea Cohen

Constable · London

First published in Great Britain 1996
by Constable & Company Ltd
3 The Lanchesters, 162 Fulham Palace Road
London W6 9ER
Copyright © 1996 by Anthea Cohen
The right of Anthea Cohen to be
identified as the author of this work
has been asserted by her in accordance
with the Copyright, Designs and Patents Act 1988
ISBN 0 09 475910 3
Set in Palatino 10 pt by
Pure Tech India Ltd, Pondicherry
Printed and bound in Great Britain by
Hartnolls Ltd., Bodmin, Cornwall

A CIP catalogue record of this book
is available from the British Library

1

The grass of the Green glistened in the early morning sunlight.

Dorothy stood at the open door of Hawthorne Cottage; the milk bottle that she held in her hand felt wet and cold. As she had picked it up she had noticed the small dark patch it had left on the doorstep of the porch. There were still 'dew slips', as she always called them, on the grass, probably made by the postman – it was still early enough for that. She looked up: the sky was a soft azure, only one or two cotton wool clouds over the houses on the other side of the Green.

Their small front garden was colourful with spring flowers; the smell of the white hyacinths near the door was pleasant. She walked down the short gravel path and closed and latched the gate – Dorothy liked order and tidiness and the milkman often left the gate open. She went back slowly savouring the morning, the jonquils and daffodils nodding to her as she passed.

Dorothy was always the first up, Michaela mostly slept till eight. As Dorothy closed the front door she heard movement upstairs; she paused to sweep up the mail with her free hand – two circulars, a couple of letters and a postcard. She again heard movement upstairs, Michaela was up. In the kitchen the table was already laid for breakfast – they always did that the night before. Boiled eggs this morning. Dorothy went towards the stove, turning on the coffeemaker on her way. She was about to switch on the ring on which the egg saucepan stood when a knock on the front door stopped her.

'I brought this, it's for you not us.'

The girl standing outside the front door was tall, almost angular. She wore faded jeans, a lumpy shapeless T-shirt, with her hair tortured into the scrunched-up crimped style that Dorothy loathed – hideous, she called it. She took the letter from the girl and glanced at it. The envelope was correctly addressed to The

Occupier, Hawthorne Cottage, Shelbourne, Isle of Wight. Dorothy turned it over; the other side was spattered with dirt.

'I dropped it – sorry.' The girl pushed her hair back. Her eyes, hard and brown, surveyed Dorothy with her neatly arranged grey hair, blouse and skirt, stockinged legs and well-cleaned flatties. 'The postman's a real pain, isn't he?' Her lips twisted in a slightly contemptuous smile which Dorothy, sensitive as always, felt was engendered by her own neat appearance.

'Yes, he does misdeliver sometimes,' she said, a little lamely.

'Sometimes!' The girl let out a short laugh, then turned. 'Sorry I dropped it, I'm a clumsy cow.' She closed the gate behind her and strode away – young, sure, arrogant. Dorothy watched her go, then turned away and sighed.

Dorothy took the letter through to the kitchen and put it on top of the other mail. She went to the foot of the stairs and called, 'Shall I put the eggs on, Michaela?' Michaela's voice, muffled as if she was struggling into a woollen jumper or had something over her head, answered her: 'Give me five minutes and then put them on.'

Dorothy went back into the kitchen and sat down by the table. She opened the two circulars – one promised a car as a prize, the other ten thousand pounds. She put them on one side and picked up the postcard, which was addressed to her. It was from Jamaica and was from Eunice. Dorothy was surprised. Eunice had been one of her staff, a colourless, nervous little woman. Jamaica! Somehow Dorothy could not visualise her erstwhile colleague going to Jamaica – Italy, France, the Costa del Sol, but not as far afield as Jamaica. The two letters were for Michaela – she got more mail than Dorothy, wrote a lot more letters, was a more enthusiastic communicator.

Dorothy and Michaela had been friends since their college days. They had always got on well. Michaela had been headmistress of a comprehensive school, Dorothy deputy head of a primary school; Michaela in Leeds, Dorothy in the Midlands. They had spent holidays together and had decided that as their retirement was at almost the same time and they were both unmarried, they would buy and share a house, divide the expenses and not be alone.

Neither had a family that would have welcomed them with open arms. Michaela professed to hate all her family – 'Toffee-nosed, over-educated gits', she called them – particularly as none of them took much trouble to keep in touch; a Christmas card was about it. Dorothy was a trace less vehement, but felt much the same about her own family.

The sharing of the house had proved most successful. It was now six months since they had moved in. The cottage had three bedrooms and, a luxury, two bathrooms, a reasonably large sitting-room, a small dining-room and a tiny morning room. (The last was given over to Michaela, who used it as a little office when she coped with the expenses of the house and her large correspondence.) These rooms and a fairly commodious kitchen and downstairs cloakroom comprised a house rather than a cottage, but both Dorothy and Michaela liked the name and so Hawthorne Cottage it remained.

Dorothy split open the white dirt-bespattered envelope and took out the contents, a white sheet of paper, without address or signature, only a short typed message right in the middle, neat and spelled out in capital letters.

Dorothy froze as she read the message – so brief, so unbelievable, so cruel.

Michaela appeared in the kitchen doorway. 'You always turn the stove up too high. It burns the bottom of the saucepan . . .' She paused. 'Oh, you haven't put them on – what's the matter?' She took the letter Dorothy handed over and read it:

WE DON'T WANT LESBIANS HERE. HOMOSEXUALS
ARE AGAINST GOD'S LAW AND ARE FILTHY

Michaela went white. 'What a load of vile crap! Whoever could have written it?'

She went to tear the letter across but Dorothy stopped her: 'No, don't do that.' She took the sheet of paper back, folded it and returned it to its envelope.

Michaela went over to the stove and switched it on. 'Ignore it,' she said, but Dorothy slipped the envelope and its contents into her skirt pocket.

'I'll get rid of it,' she said quietly.

St Barnabus was a small, rather attractive church which boasted a Norman tower. It was situated almost opposite Hawthorne Cottage, across the small triangular village green. The old vicarage, demolished several years ago, had been replaced by a modern house with a paved driveway in which usually stood the vicar's rather elderly Rover.

The Rev. Hugh Ainsworth was fortyish, thickening at the waist – not, it must be said, due to beer drinking as he seldom if ever went to the local pub and indulged in only a modest half-pint of lager with his supper, a habit of which his wife Philippa did not approve. She disliked the smell of beer and thought it was 'common'. She herself was not averse to a gin and tonic or a glass of sherry, even a vodka and tonic or two. These drinks she considered 'smart and sophisticated'. They had no children, by accident not design.

They kept up the appearance of a reasonably happy marriage and a good marital relationship. This was not easy, but they managed to satisfy the Bishop and the small congregation that all was well. But there were times, when they were alone, that their tempers frayed and marital boredom showed.

Philippa Ainsworth was a pretty woman several years younger than her husband. Being a vicar's wife had at first, by its very novelty, been enjoyable. As curate of a small Midlands town Hugh had seemed happy and relaxed, but as the years went by and he was moved to other towns – and was no longer a curate but a vicar – and at last to Shelbourne, he changed. No further step up the clerical ladder materialised, promotion to canon or archdeacon always eluded him. Now he appeared to have given up, showing little enthusiasm for his calling, and this, Philippa thought, was why his congregation had dwindled.

Philippa lived her life in a state of quiet desperation, carrying on in a similar manner to her husband, performing her duties without liking them – after all, for both of them Christianity was their meal ticket. What other job could Hugh ever be fit for if he left the Church?

This morning was no different from any other. Hugh disappeared behind *The Times* after eating his bacon and egg, toast and marmalade, drinking his coffee. Philippa, buried in her own thoughts, did not want him to talk to her. 'OK, to work.' Hugh folded up *The Times*, put it under his arm and went through to the small room which he called 'his study'. He called as he crossed the hall, 'Ring the locksmith, Pippa – what's his name?'

'Warren,' Philippa answered sharply, adding, 'I've told you his name twice, Hugh.' She began to clear the kitchen table.

'That back door lock is a nuisance – tell him to fit a new one if it needs it.'

'Yes, dear.'

Hugh, in the study, sat down at his desk. His Sunday sermons were becoming a nightmare – he could almost feel the aura of boredom welling up towards the pulpit. 'God damn them all,' he said softly and started to examine his mail. Two manila envelopes, bills probably, two circulars both promising a prize, a single piece of paper printed on one side only advertising a keep-fit class in Newport and a neatly typed white envelope – looked more interesting, only a second-class stamp though. He slit open the envelope, then wished he had done it more carefully, envelopes were expensive. He drew out the sheet of white paper: no address, no signature, just a message typed as neatly as on the envelope, in the middle of the page – in capitals. It read:

I'M SURE IT WILL COME AS A SURPRISE TO YOU TO KNOW THAT YOUR WIFE IS HAVING AN AFFAIR WITH DR BARNES.

It could not be true – his mind rejected the message. He read it again. No, no, no, she wouldn't. He looked at the envelope; the postmark, Portsmouth, told him nothing. He got up, intending to go and show it to his wife, then sat down again. Supposing, just supposing it was true! In the end he could not resist and took the letter into the kitchen. Philippa's reaction had surprised him. At first, she had appeared outraged, then, he suspected, she had found it flattering.

That same morning the health centre was busy. One of the receptionists was late and a small line of patients stood at the window. A tall, elderly man leaned on the ledge in front of the closed glass window and grumbled. 'It's me back,' he said without turning round. As he spoke his breath misted the glass in front of his face. 'I should not be kept standing here.' Two girls in the small office behind the glass window went to and fro taking files out of drawers. They were talking as they worked. One nodded in agreement, but what they were saying was inaudible in the waiting-room.

A few minutes passed and a harassed-looking young woman skidded up to the window and sat down. 'Sorry, my car wouldn't start,' she said as she slid open the window. She looked down at the big appointments book on the table in front of her. 'Your name, please?'

'Matthews,' the man grunted. 'Will Matthews. You're lucky to have a car. When I was a boy your age I walked.'

Someone moaned behind him, 'Oh, come on, Dad, we don't need your life history.'

'Which doctor?' the girl asked, pushing her hair back with a weary gesture.

'Dr Smart – and I want to see him, not that lady.'

'Please sit down.'

The queue moved up slowly; normal service was resumed.

'You were late yesterday.' The older woman, with a pile of patients' notes in her hands, looked accusingly at the girl at the window.

'Oh, all right. I've said I'm sorry.' The girl's smile disappeared, then was switched on again as she turned back to the window. 'What name? Just sit down, will you?' A buzzer went. 'Mrs Thornton to Dr Barnes, Room 2, please.'

The morning passed. More and more of the plastic chairs in the waiting-room became vacant, coughs died away and patients left clutching their prescriptions. There was no pharmacy in the village, so bus journeys or car trips would have to be taken or a friend or relative be asked to take the paper for them.

Mrs Thornton lingered a minute or two in the waiting-room. It was cancer. Dr Barnes hadn't said that, but . . .

'Mrs Thornton, another appointment?'

She turned and looked at the girl behind the window, then pulled herself together. 'No – no, thank you.' She went out of the front door into the street. She was shaking. She passed the public house. Bill Stone had planted daffodils in two large white plastic pots, each side of the front door. They bent a little in the light breeze and the sign above the door squeaked as it swayed. Mabel Thornton looked up at it. George and the Dragon. They often went there of an evening – she and Ted, her husband, met friends there. She put a hand on her breast – felt a surge of panic and walked faster along the High Street, past the coffee shop. Then she turned into the general stores and post office. Her best friend Edith ran the shop. Mabel waited by the sweet counter facing the tinned vegetables and tinned meats – she thought she would buy some soup, then changed her mind.

Edith was cashing a woman's pension in the post office part of the little store. Mabel decided she would buy the soup. Ted liked tomato soup, but her hand was shaking so much she couldn't open her purse. She couldn't bear it, she must talk about it. She wished the pensioner would go. She went to the door and stood looking down the short High Street – all so familiar, yet now so very different. She loved the place, wanted no other; even on holiday she and Ted were always pleased to be home again.

Shelbourne was a pretty village. The High Street ended with a small triangular green, in the middle of which flourished a huge oak tree – hundreds of years old, so people said. Mabel turned away from the door; the pensioner made a small purchase then left. Mabel watched her waddle past the next door and a dog barked as she passed. Two cars went by and another drove out of the small garage and petrol station further down. The garage man came out and watched.

She felt suddenly sick and turned back into the shop. 'What's the matter, ducks? You look awful.' Edith was a fat motherly woman, always cheerful and full of laughter. She often spent an evening with them at the pub. Ted liked her.

Mabel blurted out her news and began to cry. 'I'm only sixty, and I think it's cancer, Edith.'

Edith put her arm around her shoulders. 'Oh, ducks, I'm so sorry, but maybe it's nothing – I had a lump there.'

'Did you really, Edith?' Her eyes lit up with hope. 'When did you have it?'

'When I was having Tom – it was the milk.'

Mabel's tears started again. 'That's not the same. That Mary Elsby – you remember, worked as a cleaner for the Dawsons – she died of it. It was cancer. Went all over her.'

Edith was about to reply, try to give more reassurance, but her friend left the shop. 'Mabel!' Edith called in vain after her.

Mabel Thornton, like the woman she had watched, crossed the street by the garage. They had sold their car three weeks ago – Ted's eyes were not so good any more and she had never driven. She thought of Mary Elsby and the many times she had had to go to the hospital to have radiotherapy. How would she and Ted get there? She walked by Dormer Cottage, Dunroamin, Fuchsia Cottage – the big house with the bed and breakfast sign in the window – the Danbys' cottage where the garden was full of plastic gnomes. She reached her own house, Blackthorne – Ted had just got a new sign for the gate. Opposite, a red car drew out of Hawthorne Cottage. Dorothy waved, but Michaela did not look her way. They were nice ladies. She drew a deep breath, took a screwed-up tissue from her cardigan pocket and wiped her eyes. Then she went to tell Ted.

The village street was quiet – it was lunchtime. Edith shut the store from 1–2.30 p.m, her daily routine. The freshly painted red pillar box outside the shop gleamed in the sunlight. A white sports car passed, its exhaust roaring. At the police station, merely a house in the middle of the High Street, the door opened and a uniformed constable peered down the road after the speeding car. 'Young bloody Dawson,' he said out loud. The notices on the board in the office behind him fluttered in the draught from the door. Young bloody Dawson, Nigel by Christian name, lived with his father, Brigadier Dawson, in the small manor house which abutted the back of the Green. Caversham Manor was pretty, its Island stone partially ivy-covered, and in summer was rather a tourist attraction, though the Brigadier did not open it to the public. Indeed, the invasion of what he would call hoi polloi would have horrified him. He drank rather a lot, spoiled his son and, in spite of many efforts of several widowed ladies, had remained single since the death of his wife some years ago.

Shelbourne was not a big village, but was growing bigger. A small estate was gradually mushrooming into being. The fields between the High Street and the sea were being eaten away by the planners and developers. Rumours of another grocer's shop coming to the village did not dismay Edith Jevons; she had heard many such rumours before – and the fact that her store housed the post office gave her an added sense of security.

A school bus transported the few village youngsters to a school in Shanklin.

A chapel had recently appeared at the bottom of the High Street. Constructed temporarily of half brick and half red plastic, it was regarded by some as an eyesore; but the minister, who wore an open-neck shirt, sandals and a bushy red beard, blended easily into the village and had already collected a sizeable congregation. The villagers, at first startled by his breezy, easy visits, had got used to him. While Hugh Ainsworth fulfilled their expectations in manner and dress, quite a few found fault with his

12

cold and almost uncaring approach. His sermons, too, they found over-long and boring. A good few found it easier to take their problems to the new minister and, having got to know him, attended his chapel and so depleted the vicar's congregation even more.

The new minister encouraged the use of his Christian name, and his surname of Beattie was hardly even used – indeed some of his new congregation didn't even know it. He was 'Pat' to everyone, young and old. His wife was at the moment in Italy, showing off their new baby to her Italian family. He was lodging with old Mrs Pettifer in the house next to the village store, but he told anyone he thought might want to know that he was looking for a house in the village. He needed somewhere which was not too expensive, with at least three bedrooms and enough garden for growing vegetables and to keep a few chickens.

He had tried to fraternise with Hugh Ainsworth, but with little success. Although they had had a couple of brief encounters, Pat felt that Hugh retired firmly behind his clerical collar – understandable, Pat thought, but rather a pity.

So the inhabitants of Shelbourne lunched; some, watching their weight, had salads and fruit, others made their children fish fingers, chips and peas. Some retired people made more substantial lunches – the main meal of the day, so that they could watch television uninterrupted in the evening.

A few, a very few, had received something in the post that shocked them, startled them or even terrified one or two. They would not bother with lunch at all.

The postman – second post this time – had not too many letters. Second post was always light. He whistled as he delivered, avoided dogs, cursed circulars and wondered what his wife had got for his lunch.

2

Nigel Fisk was the headmaster of the school in Shanklin to which the young ones of Shelbourne were sent. He was a shy, reserved man and lived with his mother in the village in a two-storeyed house towards the bottom of the High Street. To say his mother was devoted to him was an understatement: nothing Nigel did could be wrong.

Nigel's father had been a bricklayer – or, rather, to be absolutely correct, a bricklayer's labourer; a rough, lively man and a heavy drinker. When his wife had picked a name for their one and only child he had been outraged. 'Nigel!' he screamed. 'That's a name for the nobs, or nancy boys, fairies. You must be crazy, Jane, to burden a kid with a name like that,' but Jane Fisk had persisted and Nigel it was. Even as she had first held her small, rather underweight baby in her arms she had known he would do great things. And so it had proved – top of his class at school, then college, followed by teaching in a small Welsh town. Now headmaster. Her pride in her son was so great that she felt he too must feel the same pride in his achievements as she did. Of his fears and misgivings about himself she was completely unaware. She was complacent about his happiness and well-being.

She cooked for him, cleaned for him, kept house with meticulous care and served him what she considered to be the right health-maintaining foods, whilst watching his weight. Nigel was forty now and thanks to her, she felt, had kept the figure of a twenty-year-old. Although she tried to encourage him to do so, he obstinately refused to take part in any competitive sports; long solitary walks were his only excursions, and with this she had to be content. She would never press him to do anything he did not want to do.

Jane, at seventy, still remembered her husband's brutal love-making – and even now recalled with horror, during one of these rough couplings, seeing Nigel standing watching at the bedroom door, wide-eyed, screaming, 'Don't hurt Mummy.' He had been seven at the time; she had never ceased wondering if he remembered and prayed he did not. Will, her husband, had been killed soon after that – he had fallen from a scaffold. She had not grieved for him, though she had worn black and cried at his funeral. To be alone at last with her beloved son was all that she wanted.

She often wondered if Nigel would marry before she died. He was quite a handsome man, in her opinion, nearly six foot with dark hair, and his clean-shaven face was pleasant; he was finicky about his clothes. If he did marry, what would she do then? Sell the house, perhaps, or let her son have it for his wife and family. She wondered if he were a virgin. The thought of him having sex with some stupid girl, ignorant of his true worth, was abhorrent to her. But it must happen soon, surely.

Meanwhile he went off to school in the early morning and did not return until six or even six thirty in the evening. It was a long day for him, and for her awaiting his return. The sound of his car drawing up outside their garage and the crackle of the gravel under his tyres always made her heart lift. Sometimes he looked tired and dispirited, at other times cheerful – his moods varied and she varied with them, the bonding between them was so great.

Occasionally she asked two or three friends to coffee or she would go to their houses, always hoping that a daughter or a cousin or a younger friend suitable for Nigel would appear. A female companion would be good for him – a nice girl, not a bimbo, that was what people called pretty girls these days. Someone about thirty, perhaps, or even a wee bit younger – pretty but not too pretty, domesticated, a good cook. Someone who would stay at home and look after her son as she had always done, not a career girl or one that wanted to go on working. Anyway, Jane wanted grandchildren – a boy and a girl, she hoped – who would come and see her and, if she lived to be old, do her shopping for her, and, as she grew older still, look after her. Of course, she did realise that they might move away. Nigel might get another post, but in her dreaming of the future they all stayed together.

It was at one of these coffee and biscuit visits that Jane Fisk's life changed: from being a caring, loving, if slightly domineering mother, she became a nervous, anxious defender.

It was at Mrs Delano's house – a foreign lady who had lived in Shelbourne for forty years but who still retained a trace of her native Spanish accent. She was eighty and, in spite of some deafness, a sprightly active woman.

The chat had been harmless enough between the four of them, Philippa Ainsworth, Mrs Fisk herself, their hostess and a little fat lady, Mary Harris, also a little deaf.

They had discussed whether the rumour of a new bigger store coming to the village to challenge Edith was true. The feeling was that small local shops should be encouraged, but they agreed that they charged too much.

'40p for a tin of chicken soup, dear, when I can get it from Tesco's for 32p.'

'29p,' Mrs Harris broke in.

Jane Fisk was a little bored. Nigel liked tinned chicken soup and if it had cost one pound a tin she would have still bought it for him.

15

'I'll make some more coffee.' Carmen Delano got up and went out to the kitchen.

Philippa went with her: 'I'll come and help.'

The two remaining in the sitting-room went on chatting for a minute or two then lapsed into silence. They could hear some of the conversation coming from the kitchen.

Mrs Delano's voice was louder, probably due to her deafness. 'Well, I did ask her, but she was going to the doctor, Dr Barnes.'

Philippa could just be heard replying, 'Dear Dr Barnes, he's so kind.'

'It was an early appointment, but maybe she had to wait.' Mrs Delano's louder voice continued, 'I asked Dorothy and Michaela, but Dorothy had arranged to go to Tesco's, so of course Michaela had to go with her.' She laughed, but her laugh was not pleasant. 'Women like that – augh! They make me shudder – I mean, what do they do?'

Philippa's reply could not be heard, but Carmen Delano went on: 'Well, living together like that – they are lesbians aren't they? Everyone says so.'

Another 'Mmm' from Philippa. Jane Fisk looked at Mary Harris; she was nibbling a chocolate biscuit and appeared to have heard nothing.

The kettle snapped off, something was said, the sound of pouring water, and then Carmen's loud voice again. 'Oh, surely not, Philippa. I mean, he's a headmaster – all those little boys.'

There was a distinct 'Shh' from Philippa.

'Well, I suppose he is a bit, you know, mother's boy, isn't he?' Mrs Delano giggled. 'Take these biscuits, Philippa.'

Jane Fisk had got to her feet. Her one thought was to get out, to get away from these terrible wicked lying women.

'More coffee?' Mrs Delano put the tray on to the table. Philippa put the plate of biscuits down.

'I must go,' Jane said. Mary Harris half rose, too.

'Oh, don't go. I've made more coffee, it's lovely and hot.'

Jane tried to regain control, not to let them know she had heard. She sat down on a chair nearer the door. She tried to smile, but her face felt stiff. 'Very well, just half a cup then,' she said.

Her hostess smiled again. 'Oh good,' she said. Jane let her put the cup of coffee on the table beside her. She must, she knew, try and stop her hand from shaking. It took all her self-control to pick up the cup and slowly drink the hot coffee. Then she left, even managing to thank her hostess for the refreshment.

16

On the short walk home Jane Fisk had tried to still the terrible feelings in her own body – her legs felt leaden, she could hardly draw breath, yet she was not breathless. She felt a terrible weight pressing on her. She was suffocating. Had Mary Harris heard the conversation in the kitchen? She had not appeared to – thank God for her deafness. But that terrible wicked woman, Philippa Ainsworth. How dare she – how dare she put such a scandalous lie in anyone else's mind, how dare she? And to someone like Carmen Delano, who would repeat anything she heard, who was known to be the greatest gossip in the village. And Philippa, a vicar's wife, how could she even insinuate such a thing about her beloved Nigel?

Then as Jane neared home a new thought entered her head. Did the relationship between herself and her son give rise to such despicable ideas? Could the way Nigel behaved cause people to wonder? It was normal enough to her, but to vile horrible minds . . . He had never dated a girl since he was seventeen – awful little strumpet he had picked then! Pretty but pert, common – showing herself off with her short skimpy skirts and low necks, make-up plastered on. Well, she had soon put a stop to that! He had seemed a little bit upset at the time, but he had soon got over it; had understood that his mother knew best.

Jane was nearly home now and was beginning to feel a little less shaken, a little better, but she couldn't stop her mind chasing on. Should she have encouraged him to get a place of his own? Get out more? Encouraged him to bring people, even girls, home? She arrived at her own gate. The feeling of horror, of doubt, started again. She unlocked her door, trying to marshal her thoughts into order, to reassure herself that those beastly women were stupid fools unable to assess real love when they saw it. Of course she and Nigel were perfectly all right as they were. What was the point of him moving away – he liked living with her and she liked having him. So, of course, there was no point at all in him moving. It was that woman's mind. Well, she'd show her! She would write to her to sue her for slander – or was it libel? Anything to make her eat her words, and, she hoped, choke on them. But, again, doubt crept in about improving Nigel's image.

After a pre-lunch drink – something in which she rarely indulged – she sat down at her son's typewriter in his study. She put some headed notepaper into the machine and typed: 'Mrs Philippa Ainsworth' – then she sat thinking. What could she say?

17

Nothing the vicar's wife had said had been a definite accusation – indeed, it had only been Mrs Delano's remarks that had been audible. She suddenly snatched the paper from the typewriter, and rolled in a sheet of Nigel's plain A4 paper. She had a better idea! Philippa Ainsworth was always mentioning Dr Barnes – any excuse. She knew they had even gone to a concert in Newport together. Admittedly the vicar had been in bed with flu at the time and could not go with them – but it would do.

She pressed down the capital letter key and typed away, and then addressed a long white self-sealing envelope. Then she thought of Dorothy and Michaela. What had Mrs Delano said? Oh yes, 'Michaela had to go to Tesco's because Dorothy was going.' They were lesbians, she had said. Another sheet of paper went into the machine. Jane Fisk began to feel good. The two neat white envelopes lay beside Nigel's rather old-fashioned typewriter. Only just the two! There were several people in the village she knew were not what they made out to be. Nigel had told her about the little boy, Robert Benson. His parents drank and abused him; sometimes, he had no food and came to school hungry – not because money was short, but because they were drunk or hung-over or out at the pub. Another neat envelope joined the other two on the table.

Jane had had two sherries; she knew she must eat some lunch. She set out for Portsmouth to post the letters. Second-class stamps – she slid them under the glass protecting the post office counter. 'Local,' she said. This meant she could rely on them arriving at their destinations the following day. The girl behind the glass put out a hand with long red-painted nails and drew the letters towards her – she didn't even look up at Jane Fisk.

Smoked salmon, a great treat. Jane went into the supermarket and bought a packet of real Scottish smoked salmon for Nigel's meal that evening. He adored it and for some silly reason – at least Jane thought the reason silly – she imagined it would make up a little for Philippa Ainsworth's ridiculous accusation of something so scandalous about her son. Nothing was too good for Nigel and nothing was bad enough for anyone who spoke or acted against him.

Tomorrow the letters would arrive. That would give the couple at the vicarage something to think about! Would they, or the couple at Hawthorne Cottage, consider going to the police? She felt a little shiver of fear – but she doubted they would, so even that feeling was not altogether unpleasant. Lesbians or not, one wouldn't want even the possibility discussed. The vicar was already not very popular – added to which, he was a golfing friend of Dr Barnes.

Jane detested Dr Barnes. He had once told her – well, almost told her – that she was neurotic about her son. She had asked to see him privately about Nigel, who had been attending him for an irritating skin complaint. He had been very terse – said he was not in the habit of discussing his patients' ailments with other people. 'Other people!' she had exclaimed and had pointed out to him heatedly that she was Nigel's mother. Dr Barnes had replied, 'Mrs Fisk, your son is thirty-seven years old' and had dismissed her. She had never forgiven him.

As she thought about it when preparing Nigel's meal that evening, arranging the smoked salmon and the Waldorf salad, she had wondered if she should send Dr Barnes a similar letter, too, about Philippa – but she decided against it, for the moment at any rate. Perhaps later, though. The hint she had given the vicar would implicate the doctor anyway. As she set the table she felt excited, stimulated, years younger, like a tigress protecting her young.

Nigel hesitated outside the village pub. He went there so rarely; now he had come, it was in a way to ask a favour – he wanted to buy a bottle of Liebfraumilch – and the proprietor might well say, 'This isn't an off-licence.' Nigel hoped that he would oblige him. It was his mother's favourite white wine, not his – he liked something drier, but he wanted to get something she would enjoy. It was the meal his mother had got ready for him when he reached home – smoked salmon, he did like it – and the lunch at school today had been particularly stodgy. He had insisted that such a meal deserved wine, and rather against her will Nigel had come out to get it.

He pushed open the bar door and went up to the bar. There were not many people in. He noticed the Bensons at the other end with another man he didn't know. He wondered briefly if their son Robert had had any supper left for him or whether the poor kid was having to rustle up something for himself. He acknowledged Robert's father's wave, but stayed where he was at the door end of the bar and as far away from them as he could get.

The barman and owner of the pub greeted him. 'Evening, sir. What can I get you?'

Nigel stalled for a moment. 'A – a white wine, please, dry.'

Did the man give him a quizzical look, or was it just his imagination? He wished he had ordered differently, a half of lager or a half of bitter, but he hated beer, both its taste and its smell. Nigel sipped his wine and waited until the man moved up near him again. 'Could you possibly let me have a bottle of Liebfraumilch, if you have it?'

The man nodded. 'Sure. Pub price, though.'

'Of course.' Nigel paid the man. 'Have one yourself.'

The man thanked him perfunctorily and handed him his change. Nigel wanted to get out.

Two more people came in, Mrs Jevons who ran the village post office and her husband. They greeted him and turned to the Bensons and had a word with them. They ordered their drinks and, when they had been served, sat down at a table.

The bar was small, amber-lighted and warm. The wood of the bar and the struts which ran up to the roof were well polished and gleamed as old wood does – no one was smoking. The mirror at the back of the bar reflected the bottles of spirits and the shining optics. The well-polished brass gleamed on the walls. A real country pub, Nigel thought, and wished he liked spending more time in such a place. He was just about to finish his wine when the door burst open and two young men came in. They both looked slightly high and were talking rather more loudly than necessary. One was young Dawson.

'G and T, please, mine host, doubles, lemon in one only and no ice in either.' He turned to his friend. 'Excuse me, must have a pee. Put them on the slat, Ben,' he said and made for the men's room.

His friend looked round the bar. Two more people, a man and a woman, had joined the Jevons. The young man looked towards the Bensons and then towards Nigel. His clothes looked expensive, a fawn polo-necked shirt under a well-cut jacket. He sauntered over to Nigel.

'Nice pub,' he said, picking up the gin and tonic without the lemon. Nigel nodded. 'You live here?' He shot the question. His eyes were blue, surrounded by long dark lashes. He lit a cigarette with what looked like a gold lighter. Nigel looked at the hands holding the flame and cigarette: they were almost unnaturally white, the fingernails beautifully manicured and polished. 'Ciggie?' he asked, offering the open packet. Nigel could smell the aftershave as he moved, thought the smooth, silky texture of the skin of his face looked as if he never needed to shave.

Nigel felt trapped in the man's aura. He began to feel his neck sweating and prayed that his face was not reddening. 'No, I don't smoke, thank you.' The blue eyes did not leave Nigel's face and a slight, almost imperceptible smile altered the rather thin straight lips.

Young Dawson joined them, picked up his glass and drank nearly all the contents in one gulp. He then signalled for two more. 'Join us?' he asked.

Nigel shook his head.

'Do you know something strange, old boy?' He clapped his companion on the shoulder. 'We both share the same ghastly name, don't we, mate? He's Nigel too. Don't know why they burdened us with such a name, do you?'

Nigel shook his head again, tried to smile and took the bottle from the counter. He was so acutely aware of the man beside him he could hardly speak.

'This one's Jeremy, for his sins.' Nigel Dawson sipped his second gin. His companion merely continued to watch Nigel, twisting the wineglass by its stem on the polished bar.

'Must go.' Nigel slipped off the bar stool.

'You're at the school, aren't you?' Dawson asked.

'Yes, headmaster, Shanklin Middle.'

'So-o.' The blue eyes smiled a little more widely, a little more openly.

At last Nigel escaped into the cool spring night air. 'See you again sometime?' It had not been young Dawson who had said that but Jeremy. What was his surname? he wondered. Where did he come from? He felt a cramp in his left hand and realised he was clutching the wine bottle so tightly it was hurting him. 'Oh God,' he said several times. 'Oh God, Oh God.' There had been danger there – danger in those blue dark-fringed eyes, danger in his reaction. 'One knows another,' he whispered. 'One always knows another.' If he succumbed he would be finished as headmaster of a school.

'Sorry, Ma,' he said as he entered the house. 'Had to have a glass of wine with Dawson. Couldn't very well refuse as I was asking a favour of Ben Newman.'

'That's all right, darling, no hurry.' She gave him a quick fond smile. 'Are you sure you need to open that bottle as you've had a glass of wine already?'

Nigel relaxed and the memory of those blue eyes receded and receded. 'It's for you, Ma, as well as me. Of course I'm going to open it.' He drew the cork. 'It should be a bit colder, but never mind.' He poured a glass for his mother and one for himself. They sat down and Nigel forked a piece of the salmon. 'Great stuff,' he said.

Jane, watching him, thought he looked a little pale. She noticed a few beads of sweat on his forehead; she hoped he wasn't getting a cold or something.

Nigel looked across at her plate. 'You've got much less salmon than I have.'

'I've got quite enough, dear,' she answered, then: 'Are you feeling all right, dear? You look a bit . . .' She hesitated, then settled for '. . . pale, tired.'

Nigel did not look up from his plate as he answered her. 'Fine, thanks, Ma.' As he said it, he felt that deep, deep inside he was crying like a child.

The bottle of wine emptied. Jane had only a glass and a half, but the wine helped Nigel. He began to unwind. The terrible strangling spring which those blue eyes and smooth satiny skin had wound up in him so tightly gave a little. He tried to concentrate on the Bensons – told his mother about seeing them in the pub and talked to her even more than usual about their shortcomings. 'Wonder if that lad got any supper prepared for him this evening?'

'Poor little chap.' Jane started clearing the table. 'Coffee?' she asked.

Nigel nodded, but talking about Robert had begun to tighten the spring, which seemed to screw up his entire body – his lungs, his head, his loins. The boy's fresh young face, almost a pretty girlish face, came back to him with the clarity of a photograph. The soft curly hair falling on the nape of the young vulnerable neck . . . Nigel often longed to put his arm round those young shoulders. Once Robert's form master had sent him to see the headmaster for some misdemeanour. He had stood the other side of Nigel's desk taking the ticking off, head down. 'Yes, sir,' and 'No, sir,' in a low rather husky voice. He had longed to take the boy in his arms and comfort him. He had dismissed him from his office, brusquely – brutally, he had felt.

If anyone ever knew, ever found out how he felt, what he was, how would Ma ever bear it? His life, he felt, would be over. His job would be lost, even teaching at a lower level. The control he had to maintain to remain where he was, who he was! One day would it break, would someone guess?

'What, Ma?' She had called out something from the kitchen.

'There's a good play on three. Shall we watch it?'

'Oh, yes, yes, sure,' he replied.

3

May and Jim Benson arrived home the following night at about eleven thirty. Jim Benson had promised that he wouldn't drink so that he could drive home. How many times had May listened to that promise! She felt she had a lot more sense than her husband. He, in spite of what he had said, had drunk plenty. She, because he had said he would drive them home, had had two whiskies and a beer so, in the end, Ben Newman had persuaded them to have a taxi. He would, wouldn't he, May thought. It was Ben's son's taxi and he charged extra after eleven at night. The Bensons' cottage was well out of the village, by at least two miles. Jim was no walker, so the taxi it had been. Now he was cursing about the cost of the fare. 'Bloody scandal. No meter, so how can you tell what he is charging is right?' He muttered and grumbled his way into the kitchen.

'Want more grub?' May asked. Drinking always made her hungry.

'Yes – well, I dunno, what can we have?'

'Bacon and egg and fried bread do you?'

'Yeah, yeah.' He slumped down in a kitchen chair and tapped his fingers on the table gloomily. 'Ten bloody quid for that fare – daylight robbery!'

'You could have walked,' said May, but he did not answer.

May cleared a space on the cluttered working surface. A letter fell to the floor and two more lay on the surface. She shuffled them together and threw them on the table in front of Jim. 'Mail – this morning's,' she said.

'Ugh,' Jim said. He spread the letters out in a fan. He hated letters, hated dealing with them. He was a laborious writer and left everything to his wife as a rule. Christmas cards, birthday cards, bills, relatives' letters, were all left for May to deal with. However, one letter in front of him stirred a faint interest: the white envelope bore a second-class stamp. One of the others was obviously his garage bill. 'Well, sod that,' he said, throwing it aside. 'Got any beer?'

May opened the fridge, looked in and banged it shut. 'No.'

'Well, why don't you keep some in?'

May replied, a trace irritated, 'I do, but you pour it all down your neck. There were four in there yesterday.'

He grumbled, 'Well, yesterday's not bloody tonight, is it?' He slid his thumb along the sealed flap of the white envelope, tearing it open untidily. He carefully opened the sheet of paper and read the message. 'Look at this. Look at this,' he shouted, jumping up from the chair. 'What sod sent this?' He was furious. 'I'll take it to the bloody police.'

He pushed the sheet of paper into May's hand. She wiped her other hand down her skirt to get off the bacon fat and read the letter. He watched her read, his face red with rage; the words typed on the neat white paper had quite sobered him. The typing was in capital letters in the centre of the page – no address, no indication as to who had sent it. May picked up the envelope and looked at the postmark. 'Isle of Wight,' she said. 'That tells us nothing at all.'

YOU SHOULD SHOW MUCH MORE RESPONSIBILITY
TOWARDS YOUR SON ROBERT. REGULAR MEALS,
BE THERE WHEN HE RETURNS FROM SCHOOL. HE
IS NOT A HAPPY CHILD. MEND YOUR WAYS.

'The cheek of it – the goddamned cheek of it.' May could hardly contain herself; her voice rose to a screech. 'That little bugger has been shooting his mouth off telling people we neglect him.' May was tearful.

'Where is he, upstairs?' Jim's voice was more controlled.

The fried bread began to burn and May turned back to the stove and placed it on a plate. She put another slice of bread in the pan and turned down the stove a little. 'Leave it a minute, Jim. No need to let it ruin our supper.' Jim sat down, picking the letter up again, reading it and muttering to himself. There was another sizzling sound as May cracked the eggs and dropped their contents into the hot fat. 'One's broke,' she said.

'You can have that, I don't like 'em broke,' Jim said.

She banged the plates down on the kitchen table, brought the frying pan over and lifted the eggs out on to the plates, covering the burnt fried bread. They both ate in silence, eyeing the now grease-marked letter beside them.

'Can I have some bacon and egg, Mum?' Their son Robert took them by surprise, standing in the kitchen doorway.

'Why aren't you in bed and asleep?'

'I was, Dad, but I smelled the bacon and thought –'

'Well, you thought wrong,' his father interrupted him harshly. He continued, 'What do you know about this? Who have you been snivelling to?'

The boy read the letter slowly, mouthing the words, his fair hair falling over his eyes as he read, so he pushed it back. 'I haven't, Dad. I haven't said anything to anyone.' Then a defiance crept into his manner. 'Anyway, I never get a supper, do I? Not like you're having.'

His father cleared up the bacon fat on his plate with a piece of bread, put it in his mouth and leaned back in his chair chewing slowly. 'You nasty little bleeder, you have been snivelling to someone.' He got up.

'Now, Dad,' May said loudly, 'the boy can have some bacon and egg if he wants it. Won't take a minute.'

But Jim Benson was in no mood to listen. Robert cowered as his father approached him and struck him a blow on the face with a clenched fist. The boy yelped in pain, turned and ran up the stairs. His bedroom door banged. Jim made as if to follow him, then changed his mind and came back and sat down at the table. 'We'll take this letter to the fuzz – I'll find out who wrote it. "Mend your ways" – sounds like a woman to me.'

May had put the kettle on. 'Cup of tea?' she asked.

'Yeah, the bacon was too salty, don't know why you can't get decent bacon.'

May sniffed. The kettle clicked off and she poured the boiling water into the teapot. 'Wait till it's mashed,' she said. 'You hit him on the eye, it was cut, bleeding. There was no need for that.'

Jim turned on her. 'Shut up, woman. I did not, it was not bleeding.'

'It was,' said May, but she said it quietly; she did not want to

25

inflame her husband's temper any further. He was frightening sometimes – broke six dinner plates once; just picked the lot up and threw them on the kitchen floor.

May looked round the untidy room. The letter was right in a way. He wouldn't take it to the police, she knew that, there was too much truth in it. He was all talk – couldn't keep a job and fell out with the boss and his mates with that awful temper of his. He was carting earth at the garden centre at the moment, but how long would that last?

May sighed as she poured the tea.

'Could be that bloody vicar's wife,' Jim muttered suddenly.

May shook her head. 'No, vicars' wives don't act like that.' Her tone was so positive that he gave way.

'Well, maybe not her, but it's some bloody busybody he has been lying to.'

May emptied her cup. 'Well, you shouldn't have hit him like that, you're always doing it. Now he'll have a cut eye to make it look as if we beat him up. I'll go and see.' She went upstairs.

The light was on in Robert's room; he was sitting up in bed reading. If he had been crying it didn't show. As May came into the room he looked at her sullenly. His left eye was slightly puffy and a slight shallow cut ran the length of his eyebrow. May crossed the room and sat down on the bed. 'You need a haircut,' she said. 'Does your eye hurt? Your dad was mad, see – we had the letter.'

She paused and Robert burst out with his own troubles. 'You're all on at me. Mr Fisk for breaking a window – I never done it. Old Maston said I trod on his toe on purpose. You're all on at me.'

His mother got up – the beer, the fatty meal and the hot tea had given her heartburn. She burped and hit her chest with her clenched hand. 'I'll bring you up a bacon butty,' she said.

'Oh thanks, Mum.' The boy's face lit up, all the sullenness gone. His eyes met hers.

'Your dad didn't mean it, Rob.'

The sullen look returned. 'Oh yes, he did – he always means it, Mum, and I hate him.'

'Now, speak like that and you'll get no bacon butty.'

May went downstairs. Robert sat listening – the smell of frying bacon wafted up the stairs. He relaxed and felt better, but the hatred of his father remained with him.

26

4

The atmosphere in Hawthorne Cottage between Dorothy and Michaela had suffered a sea change. A week had passed since the 'horrible letter' (Dorothy's words) or 'the bloody stupid letter' (Michaela's words) had arrived. Their different descriptions of the letter indicated the differing effect it had on them. Michaela carried on as usual, but she watched Dorothy with some anxiety, hoping against hope that as the days went by she would forget the words on the sheet of paper and realise that poison pen letters were not all that uncommon in villages and should be ignored. As she constantly said to Dorothy, such people were probably paranoid and not worth bothering about – they just needed something to colour their otherwise, no doubt, dull and empty lives.

This argument did not work. Dorothy grew more and more quiet, would not eat and refused to go out. 'Supposing I meet the very person who wrote the letter and I won't know it?' As obstinate as a mule, Michaela had dubbed her.

She did manage to persuade Dorothy to go to Tesco's with her and of course they had met someone from Shelbourne, a Mrs Billingham, a fat genial lady with a loud voice. She greeted them with enthusiasm, asked them where they were going and to come to her for a snatch and grab lunch, as she called it. She pointed to her trolley. 'Will you look at that load, and I'm only shopping for little me. Mind you, the toilet rolls take up a lot of room and I like to lay a good stock in.' She laughed loudly.

'Very wise of you,' Michaela answered.

Mrs Billingham went on to say, 'Of course, it's even more shopping for you – there are two of you. It must be nice if you find someone you want to live with.'

Dorothy's face had warned Michaela that they had better part company with Mrs Billingham but fast.

'There you are, I told you – she was hinting, wasn't she? I could tell by her expression.'

Michaela looked round to see if the large lady was out of earshot. 'Of course she wasn't hinting anything, it was just an ordinary remark.'

Dorothy would not agree with her. 'Mrs Billingham thought the same as the letter said – probably the whole village does, too. It's no use, I can tell how people are thinking.' She stood for a moment looking at the shelves but, her companion thought, seeing nothing.

'Come on, Dorothy, let's get two large baking potatoes for tonight's supper.'

Dorothy followed her towards the vegetable section, but would not give up the argument. 'You take everything in your stride, Michaela – you're different.'

Michaela chose two big clean potatoes, put them in a plastic bag and into the trolley. 'You know it's not true, Dorothy, and I know it's not true, so what the hell does it matter what anyone thinks?'

'It does to me. I can't look anyone in the face any more.'

'Oh, do give up,' Michaela had snapped back, wanting to forget it and go on with their own lives.

Try as she would, though, a small doubt was creeping into her mind. Why should Dorothy continue to be so upset? Had she a tendency toward the very thing the letter had suggested? On the face of it Dorothy was a very meek and mild sort of woman, whilst she herself was more domineering. Never, during the time they had spent together, at first on holiday and now during the six months they had been living together, had anything occurred – but to the outsider how did it look? Had the letter sown doubt in her companion's mind? Michaela began to wonder about her greatest friend. So the atmosphere began to change a little and a reserve began to creep between them that had never been there before. To her dismay Michaela saw that this change, this discomfort between them could, unless she destroyed it, bring the relationship to such a state that they might have to part. The very thought of it . . . their shared possession of the house, their contented life together, the amicable arrangement of their expenses, their routine – all would be sacrificed, all because of this bloody godforsaken man or woman who had sent that letter. If she knew who it was she felt she could cheerfully kill him or her. It did cross her mind that in stories and novels there were always several poison pen letters; never, as far as she could remember, just one. Who else had had one, she wondered, if anyone. How could she find out? She could not really think of a way round such a problem.

The immediate worry, however, was centred around Dorothy.

Her depression seemed to be getting deeper and more obvious. 'Why don't you go and see Dr Barnes and ask him for a tonic – something to improve your appetite, dear?' Michaela had suggested.

Dorothy's reply had been 'No!', so sharp and so uncompromising that Michaela had decided to say no more. 'What! Tell him that I've been accused of being a homosexual and need some medicine to make me feel better?'

As the days went by nothing had improved. Life had changed totally for both of them. The letter had destroyed the contented companionship and left in its place an unhappy distrust.

Mrs Thornton was in hospital for a lumpectomy. The surgeon had recommended immediate removal and a bed had been available. Except for a small cut in her breast, which hurt a little when she moved her arm, she felt none the worse. Ted had been to see her that same evening and he had been amazed and delighted to find her sitting in a chair by her bed. Ted had never been a demonstrative man; he had kissed her cheek almost shyly when he arrived. He was carrying the traditional bunch of flowers – in this case daffs – and a bottle of her favourite soft drink, Robinson's Lemon and Barley.

'Really, Ted,' she said, 'you need not have bothered with all this, I am coming home tomorrow.' She was pleased with the flowers, nevertheless. 'I am going to Southampton for some more treatment, and they hope that will be all it needs.'

'How do you feel, Mabel?' Ted asked.

'Fine. They say the radiation treatment may make me feel a bit rotten, but that will soon go off. Sit down, Ted, for goodness sake – you make me feel nervous standing up, all the other visitors are sitting down.'

He did so, but he soon left once he had assured himself that his wife had got through the surgery so well. Before he left he tried to please her by thinking up something to tell her. 'Miss what's her name sends you her best wishes for a good and quick recovery.'

'Miss who?' Mabel asked.

'The Hawthorne Cottage lady.'

'Oh, Michaela.'

Ted shook his head. 'No, the other one. She didn't look at all well, she looked sort of all over the place.'

Mabel smiled. 'Whatever do you mean by that, Ted – "all over the place"?'

Ted replied, 'I don't know – sort of muddled in her mind, like.'

Soon after that he took himself off, walking self-consciously down the ward. Mabel watched him go, then relaxed against her pillow. She had left a nice steak and kidney pie in the freezer for him to eat that night and there was a chicken pie, toad in the hole and lots more, just in case anything had gone wrong and she had to stay in longer than expected.

The ward television came on and the news started. 'Time for bed now, Mrs Thornton.' A nurse helped her in – it was nice to get into bed. She felt a bit tired, but it was so good to know that the day was over and everything was all right. It was sad that she and Ted had no children, but it meant a lot to be together. She didn't want to die yet and according to the doctors she wasn't going to. She watched the television.

Philippa Ainsworth felt restless and dissatisfied. She would have liked to have gone to the mainland and bought a really gorgeous, expensive summer dress, exceedingly short – one a vicar's wife would never be expected to wear. Her figure, she considered, was very good; her breasts high, small, well-shaped and firm, her stomach as flat as it had been when she was eighteen. Her bottom, too, was as firm as a girl's – perhaps dropped a tiny bit but, after all, what could you expect, she was eighteen no longer. She wondered, as she had before, what Dr Barnes would be like in bed. She tried to imagine it, but she couldn't – after all, she had never thought of him in that way, just as a doctor. She had met his wife on one or two occasions. She was nothing special, quite pretty, a jolly hockey-stick type of girl, rather horsey. Come to think of it, his young daughter had a pony and she rode in gymkhanas.

The letter, she was pleased about. Poison pen letter, she felt, did not apply. She remembered her husband's surprise at the contents – that had been an insult!

He had probably put it in the drawer in his desk which he kept locked – sometimes he forgot to lock it. Philippa was determined to get hold of it. She wanted to reread it, show it to someone – but to whom? Carmen Delano, it was well known, couldn't keep a secret for five minutes; should she show it to her? That would really shake her and all those to whom she spread the news.

Philippa felt a little thrill at the thought of it. She could almost hear Carmen's telephone clack, clack, clacking away – 'Do you know what, Philippa Ainsworth has had an anonymous letter about her affair with Dr Barnes' – clackitty, clack, chatter, chatter. 'Oh yes, she denies it, of course – well, she would, wouldn't she? But I say, dear, there is no smoke without fire.'

God knows, Philippa thought, there is little enough in this damned village for anyone to gossip about. Wait a minute, though – suppose Carmen had sent it? No, that wasn't her style. Who had, though?

The day came, sure enough, when Hugh left the drawer un-locked and, just as she had thought, there was the letter. She took it out, turned the lock and dropped the key on the carpet directly under the drawer in the desk. She opened the letter almost rever-ently, reread it, then put it into her handbag. It was wonderful, quite wonderful, that anyone should have written such a thing about her; it made her feel young again. She hadn't fancied Dr Barnes, but after the letter she was not so sure – an affair with anyone would be such a delightful cure for her boredom. At the moment her own opinion of her charms was at an all-time low. The letter had given her a boost which, as Hugh's wife, she badly needed.

Philippa arranged her little plot with care. She wanted Carmen on her own, not at one of her chattering gossiping coffee morn-ings. So she dropped in one morning, a particular morning when she knew Carmen went shopping. She guessed pretty accurately when Carmen would return and rang her door bell about ten minutes after she had seen her enter her house carrying a couple of carrier bags.

'Well, hello, Philippa, what a nice surprise. Come in. I was just going to make a cup of coffee.' The welcome was genuine. 'You don't mind mugs, do you?'

After a few minutes Carmen produced two steaming mugs. 'Sugar?'

'Yes, two spoonfuls, please – I'm in shock!' Philippa smiled and sat down at the kitchen table.

Carmen sat opposite her. 'In shock, dear?' she asked. 'What's happened?'

Philippa opened her handbag and took out the letter, unfolded it and handed it across the table to her friend. She managed to get a touch of drama into her action – this, however, was slightly spoiled by Carmen having to get up, fetch her reading glasses from the Welsh dresser and put them on. Then she read the small amount of typing in the middle of the large sheet of paper. Behind the glasses Philippa watched her friend's eyes widen. She read the message twice, then looked up at Philippa. 'This was sent to the vicar?' Her companion nodded, waiting for the inevitable question. 'But it's not true of course, is it?'

Philippa was glad that the question ended 'is it?' If the query had ended with the words 'of course' she would have been deflated and furious. 'Oh no, Carmen, it's not true.' She hoped she had managed to infuse just that note that would leave a faint possibility of the letter being true. She drank the rest of her coffee.

'What are you going to do about it?' Carmen asked.

Philippa shrugged her shoulders. 'What can I do? Anyway, it was sent to Hugh, not me. That coffee was delicious, Carmen.'

'I'll make some more,' said Carmen, handing the letter back and switching on the coffeemaker. 'Who sent it, that's the question? Will the vicar go to the police?'

Philippa shook her head. 'No, it wouldn't do to let them see it. I don't think Hugh would want that. I've only shown it to you because I knew you wouldn't say a word.'

There was a long pause. 'No, you know you can trust me, dear. I won't tell a soul.'

They went on discussing the letter and Carmen made several wild guesses as to who it could be. 'I feel it's a man,' she said eventually, draining her mug.

'Do you really think so?' Philippa got up and put the letter, just as carefully folded as before, into her handbag. 'I must go. Glad I told you, Carmen dear. I felt I must confide in someone.'

At the door Carmen looked up and down the village street. 'Would you imagine, in a quiet place like this? And that Dr Barnes, I would never have thought it of him.'

Philippa clasped Carmen's gesticulating hand. 'But it's not true, Carmen. It's not true,' she said.

Her friend looked at her rather blankly. 'Of course, I was forgetting, it's not true. But it makes you think, doesn't it? That's what's called a poison pen letter, isn't it? So there must be someone wanting to make trouble!' She suddenly realised she was getting into rather deep water and retreated into her house. 'Bye-bye then,' she said.

'Bye-bye, Carmen, and thanks so much for the coffee.'

She shut Carmen's small wrought-iron gate, checked the latch carefully and started her way back to the vicarage. She felt well satisfied with her visit. Soon, Philippa hoped, that quiet village Carmen had talked about would be looking at her with different eyes. Maybe she would improve her appearance a little – get the hairdresser to retint her hair, cover up the few grey flecks, buy new make-up. She looked at her hands; they were well shaped and her nails were pretty. She would get some dark red nail varnish and stop using old-fashioned colourless stuff. Hugh hated painted nails – yes, she'd definitely get some!

When she reached home Hugh was still out. The key was on the floor where she had dropped it. She popped the letter back into the drawer, picked up the key and put it in the keyhole, but left it as it was, the drawer unlocked. She looked at Hugh's tidy desk – the sermon notebook with the last page half filled with his neat writing. Next Sunday's boredom . . . ! Perhaps a smarter, sexy wife might do his image good!

Philippa started to get lunch ready, wondering as she did so how many of her friends Carmen had telephoned. Perhaps she had even slipped out to tell the fascinating news – swearing each one not to repeat a word. Would the silly woman get round to Dr Barnes? She hoped so. He would know it was totally untrue, of course, but he might look at her with a trace more interest – perhaps even a little admiration. His wife was quite an attractive woman, though, well dressed, slim. Still, men liked a change, there was no doubt about that. Of course, not that she was ever likely . . . She scraped a carrot with a degree of viciousness that was hardly necessary.

The George and Dragon was almost empty; it was only seven thirty and its patrons usually started to come in at around nine – after they had been home, cleaned up, and had their tea or supper, whatever their evening meal was called.

Nigel Dawson and his companion Jeremy were at the far end of the bar, frozen out of the Manor by the Brigadier, who had had a little too much to drink before dinner. He had suddenly turned on the two of them, in front of the housekeeper, and said, 'Get out, you two fucking fairies – get out. I've had enough of you both.'

Even Nigel, used to his father's outbursts, had been intimidated by this tirade. 'Come on – let's go to the Dragon and have a jar.'

As they had left the house the old man had shouted, 'And don't bloody come back.'

'Oh sir, casting us out, hungry, into the cold night.' Jeremy had fluttered his eyes at him, which had further enraged the old man, causing him to shake his fist at him.

They had climbed into Nigel's car and arrived at the pub.

'Alas, why couldn't your father have started the anti-homo routine after we'd eaten?'

Dawson was in a bad temper. He looked at Jeremy and his brows drew together in a frown. His eyes looked slightly contemptuous. 'The last straw for Dad was that blue eyeshadow you're sporting – what's the bloody idea?'

Jeremy took a long final swig of the beer. 'Just wanted to look lovely for you, sweetheart.' He pursed his lips in a kissing gesture. 'May I have a G and T, please? I hate this manly stuff.' He pushed the tankard away with the top of his finger.

Nigel ordered two gins and tonic, signalling to the proprietor, who pushed one glass and then the other up to the optic, added a slice of lemon to one, then tonic to both. He carried the two glasses over and placed them in front of Dawson.

'Thanks so much, mine host.' Jeremy picked up his glass by the stem and sipped, his eyes fixed on the barman, smiling. Nigel knew Jeremy in this mood only too well. He could make himself a damned nuisance to everybody and enjoy every minute of it.

Ben Newman went to the other end of the bar – as far away as he could get from Jeremy. Suzie, his live-in girlfriend, was just passing two glasses of foaming bitter across the bar. She took the proffered money, rang it up in the till, then turned to Ben and saw his expression.

'What's up with you?'

'It's that bloody pansy with young Dawson. He's covered in make-up – his face, I mean. I've a damned good mind to ban him!'

'Oh, come on, Ben, don't be like that. He's only a faggot, a fairy, or draggo, that's their business.' She wiped the counter.

Ben continued, 'What must the Brigadier think?'

Suzie served half a pint of lager and came back to Ben's side. 'That's the Brigadier's business, not ours. They're very good customers – always pints or doubles. We need the loot over the counter, that's what we need.'

Ben nodded; she was right, of course, but it got up his nose even to serve them. 'When I was a boy –' he began.

'Oh, I know – a pint cost elevenpence, you could get a pair of boots and a dinner and still have enough money to go to the pictures out of a pound. Do give over, Ben!'

He smiled at her and went on serving more amiably.

Meanwhile the Brigadier's son was rapidly losing his temper. As he watched the slightly lipsticked lips sipping the gin he began to think, Have I had enough of Jeremy? He was getting insufferable. Two years they had been lovers – was it over? 'Oh shut up, Jeremy.' Two more double gins and he was getting rather drunk. They both were.

'No, dear, I won't shut up.' Jeremy touched Nigel's lapel, drawing his fingers gently down the material. 'That nice man you introduced me to, your namesake – he was attracted to me. One look and I think he was hooked. I could see him begin to tumble as I eyed him.' He smiled and looked down at the drink. 'Who was the wine for? Not a girl – I'd take a bet on that. Got a ciggie?'

Nigel passed him one. It was useless to try and pin Jeremy down – he was like an eel, twisting away and changing the subject, usually to a more irritating one.

'I tell you what, sweetie, I'm going to telephone and ask the other Nigel – the nice one – to join us here right now. You'll see, he'll be no trouble.' He felt in his pocket for change. 'What's his number? Where does he live?'

Nigel finished his drink. 'Down the High Street somewhere, with his mother.'

'That figures, dear. Fisk, wasn't it?'

Dawson nodded.

'I'll look it up.' Jeremy sauntered away, throwing a sweet smile at Suzie, who smiled back at him.

Jeremy ran his finger down the Fs in the phone book. There it was – J W FISK – not even his own telephone number, poor sod. What did he do for a living? Nigel had told him, but momentarily he had forgotten. Then he remembered – he was headmaster at a local school. Well, well, he should be so lucky . . . He pressed the digits, admiring the shape and the polish of his nail as he did so.

After about six rings the receiver was picked up. 'Yes?' It was a woman's voice.

'May I speak with Nigel, please?'

'Who is it? What name shall I say?'

Jeremy coughed but did not answer. He heard the woman's remark as she left the telephone: 'It's for you, Nigel.' Jeremy waited.

Jane Fisk came into the sitting-room, where Nigel was watching the news – or rather the weather forecast as the news was over. He turned to her. 'Who is it, Ma?'

'He didn't say. I asked but he didn't reply.'

'Oh bother, I hope it's not the new caretaker being over-zealous and something is wrong at the school.'

He got up and went out into the hall, leaving the door open behind him.

'Yes, Nigel Fisk speaking.'

There was a short silence. Jane heard Nigel put the telephone receiver down on the little table. Then he came and shut the sitting-room door. Jane was surprised – they had no secrets from each other; never had, as far as she knew. For a moment Jane thought it might be a girl. Then her son came back into the room; he looked pale, flustered.

'It's a friend. I have to slip out, Ma. I won't be long.'

Jane Fisk did not want to question him, but could not help herself.

'No, Ma, it was a man not a girl.'

'I know,' she smiled, 'but a friend could have a sister or a girlfriend he wants you to meet, couldn't he? I was just hoping you'd met someone nice.'

'No, it's nothing like that, Ma. It's a friend of Nigel Dawson.'

He went out into the hall and picked up a light anorak. She followed him. 'You don't mean that dreadful Jeremy? I don't know what his other name is.'

He shrugged on his anorak. 'For God's sake, Ma, they have only asked me to go and have a drink with them.' He stood for a moment in the doorway and ran his hand over his hair. 'Sorry to have interrupted the news, Ma.'

'You haven't, dear, it's over – you were watching the weather forecast.'

Their eyes met and lingered for a moment. 'Oh yes, of course, I forgot.'

'Nigel, don't get mixed up with those two – you know their reputation!'

'I told you, Ma, I'm just going to have a drink with them – not sleep with them!'

He went out of the front door, not actually slamming it but closing it a little more firmly than usual. She heard his steps go down their short garden path.

Jane sat down heavily, then leaned forward and switched off the television. In his haste Nigel had put the remote control out of her reach. Not like him, he was so meticulous about such things . . .

She sat for some time gazing at the blank screen. She could feel worry mounting in her, an awful acute anxiety. Nigel Dawson was homosexual – the whole village knew that. It was such common knowledge that it had almost ceased to be talked about. In so many walks of life these days such things were accepted. Doctors, priests, police, civil servants – and, indeed, gays as they were called seemed to be better hairdressers, couturiers – but no one, she felt, no matter how tolerant, would want his son at a school where the headmaster was a known homosexual. No parent would.

She got up, impatient with her imaginings. 'For goodness sake, he's only gone for a drink.' She felt she had to move about. She switched on the radio. In the kitchen she got out the two mugs they had their night drinks in – Nigel had Horlicks, she Ovaltine. Good God, was that normal or natural for a man of forty? Could other people see – was it so obvious to them? How could Philippa Ainsworth guess? That conversation with Carmen? Was there some other clue – something going on at the school that she, his mother, knew nothing about? She put Nigel's mug back in the cupboard and left her own on the work surface. The action seemed to her to be a symbol, a sign. How could she help him? She began to plot, sitting down again in front of the blank television. Although the spring evening was warm she felt very cold.

Should another of those letters be sent? But who to? Nigel Dawson? His friend? The Brigadier – if he received one, would he expel his son and the friend, forbid them the house? Then they might take off to London. The Dawsons were well off, so people said – he could afford to buy the pair some sort of accommodation. She felt the Brigadier might be longing to see the back of his son and any of his so-called friends. He was seldom seen in the village now, perhaps because of their actions. Nigel's sports car roared through the village while his father, on the rare occasions he did appear, drove an old, grubby Rover, large and slow. People said the old man was only interested in his bit of rough shooting. His wife had been a quiet, rather snobbish lady, not particularly liked.

Nigel Dawson had always been a problem, even to his mother. Educated at public school, he had been caught smoking cannabis and been expelled, but let off with a caution by the police.

All these thoughts added up in Jane's mind to the 'rightness' of an anonymous letter to the Brigadier. It might precipitate her son's rescue – something had to be done!

5

At Hawthorne Cottage Michaela was talking to Dorothy.

'This relationship is going to be ruined, Dorothy, if you continue like this. Some stupid person sends a stupid letter and you go to pieces.' Dorothy sat mute on the settee. 'Even if it were true, would it damn well matter? I mean, it's our business, no one else's, for Pete's sake!'

Dorothy looked out of the window: the sunny spring weather had given way to a fine misty rain. As Michaela made for the door – she was going for a walk and to post two letters – Dorothy at last spoke.

'It's no use, Michaela, everyone's not the same. You can cope with things, I can't; I never have been able to.'

Michaela made an impatient noise. 'Oh, come on, what do you want to do – move?'

Dorothy shrugged. 'Probably,' she said. 'I can't go out without seeing someone or meeting someone I think might have written that letter.' She twisted her handkerchief in her hands. 'Or thought that awful thing about us.'

Michaela could stand no more. Impatient by nature, she was unable to keep her temper. 'I'm going out. Do you want to come?' She had on a mac and a waterproof headscarf tied under her chin. Her face, devoid of make-up, was pink-cheeked, healthy-looking. Michaela looked as if she enjoyed life.

Dorothy shook her head. 'No, I won't come. I'll have tea ready for you when you get back.' She did not get up and she did not look at her friend, but continued to stare out at the rain.

Michaela slammed the front door, thrust the letters into her mackintosh pocket to keep them dry and walked down the path, not bothering to shut the gate behind her. She was furious. Since the beastly anonymous letter had arrived days ago Dorothy had behaved, in her opinion, like an idiot. She wouldn't eat, couldn't sleep and would hardly ever go out at all. She had ventured out with Michaela only once after meeting Mrs Billingham in Tesco's; they had gone to Gateway's in Ryde, but unfortunately they had met Carmen Delano, who had greeted them with enthusiasm and asked why she had seen so little of them lately and would they come to tea one day. Dorothy had acted like a shrinking violet – indeed, had barely spoken. Admittedly Carmen was known to be a bit of a gossip, but her manner had certainly not given the slightest sign that she thought of Michaela and Dorothy as anything more than good friends. When at last they had parted Dorothy had almost forced Michaela to go home. 'She knows, and she's the biggest tittle-tattle in the village. She'll have heard what people are saying about us; perhaps she wrote the letter.' Carmen's comment during their conversation that 'Dorothy looked a bit peaky' was true enough – she looked most unwell, she was pale and had lost weight.

Two things occupied Michaela's mind as she strode along, enjoying the soft gentle rain which was making the earth and grass smell delicious. She would like to get Dorothy to the doctor; she had suggested that already and the idea had been turned down flatly. Dorothy, though so quiet and reserved, could be as stubborn as a mule when she felt like it. The other thing on her mind was that maybe a visit to the police would be advisable; this idea she did not much relish.

She posted her letters in the pillar box at the corner of the Green. On the way back she passed the new minister, his head dipped against the rain. He smiled as he passed. 'Do the gardens good,' he said.

Michaela smiled back. 'Yes indeed.'

He seemed a nice fellow, though his clothes were perhaps a bit weird for a vicar – no, not vicar, minister he was called. She was not particularly 'in' as to church and chapel matters, but the chance meeting did give her an idea. Why not go and have a word with Hugh Ainsworth? They had met him and his wife a couple of times at church and shaken hands with him on the way out, so perhaps he would remember her and think of her as one of his flock, if a somewhat straying one. Worry about the condition Dorothy was getting herself into made Michaela feel she must talk to someone about the letter. After all, vicars should know a lot more about the villagers than most people. He might even have some idea who could have sent such a message. He might know who in the village could type, who owned a typewriter. Perhaps, though, he might not even want to guess at the sender, she didn't know. Still, at least it would be someone to talk to. She hadn't got the letter now, but she could easily describe it, acquaint him with the accusation it had contained, even tell him the postmark.

By the time she got back to Hawthorne Cottage Michaela had made up her mind – the vicar was to be her confidant. She would have to telephone him from a box outside the cottage and not tell Dorothy what she was thinking of doing. After all, apparently Dorothy's aim in life was that no one, absolutely no one, should know about the letter, ever. She thought irritably that the way her friend was behaving would make anyone think that they were in fact lesbians; her behaviour was little short of irrational. If she went on in this frame of mind she would end up with a nervous breakdown. Michaela felt she would really love to expose this wicked letter-writer and make her or him eat their words – even get him or her imprisoned.

The following morning she had not changed her mind. She made the telephone call and arranged to be at the vicarage at three o'clock that afternoon.

When Michaela came out of the vicarage she felt confused, a state of mind most unlike her. She had told the vicar, Hugh Ainsworth, about the letter. She had taken the trouble to write out the words that had been typed and she was sure she had done them correctly. He had read it and for a moment had been completely silent. Then he had asked her rather hesitantly about the postmark and when the letter had arrived, but the reaction which had struck her most forcibly was that he had not appeared to be surprised. He had dropped the copy of the letter on the desk in front of him, put his fingers together and looked at her over the top of his hands – an almost theatrical vicar-type posture, Michaela had thought. She had found herself watching him, expecting something, an expression of disgust or dismay – but no!

'Well, how very upsetting for you,' he had finally said.

After a pause which Michaela had felt was minutes long but which had probably been only a second or two she replied, 'Certainly it was upsetting, and particularly to my friend. She is so affected by it that she is unable to eat or sleep.'

He had nodded slowly. 'Yes, most upsetting.' He picked up the copy she had handed to him and read it again. Michaela had the feeling he was playing for time. 'Yes, very nasty, but I believe this kind of thing is not uncommon in villages. They do –'

She had interrupted him rather irritably: 'Yes, yes, vicar. I am well aware that poison pen letters do exist, but I came here to ask your advice. What should we do about it? Go to the police, take it to our lawyer?'

He had looked up quickly then: 'No, no, I don't think so. I really don't think that it would be . . . Well, it would be like using a sledgehammer to crack a hazel nut – isn't that the expression?' He looked back at the piece of paper she had given him. 'I should just ignore it, forget it. It's obviously from some poor sick person. Yes, I think I'm right, it's best forgotten.'

'That's easy to say, vicar, but I think perhaps this person should be apprehended. What if more are sent, or have been sent?'

Hugh Ainsworth had got to his feet as if the interview was over. 'Oh, I don't think there will necessarily be any more . . .'

Michaela had jumped on him – she smiled as she recollected. 'Oh, you mean that this one was the only one that was necessary to be sent then, vicar?'

He had realised his mistake and had hastily tried to correct it. 'Oh no, of course there may be others. I don't mean that this might be the only one, but . . .'

'Oh, I see.'

She had got up, walked across the study and opened the door before he had time to reach it to open it for her.

Philippa Ainsworth was standing right up against the door. She had obviously been listening, Michaela was sure of it.

'Oh, I was just going to knock and ask if you would both like a cup of tea, Hugh,' she said, her face going a rather dusky pink.

Michaela had been about to refuse, but had then thought better of it. 'Yes, how nice of you.' She heard the kettle flick off in the kitchen as she spoke, so Philippa might have had the idea in mind when she stood outside her husband's study door.

It was when the three of them were sitting at tea, Michaela, Philippa and Hugh Ainsworth, that Michaela had felt muddled, indeed bewildered. Philippa's attitude was coy, girlish, totally unlike herself. She was certainly more smartly dressed than usual

– her long painted nails were displayed as she dispensed tea and biscuits. Now and again she would give the coy look towards her husband, but he seemed embarrassed by it. What had been going on? From a dowdy, rather downtrodden little woman, Philippa Ainsworth had completely changed. What had happened? Michaela was baffled but intrigued.

She would have to tell Dorothy that she had shown someone the letter – that, she felt, was only fair – but she knew her friend, who took life far too seriously, would be outraged.

The thought of Dorothy took her back to that holiday they had taken together in Switzerland some years ago. Dorothy had succeeded in ruining the whole time abroad because of an unfortunate incident that had happened at her school, trivial really, but not to Dorothy. Michaela had sympathised with her friend, but had got absolutely sick of hearing the details of the worry again and again.

The facts were that a small boy in the playground of Dorothy's school – a right little bullyboy, by the sound of it – had purloined a pair of scissors from the teacher's desk, which should have been locked, and had pulled a small girl down on the ground and cut off her pigtail. The parents had of course been livid; the small boy had been sent home in disgrace. Dorothy had heard that his father had tanned his backside: indeed, he had told her so himself, pleased that he had done so. Dorothy had been further distracted for she did not agree with any form of corporal punishment. Michaela's remark, 'Serve the little bugger right,' had not gone down well, but Michaela had been so browned off with her friend's depression she had said several things she didn't even herself believe.

So this new worry was not going to be shrugged off easily. Dorothy was taking it very hard. Michaela appreciated her friend's nature was not as tough as her own. She must, she knew, make allowances for Dorothy's extreme sensitivity.

She pushed open the gate, closing it carefully behind her – Dorothy might be watching, she grinned to herself. Inside she called out, 'Dorothy, I'm back.' No answer. She was pleasantly surprised. Dorothy had been writing a letter when Michaela left and she may have gone to the post and on to the general store. Michaela had hinted they were out of cornflakes . . .

Michaela took off her headscarf, threw it on the little table. She looked at the kitchen clock, four fifteen – she would make the tea.

She was still thirsty and the tea at the vicarage had been rather weak. By the time she had made it Dorothy would be back. She put the kettle on, got out two cups and saucers, and placed Dorothy's sweeteners beside her cup. By the time the tea was made Dorothy had not returned. After five thirty Michaela began to worry, only a little. She might have gone to Tesco's on her own. She went out of the front door and round to the garage – no, the car was there . . . Carmen's – perhaps that was where she had gone; maybe she was trying to solve what was to her an awful problem. By six o'clock Michaela was more than slightly anxious.

She went upstairs to fetch a cardigan; the evenings were not yet warm. At the top of the stairs she stopped. Dorothy's bedroom door was open and she lay on her bed curled up, her face pillowed on her arm . . . There was saliva running from her mouth down over her arm, wetting her blouse sleeve. 'Dorothy!' Michaela walked into the room and up to the bed. 'Dorothy, wake up, old girl. You needed a good sleep.' Then she saw the two empty aspirin bottles on the floor.

Jane Fisk was troubled – no, more than troubled, she felt at times almost distraught. Nigel was going out most nights now after supper, sometimes taking the car, so his visits were not always to the Dragon. She would not ask him and he made no attempt to tell her, he just said, 'Won't be long, Ma,' or 'Don't wait up, I may be late.' She was certain, or almost certain, he was meeting either Nigel Dawson or that Jeremy, whatever his surname was – she had no idea.

The afternoon that Michaela visited the vicar, Jane had taken herself for a walk although it was getting dark. She had no particular destination, but she felt she might go and ask Michaela and Dorothy to tea. She would like to see if they mentioned the letter and if they did how much it had meant to them. In some ways she hoped they wouldn't and in some ways she hoped they would. She was beginning to despise herself for having written and sent the letters. Perhaps she was beginning to believe the gossip she had heard about her son at Carmen's coffee morning – perhaps it had not been wrong. Nigel was queer – a pansy – a fairy – gay – horrible, horrible words; horrible terms that ran through her life like filthy water, polluting a once clean and sweet river.

43

As she neared Hawthorne Cottage she noticed the front door was open and the light in the hall was throwing a stream of brilliance down the garden path, lighting up Michaela who was standing at the gate, gazing down the road. She turned to run back into the house, not seeing Jane. She looked panic-stricken.

'What's the matter, Michaela – is something wrong?'

Jane followed her into the garden, but Michaela did not stop, only called, half turning her head over her shoulder, 'It's Dorothy, she's taken an overdose.' She disappeared through the door.

Jane saw the glare of headlights turn from the left, skirting the Green, a blue light flashing.

'Stop it, Jane, please. Stop the ambulance!' Michaela called.

Jane stepped to the edge of the path and waved her arm wildly and the ambulance stopped. Back doors opened. 'An overdose,' Jane managed to gasp out. She spoke as if she had no breath in her own lungs and the strength in her legs had gone. She leant on the little fence that bordered Hawthorne Cottage; all she could think of was that that dreadful letter she had written might, well might, have caused this.

It seemed in very little time, very quickly, that the paramedics had carried their burden down the lighted path and loaded it into the ambulance. Michaela looked around her, still distracted. Jane pulled herself together. 'Go with her, Michaela. I'll lock up, get my car and follow you, then I can bring you back.'

'Thanks, Mrs Fisk . . . Jane. Thank you so much.'

Michaela got into the ambulance after Dorothy and slid in. The doors closed and Jane was left standing in the path herself now, alone, in the beam of light. She watched the ambulance going round the bend of the road and then heading back towards St Mary's Hospital.

Jane locked the cottage front door after checking the back door, leaving the hall light on but switching off those of the kitchen and bedroom. She then walked back to her own house to get her car. It was five to seven. Jane wrote a hasty note to her son, put it under a mug on the kitchen table where he couldn't miss it. He would get no supper unless he got his own – maybe he wouldn't come back at all. Jane felt so shattered about what had happened, what might have happened, at Hawthorne Cottage, that her feelings about her son were for the first time pushed into the background of her mind.

She drove to Newport, steadying her thoughts as well as she

44

could as she manoeuvred her car round the country lanes and then into the more urban area of Newport. If Dorothy died, if the cause of her death was the accusation made in the letter, she would never forgive herself – never, never!

At the hospital she was directed to the casualty department. Michaela was sitting on one of the blue plastic chairs that stood in rows in the large waiting hall. There were very few people, about five, sitting there. They were all, with the exception of Michaela, looking composed; indeed two of them were thumbing through magazines.

Michaela looked up as Jane approached. 'They've taken her through there.' She gestured towards two frosted glass doors, over the top of which was a lighted sign, black letters on green, which read 'No Entry'. 'They told me she would have to have a stomach wash-out. I brought the bottles and gave them to the nurse – they were empty. She might have to stay in.'

Jane thought Michaela looked tired and old, whereas whenever she had met her before, at coffee or in Tesco's, she had always envied her for looking so much younger than she imagined her years to be. I'm responsible for all this, she thought.

'It's so good of you to come, Mrs Fisk.'

'Please, not Mrs Fisk, Jane.'

Michaela nodded. 'It means a lot to have someone with you. You feel so alone sitting here.'

Jane hardly knew what to say. 'Has she any relatives who should be told?'

Michaela shook her head. 'Not close ones; no one I feel she would want to be alerted, unless of course . . . ' The stout-hearted Michaela suddenly burst into tears, apologised and mopped her eyes. 'Sorry, I'm being so damned ridiculous,' she said at last. 'But I didn't know she was so got down, upset . . . '

'What about?' Jane almost prayed that there was some other cause – a friend's death, anything.

'Oh, I don't suppose it matters now, my telling you.' Michaela wiped her eyes again. 'We had this beastly letter saying we were . . . you know, lesbians. I didn't care. It's not anybody's business. I don't mind what people think, they can think what they like.'

Jane put out her hand; it hovered above Michaela's hand, then she took it away. She felt like Judas. They waited in silence for about ten more minutes, maybe more, then a nurse came out through the frosted glass doors and approached.

She looked uncertainly at Michaela then at Jane. Michaela stood up. 'Is my friend . . . ?' she asked.

The nurse smiled reassuringly. 'She has been taken up to the ward. She is conscious. You may go up and see her, but only one of you and only for a few minutes. Julie will show you where to go.' She gestured towards the very young girl in a striped uniform behind her who also gave a rather reassuring, switched-on smile.

Julie led Michaela to the lift. They got in, the girl standing behind her, occasionally looking sideways at her, under long lashes.

'Are you a nurse?' Michaela asked, not out of real curiosity but the silence was oppressive.

The girl shook her head. 'Not yet,' she said and as she said it the lift doors silently slid open and they emerged into a white corridor. 'This way.'

Michaela followed the girl for some way down the shiny silent floor, then turned right into a ward marked 'Eastern Ward'. There were only six beds, three each side. All were apparently occupied, judging by the things on the lockers beside them – flowers, Lucozade, glasses, water jugs – but the little ward was empty of patients. Only one bed had curtains drawn around it. Julie swept back the curtain and there was Dorothy.

She was propped up in bed, the sheet neatly folded across her. Her face was pale, her mouth looked slightly puffy. She began to weep the moment she saw Michaela.

'Oh, they did this awful . . . they put this thing down my . . . It was a stomach wash-out. It was awful, Michaela,' she wailed. 'Awful! It was so humiliating, they –'

Michaela cut her off, interrupting her almost brusquely. She felt an emotion that was so mixed up she hardly knew how to handle it – pity mixed with irritation. 'Well, you took the aspirin. What did you do that for?'

She sat down on the stool drawn out from under the bed and put out a consoling hand to take Dorothy's, but she drew it away quickly. Oh God, thought Michaela, she's still thinking of the lesbian bit. That bloody letter. I could kill whoever wrote it!

She was only there for a few minutes and said little to Dorothy, and the little she did say received no answer at all – her friend just turned her head away.

The nurse came in. 'I think your friend should rest now.'

Michaela turned to the nurse; she felt completely at a loss. 'Oh yes, of course.' She did not attempt to take Dorothy's hand or even try to touch her again, but left the room.

'She'll be OK – probably see the psychiatrist tomorrow. Then she'll be able to come home, I expect.'

Michaela repeated, 'Oh yes. Of course,' and followed the nurse back to the waiting-room.

Jane stood up. 'How is she?' she asked.

Michaela shook her head. 'She looks pretty awful and hardly said anything to me. Wouldn't even let me take her hand, but I suppose she's all right.' She shrugged. 'I don't know how all this will turn out. We had such a happy relationship . . . Not now!'

Jane took her arm. 'Well, let's get back. You can do nothing more here tonight.'

They drove home, locked in their own thoughts. At the gate of Hawthorne Cottage Michaela turned to Jane. 'Who could have done this? What kind of people write these letters? What pleasure . . . what kind of kick do they get out of it?'

'Someone with troubles of their own, I expect,' Jane replied very softly.

Michaela pulled down the handle of the car door. 'But how would it relieve them, or make them feel better, to make someone else miserable?'

Jane sat for a moment saying nothing, then she turned to Michaela. 'I suppose,' she said, 'people who feel impelled to write these letters to hurt or even destroy are hurting so much themselves they lash out.'

Michaela did not reply for a long time. 'It's gossip,' she said eventually 'gossip, malicious gossip, that's what I believe causes poison pen letters.'

'You may be right.'

Michaela opened the car door. 'Thank you again, Jane. Thank you so much.'

Jane put the car into gear, watched Michaela walk up the garden path and open her front door. Then she drove back to her own house and put the car away. In the kitchen the note was still on the table under the mug where she had left it . . .

Jane sat down at the kitchen table. She felt unutterably tired and as if she had fought and lost a long, long battle. Dorothy – Dorothy was ill in hospital and it lay heavily on her conscience.

In three days' time she would be seventy years old. She seemed to be seeing herself, coming to terms with herself for the first time.

How long had she fought off the idea that her son would never marry; that she would never have grandchildren? How much was it her fault? Why had she pushed away, disliked every girl he had met at school, at college? What was it in her that wanted him to stay with her, be her child, her boy, safe by her side? Was it, she wondered, a reaction to her husband's brutality? She shook her head. No – not that. It was no use trying to blame it on her husband; it was all her. When would the rumours, the gossip she had herself heard at Carmen's leak like a flood, a torrent, and engulf her son – drive him out of the profession that he loved and she was so proud of? She hurt as if she was wounded.

The small piece of paper under the mug on the table in front of her was symbolic she thought. Something held down, captive. Probably the way Nigel felt – the way he must have felt, perhaps acutely, for so long, knowing that the feelings he had were so strong that one day they would break through his self-built wall of restraint and he would be caught caressing some young boy, at school perhaps or in some public lavatory. God forbid that was how he felt!

Jane felt tears running down her cheeks, although she was not conscious that she was crying. She reproached herself for thinking of her own suffering, her own apprehensions – how about his? She put her hand out and pushed the mug aside. The slip of paper stirred a little in the draught from the door, slid across the table and fell to the floor.

This was not the first time that Nigel had not come home for the evening meal with her. Perhaps he had telephoned whilst she was at the hospital? Where was he now, who was he with? Jane got up, picked up the piece of paper from the floor, screwed it up and threw it in the bin. Was he with Jeremy? Was he still at the school? Would he come home at all, ever again? And was it all because of her?

Writing these letters had been a stupid, irrational action, triggered by anger, fear, jealousy; by a wish to deny something she had known or half known but which would one day burst out and prove the gossips right.

She had sat at the table for so long that she had grown cold; as she got up her limbs were stiff. She felt empty and old. The kitchen clock, its second hand ticking round, was the only sound in the house. It read ten to nine. She made coffee – she

48

wanted nothing to eat. She went into the sitting-room, switched on the television and watched the news, forgetting it by the time she had reached the end. She switched the television off, put down the empty coffee cup and shook herself. 'Positive thinking,' she said aloud. 'Positive thinking.' Whatever Nigel did, however he behaved, she loved him. She was all he had; he was all she had, her son, no matter if he was . . . different. Together they would hide the fact for as long as they possibly could.

6

It was the day that Nigel Fisk, successful teacher and headmaster, recognised that, when the fates take over, there is little one can do. His carefully laid plans, successful enterprises, controlled actions, were swept away by a tide of events which made that control no longer possible, no longer even desirable. By the end of that day he felt he was destroyed or perhaps reborn. He could not, no matter how he tried, decide whether he was at last released or forever imprisoned.

It started at assembly. The morning had, up till then, been as usual. He had got up, shaved, bathed, frowned at his reflection in the mirror, noted for the hundredth time that his hair was receding, making his forehead look higher, making him look older. Downstairs he had eaten breakfast – cereal, cold milk, tomatoes on toast (not his favourite, but his mother watched his cholesterol intake – bacon on Wednesdays, vegetarian sausages on Thursdays, tomatoes on toast on Fridays). He was grateful for all the care she took – the decaffeinated coffee, the carefully aired clothes, the beautifully ironed shirts, fresh and clean every morning. For Sunday breakfast she relaxed, bacon and egg. This morning, as he had finished his second cup of coffee, he had glanced through the *Telegraph*, folded it neatly ready to take to school with him; his mother favoured the *Daily Mail*, so they had a paper each. They discussed briefly the documentary he wanted to see that night. His mother would mark it in the *Radio Times*, he knew, so it would be remembered. They would watch it together. He paused there in his thoughts.

No, he wouldn't go out, he had gone out several times lately – he would have a drink at home. He and his mother often enjoyed a gin and tonic together. Their routine was as inevitable as death, yet until now he had determinedly not found it oppressive – not until he met Jeremy. Jeremy with the long-lashed blue eyes, the caressable smooth skin, who trailed danger for Nigel like a drag hunt.

As he had walked into the hall for assembly, the chattering had died away. He mounted the dais at the end of the hall, smelled the familiar smells of perspiration, unwashed socks, feet, peppermints, chalk, the fustiness of clothes worn too long and washed too little. The girls always looked cleaner, brighter, than the boys, the girls who giggled more, fidgeted more, used perfume strong and musky – the older taller girls already trying to attract capture. A few countries were represented in the small Island school, not as many as in the mainland schools, but here and there a small Asian face looked up at him, skin pale, pale gold. He started the usual prayer and then he saw him . . .

Nigel had difficulty in continuing the hackneyed assembly prayer. He knew he paused – hesitated. It was Robert Benson. Two rows back he was clearly visible. The spring sun shining through the window lit his fair hair like a halo; beneath it the rather babyish face was bruised, the eye and cheekbone were discoloured, and across one eyebrow was a gash about an inch and a half long. Nigel felt a stab of pain in his chest, a strange pain, a spasm. A boy in front of Robert Benson suddenly moved and hid him from Nigel's view. He hesitated again. The sports master moved closer to him – he had a short announcement to make about the games session and wanted to be near the centre when Nigel finished. He was thick-set and tall, his hair – Nigel always thought, too long, too unkempt – fell over his forehead in an untidy fringe. He took out a piece of paper from his jacket pocket, looked at it and at Nigel. 'You all right, Mr Fisk?' he asked.

Nigel turned to him. He wanted to say 'Perfectly', but he had to clear his throat before he could speak, then he managed it. 'Perfectly all right, thank you,' he said and moved away from the lectern to make way for the PE teacher. His eyes searched for the fair-haired boy, but he was still hidden by the boys in front of him.

Back in his office Nigel sat down at his desk. He picked up his pen and tried to stop the shaking of his hand. He closed his eyes for a moment, but the fair-haired boy's face and Jeremy's blue eyes seemed to superimpose on each other. He opened his eyes to try and clear the vision. He felt terribly afraid – afraid of his own feelings and afraid of what he was about to do. He picked up the telephone and asked for Robert Benson to be sent to his office.

As he replaced the receiver Nigel was conscious of a strong, strange premonition of danger. He closed his eyes. He felt as if he had pushed a snowball from the top of the hill. Behind his closed lids he watched, visualising it rolling away from him, gathering snow and rocks as it bounced and rolled down the deep descent, getting bigger and bigger, ready to crush, kill and demolish all before it, all that got in its path. It was like a waking nightmare, over in seconds; he opened his eyes before he had time to see the great object crash to the bottom of the hill. The vision, dream or whatever the illusion was, had been so real. Nigel hardly dared blink in case the picture came back to him. He fixed his eyes on a vase of bluebells on his desk; he had not noticed them when he had entered his office. His secretary, a middle-aged rather bossy woman, was always putting flowers on his desk, usually wild flowers. Sometimes she would draw his attention to them, telling him the Latin name. She was quite a botanist. But the bluebells brought new thoughts, they were the exact colour of Jeremy's eyes. He picked up his pen and found his hand was still shaking.

There was a light tap on the door. 'Come,' he said. The boy stood at the half-open door, his hands still clutching the door knob. 'Well, come in, Benson. Close the door after you.'

The boy came forward, turning to close the door carefully behind him, then walked slowly across the space and stood opposite Nigel. He looked apprehensive as the pupils did when sent for by the head, expecting a ticking off. Nigel surveyed the boy, hesitating before he spoke, taking in the sullen look, the almost pouting moist red lips, the curly hair, looking darker without the sun from the assembly hall window lighting it up.

'I never did the lavatory window, sir – it was just the cricket ball, it . . .'

The speech surprised Nigel. He held up his hand, dismissing the broken lavatory window with a waving motion. 'No, it's your face. How did you get that black eye? Were you hit in the playground?'

Robert shook his head. 'I – I fell down, sir,' he said, those red lips setting in a straight obstinate line.

'Oh, I see. Or walked into a door perhaps, Benson? Tell me the truth.'

The boy shuffled his feet, the dirty trainers making a soft rustling noise on the floor. 'It was me dad. He said I had been snivelling to people about not getting enough to eat and being left alone.' He paused. 'Stuff like that, sir.'

'And had you – not been getting enough to eat?'

The boy showed a little more animation. 'Well, sir, no, sir, it was . . . it was this.' He pulled a piece of paper from his pocket and thrust it at Nigel.

'Who sent this?' Nigel read the neatly typed message, noted the grease marks.

'They were having bacon and eggs, a fry-up, and I came down to see if I could have some and he hit me.' He began to cry, rubbed his eyes. Nigel came round the desk and handed him his clean morning handkerchief. The boy took it, but did not unfold it, just rubbed his nose and eyes, then handed the folded square back. 'No, keep it.' Nigel shook the white square open and handed it back to the boy.

Robert Benson looked up at Nigel. 'It was all right, sir.' He sniffed and used the handkerchief again. 'Mum brought me up a bacon butty. He's like that, Dad, he hits out. Mum gets it sometimes, but she hits him back.' He smiled.

The smile was too much for Nigel – he put his arm round the boy's shoulders. Robert wiped his eyes again with the handkerchief. Nigel's arm slipped down to the thin waist, then lower. He felt the firm, round, warm buttock – was aware and terrified of his own excitement. There was a knock on the door and it opened.

Hewitt, the deputy head, stood rather as the boy had, half in, half out of the door, still holding the door handle. He peered at them through his thick lenses, murmured a faint 'Excuse me, headmaster, but a slight problem needs to be brought to your attention.'

Nigel released the boy. 'Wait outside, Robert, I'll call the school nurse.'

Robert edged past the deputy head who drew back to let the boy pass, then entered the room, pushing the door shut behind him, clutching in his hand a large sheet of paper, which Nigel recognised as the rota – a problem with that was always a problem indeed. He thought that if Hewitt had leapt to any conclusion, or even taken in the scene he had just witnessed, he gave no sign of it.

'What is it?' Nigel went round to his desk chair and sat down. He felt curiously calm and resigned. Before Hewitt spoke, his thoughts were clear. Well, if the man had deduced anything . . . so be it.

It soon became obvious that the deputy head had hardly noticed who the boy was. In fact the problem was a small one: the history master had an attack of migraine. Usually if he took an hour or so, lay down in a darkened room in the sick bay, took pills supplied by the school nurse, he was able to return to his class only missing one session. This settled, Nigel telephoned the nurse to let her know the migraine sufferer would be up shortly and would she please come down to his office to see a boy with an injury. Hewitt left.

Nigel sat looking at the bluebells, seeing only their blueness. He had always imagined that decisions were taken after much thought – at least in his case. He had always been cautious, took after his mother; she was always sensible, rational. Now he knew he had taken a decision because of the bluebells, because of a child with a cut eye. He knew he had at last allowed himself to be himself, refused to hide any more. 'Out of the closet,' he said aloud.

The school nurse came in; she looked at him rather accusingly. 'I did knock, headmaster,' she said, pushing up her glasses. Her face was fresh and young, her hair cut short; it shone with health, its curls dark copper. 'Is that the boy outside with the black eye?'

'Yes, see what you think. Bring him in.'

Young Benson had stopped crying, though he still held the white handkerchief in his hand. The nurse took the boy's arm. 'What's this? Been fighting?' Robert shook his head and looked at Nigel as the nurse led him over to the window to get a better view of the injuries. 'Well, it looks as if it's on the mend now, but maybe I ought to take him to Casualty just in case.' Nigel nodded, got up and again put an arm round the young shoulders and gave the boy a little squeeze, then put a hand up and stroked the fair hair from the white forehead. It didn't matter any more. The school nurse, however, obviously thought the gesture caring and natural. She gave him a warmer than usual smile and the two left the room.

There were many things Nigel should be doing. His desk was

neatly arranged by the lady of the bluebells, his secretary: letters to be answered, parents to be advised, the agenda for the next governors' meeting to be checked. The PE master was leaving; some applications for the post needed to be assessed, but Nigel could do nothing. He felt as if the world outside was for the moment nothing whatever to do with him. He had a feeling, too, that he was approaching something fearful yet thrilling. He got up and stood by the window. Boys and girls were pouring out into the large square for break. The square was surrounded by a low wall, out of which sprouted symmetrical rows of black railings. Through them he could see cars passing, people walking by, women carrying plastic bags, a man with a briefcase, another with a dog. What were they all? Salesmen, bank clerks, a double glazing salesman, perhaps? All the things a man could be without worrying that women meant nothing to him, men everything . . .

Some boys, yobs already, pushed and yelled, kicked and shoved, making other boys' lives a misery. Girls huddled together, some smooth-haired, some frizzy-permed, some red, some gold, some dark, some foreign – the scene was so familiar but Nigel felt that in some way he was seeing it for the first and then again perhaps for the last time. The quiet ones . . . a boy stood near his window leaning on a buttress of red brick, isolated from the crowd, white-faced, thin, his eyes vacant, watching nothing. A ball, kicked hard, hit the wall near him. He didn't stir, appeared not to notice. What was he thinking? Why was he so withdrawn, so still?

Nigel felt more aware, more sensitive to his surroundings, than he had ever felt before. Nearly forty years old, twenty-five years of knowing, suppressing, denying. It was over now. What would he do if his job had to be sacrificed? He enjoyed it, but he supposed something must give.

Resolutions made that day trailed about him like an aura. His colleagues, the pupils, the dinner ladies, but most of all his secretary, noticed and were conscious of his abstracted yet exhilarated manner. One of the dinner ladies summed it up to anyone who would listen. 'He's in love, mark my words. He'll be getting married – engaged. I don't know who she is, but . . .'

Nigel heard his secretary answering a question as he passed the staff room. She did so in a rather lofty manner, as one who knows but certainly is not going to tell. 'It's not my business to gossip,' he heard her say, and he smiled as he passed. If only he could tell them he was in love with eyes as blue as a summer sky and as dangerous as fire.

His plans and resolutions, though formed quickly, were firm. He must move, find a flat, a small house in or near Newport – something to offer Jeremy, if it was to be Jeremy, if Jeremy would . . . He must tell Ma; how would she take it? He could almost hear her say, 'But why, Nigel? Aren't you comfortable here?' He tried during the day to dream up explanations for her. 'I wish to be alone' – that was hurtful. He wished to entertain his friends more – stupid, his mother knew how few friends he had. His mother's life and his own were so intertwined in routine and in knowledge of each other's actions, so intimate. If she couldn't sleep she was in the habit of going downstairs and making herself a cup of coffee and bringing it back upstairs to bed. Her actions, though quiet, always wakened him and the conversations in the morning would always be the same. 'Did you have a bad night, Mother?' 'Oh, did I disturb you? Sorry, dear.' 'Oh, it's not that, Ma, I heard you and I just wondered.' 'Yes, I couldn't sleep, so I came down and made coffee.' Always, always the same. 'Would you like pork this weekend, dear, or shall I cook a chicken?' He never chose, he was not particularly interested in food. 'Well, I'll get a chicken then . . .' or pork . . . or beef . . . or turkey . . . or duck . . . Good God, how had he stood it all these years? He felt ashamed of that thought; he had stood it for there had been no point in moving – no one to go to, no one to love.

The day passed and he was thankful when it had ended. He put his letters ready for his secretary to post – that was usually his last task of the day, except for locking the drawers of his desk and closing his office window; even though there was a caretaker he always took that job on himself. As he did so he wondered how he would get in touch with Jeremy. Go to the Dragon this evening? He needn't have worried. As he rounded the corner of the school to the car-park, he saw his red Peugeot, freshly cleaned by the janitor for the sum of ten pounds and done once a week, shining in the sunlight. Beside it, his hand resting on the handle of the passenger door, was Jeremy.

'I thought you'd never come, Nigel dear. Those awful brats stampeded out ages ago.'

Nigel stood looking at him; his heart was pounding, he could hardly speak. Jeremy went on, drumming his white fingers on the car bonnet, 'The Brigadier threw me out – got some letter about me or something. I'm sick of Nigel. I felt like a new Nigel.' He smiled and Nigel found the smile sweet.

The 'new Nigel' unlocked the car door. Once inside he leant across and unlocked the passenger door. Jeremy had a way, Nigel noticed, of curling his legs and curving his back as he got into the car, rather like a cat. It was a graceful movement, neat. His eyes met Nigel's and they were full of amusement. 'Am I in order, New Nigel, getting aboard?'

Nigel started the engine. 'Yes, you're in order, Jeremy.' He drew out of the parking place. 'Where are you staying?'

'Nigel gave me some money. I've booked in at Anchor House outside Newport – for a couple of nights anyway. As to the future, I rely on the fates, New Nigel,' he said, smiling again, and he put out a hand and covered Nigel's on the steering wheel.

They drove to Newport, Jeremy directing Nigel through unfamiliar streets. Anchor House was more a boarding house than a hotel. The sign outside read 'Anchor House Guest House. Rooms en suite.' Inside there was a small reception area which had once been the hall of the house. This was divided by a hardboard partition and a counter, on which was a press bell and an open book, presumably for registration. There was no one behind the makeshift desk. They went up the carpeted stairs. As Nigel followed Jeremy nothing was said – no communication of any kind took place between the two men until Jeremy put his key in the keyhole of the white-painted door. Then he turned to Nigel. For a moment his blue eyes were serious, his mouth unsmiling. 'OK. You want this, New Nigel?'

There was a second's hesitation. Through his head went the words, 'I can walk out of this situation now, at this moment, but I have walked out of it for twenty-five years and I can't any more.' He followed Jeremy into the neat single-bedded room and the door closed behind them.

Jane Fisk wakened early. She opened her eyes and looked at her little bedside clock: twenty past six. She had had three hours' or less sleep. Nigel had come in at about 2 a.m. Why did she say 'about'? The luminous hands of her clock had read ten past two.

She could not sleep again now. She couldn't cuddle down as she usually did at an early morning waking and go to sleep again until eight. She got out of bed quietly and went to the bathroom.

The sight of herself in the rather harsh light of the strip lighting bewildered her. She prided herself that her seventy years sat easily on her. She walked well, back straight, used a little make-up (foundation, a blusher, lipstick, a trace of eyeshadow); she used glasses for reading and driving. This morning the woman in the mirror looked grey and lined. She filled the handbasin with warm water and held the face flannel to her face, covering it, standing like that until the flannel cooled on her face. Then she looked again into the mirror, took off her hairnet; she was proud of her white hair, never missed her weekly hair appointment – shampoo, conditioner and set. This morning the restless night had not improved yesterday's set, but surely the lines under her eyes were new; her mouth looked blurred, too.

She cleaned her teeth, finished washing, then went back to her bedroom. Saturday morning was – or had always been – a pleasant, relaxed morning; no school for Nigel. Sometimes he brought work home with him, but that could be done at any time over the weekend. He usually went for a walk on Saturday morning or played golf, though he had never seemed to be keen on the golf club – but then he had never been a mixer, even as a child. She finished trying to repair her face and hair. The sun was shining now, a fine spring day. She went back into the bedroom, folded back her bedclothes, put on her watch and some pearl ear-rings. She picked one of her smarter dresses. She knew that this morning there would be a confrontation between them, between Nigel and herself, but she was determined to be relaxed, understanding, not surprised – even acting as if she was expecting whatever he was going to say. On the other hand, perhaps he would say nothing, perhaps he would decide to tell her nothing – although she doubted it. She put on a spot of perfume, just on her wrists, and wondered at herself for doing such a thing, then realised she wanted to convince herself that she was a woman poised and in charge of herself, perfectly capable of living alone, if that was what he wanted, and of living her own life.

She went downstairs and put the kettle on. It was now eight o'clock. Her thoughts were a little more chaotic. If he intended to move away what would she say? If he wanted her to move – no, she felt he would not do that. She would miss him of course, but . . . As she laid the breakfast table she began to wonder if she was assuming too much. Just supposing it was Jeremy that he was going to live with – or could it be someone else, a woman even?

She interrupted her thoughts and picked up the telephone. Michaela answered. 'No, it's not too early, I haven't slept anyway. I haven't rung the hospital yet, I thought I'd wait until later.'

'Let me know,' Jane said before she put down the receiver. She went back into the kitchen, took out the bacon and two eggs from the fridge, bent down to the cupboard to take out the frying pan. She was about to run a little oil into the pan when Nigel interrupted her: he must have got up early as well, as he was shaved and dressed.

They stood facing each other, both silent. Jane felt as if she was seeing her son after a long absence. He looked pale. She noticed for the first time – or was it the first time? – how his hair was receding and there were tiny flecks of grey over his ears. His eyes looked set deeper into his head, dark shadows under them. She felt a look of concern coming over her face and then tried to banish it with a smile. He had on his usual relaxed Saturday clothes and yet he looked tense and uncomfortable.

After what seemed minutes, but was probably only seconds, he spoke. 'No breakfast thanks, Ma, just coffee.' The smell of the percolating coffee filled the room. 'Smells good,' he said and sat down on a chair at the kitchen table.

Usually he fetched the papers from the hall, but this morning, no.

'Just a boiled egg and toast, dear?' Jane suggested.

He only shook his head, then was silent. She poured two cups of coffee and put one in front of him and beside it the milk – she always kept the top of the milk for his coffee – and some sugar.

'I hope I didn't disturb you, I was late in, Ma.' He stirred the coffee round and round and did not look up.

'No, I wasn't asleep.'

'I was with Jeremy, Ma – the Brigadier threw him out. He had had some anonymous letter . . .' Jane felt her heart give a lurch – her letter again. More was to come. 'I had a day of it,' Nigel went on. 'Anonymous letters seem to be in vogue. Robert's father, Benson – he hit the boy because some ill-advised fool had sent him a letter saying he was mistreating his son, not feeding him, or something – so of course he hit the boy, blamed him. I had to send Robert to hospital.'

'Why Jeremy, how . . . ?' Jane asked hesitatingly as if she was probing into his business and it was nothing to do with her.

'Then Jeremy was waiting for me outside the school. When I came out, I . . . There he was.'

This did shake Jane. 'Good God, Nigel, do you realise what this could do to your . . . That notorious young freak?'

It was the wrong word and she regretted it the moment it was out. 'He's no freak, Ma, unless you call me one, too – I . . . I seem to be very fond of him.' He put his head in his hands and suddenly broke down. 'It's been so long, Ma – so long.'

Jane broke down, too. She came round the table and cradled her son's head in her hands and pressed it against her. 'I shouldn't have said that, darling. I shouldn't have said that.' She held Nigel tightly in her arms, then let him go and looked down at his face. Perhaps she had never, she thought, felt closer to anyone than at that moment. His eyes, grey like hers, looking into hers. She had worked so hard, so hard to get him where he was. He had responded to her urging, of course, but he had done it. Headmaster – wasn't that worth hanging on to? What about that proud position now?

At last she reheated the coffee, made more and they sat and talked. Where would he live? Somewhere outside Newport – rent a house or flat for Jeremy and himself? Keep the relationship secret? When Jane said that, Nigel shrugged his shoulders. 'Well, Ma, if I can I will. I'm not ashamed of it, it's my business and Jeremy's.'

Jane gazed into the distance, almost talking to herself. 'We need a screen, dear,' she said, but did not enlarge on the remark. She was for some strange reason beginning to feel younger again, purposeful. He, her son, needed her now – more, probably, than he had ever done before. A plot began to form in her mind vaguely – hardly a plot at all, just a suggestion of a plot. 'What, dear?' She had missed that last remark her son had made.

'Will you mind living alone, Ma, here?'

She shook her head. 'No,' she said. Though she sounded positive, inside she was not quite as sure, but she knew that keeping what her son was doing . . . her plot would help pass the time. When she had made it concrete she knew she would have quite a bit to do.

After Nigel had left she sat thinking. She had a son who was now a self-confessed homosexual; many mothers, she was sure, had the same problem, but not many had a son who was also a headmaster. That he was safe with and among young boys had surely been proved, nearly a quarter of a century of proof. Then the gossip – that must be stilled. She didn't regret any of the letters she had written to Hugh Ainsworth and Mr Benson, Dorothy and Michaela – well, perhaps that one had caused more ripples on the waters than she had intended, but – she smiled to herself – any ripples, in the village at least, would give the gossips something else to think about and now she herself would give them further food for thought. She got up, collected the coffee cups and washed them up. Nigel had not said if he would be back for lunch, but that no longer mattered. She could prepare a lunch for him if he came back; if not, it would not be necessary to do so, only to prepare one for herself. The sooner she got used to that, well, maybe the better. Meanwhile she would go out and call on Hawthorne Cottage to ask if Michaela had telephoned the hospital and to find out how Dorothy was.

As she walked down the road towards the cottage Jane was conscious more and more of how her life was going to change; that she would at last not be a mother, devoted to serving her son, waiting for Nigel to come home, preparing his meals, doing his laundry, ironing his shirts, seeing that his room was neat, the bed changed – the house warm just for him. A thousand and one things that had made her life busy on his account. Was this so terrible? Now she could be herself at last; maybe go to the painting classes at Newport that she had thought about, but Nigel had come first. Now it would be her life. The fact that he would be dependent on someone else was not as horrifying as she had imagined it would be. When he had clung to her that morning and she had hugged him to her, as she had when he was a child, her feeling had surprised her. She was sorry – sorry for his suffering, but not overwhelmed by it. He was on his own now; she was on her own. She felt – she searched for a word – emancipated.

As she walked up the path of Hawthorne Cottage to the front door Mrs Thornton passed. She waved and smiled. She would have to see more of Mrs Thornton – she seemed a nice woman and she had been in hospital recently and had something or other done, she wasn't sure what.

Michaela greeted her. 'How nice of you to come, Jane,' she said. 'Not much news of Dorothy yet. I'm to ring again at twelve. Do come in.'

Jane went in and sat down.

'I'm making coffee with a dash. Yep – a good dollop of whisky. I feel I need it. Will you have one too?'

Jane was about to say no, then changed her mind. 'Never tried that,' she said.

Michaela went off to the kitchen and soon returned. The coffee was hot. The whisky made it smell fragrant and spicy. Jane sipped it. 'Delicious,' she said. 'I didn't know I liked whisky.'

Michaela laughed. 'Good. Glad you like it, it's a great pick-me-up.'

Jane was for a moment quiet, then it seemed something clicked in her head and the plot – till now hazy – formed sharper outlines. 'I need this, too,' she said. 'My son Nigel has just told me that he is moving in with a girlfriend.' Michaela's look of astonishment pleased Jane and she chose to misinterpret the surprise. 'Well, it seems to be the thing now, doesn't it? What can I say? He's old enough to know his own mind, and marriage these days, well . . . I believe the girlfriend is over thirty.'

She had nearly finished her coffee. Michaela still looked surprised. 'You'll be all alone, then?' she said.

'Yes, I'll be all alone.' Jane drained the cup.

'You driving, Jane?'

Jane shook her head. 'No, I walked here.'

'Let's have another?' Michaela took the cup from her visitor's unprotesting hand and went out of the room. Jane leaned back in the comfortable chair; the whisky had warmed her. The plot had started. How long it would last, and whether her son was man enough to help her keep it up, was all in the lap of the gods. 'I shouldn't,' she said as she took the second steaming cup of coffee from Michaela's hand.

7

Philippa Ainsworth was going to see Dr Barnes professionally. She had at first had difficulty thinking up a reason, but now she had one prepared. As she made up her face sitting in front of her dressing-table she felt vaguely excited – after all the letter had said . . . She wanted badly to see Dr Barnes – Eric. She wanted to see Eric's reaction to her entering his surgery. She knew, and presumably he knew, that there had never been as much as a glance between them, but whoever had written the letter must have thought . . . well, that there was something going on between them. He might have mentioned casually, or maybe not so casually, that he thought she was attractive; or in church had been seen to be looking at her with more than usual interest, even admiration . . . She threw her lipstick back into the box – it wasn't the right colour to go with her new smart red jacket. She tried another; better but not quite right. When she had bought the coat she should have got a lipstick to go with it. She drew her lips carefully, making the lower one a little fuller than it really was, then blotted her mouth with a tissue – it wouldn't do to put on too much, too thickly.

Silly time to have an appointment and dress up – nine thirty – but it was all she had been able to get. Her plan was to ask Dr Barnes if it would be a good idea to have a flu injection to prevent – she was going to say – her innumerable colds. Spring was not the time to get the injection, but it was a good excuse. After all, she didn't want to consult him about her menopausal symptoms – that would put him right off. Thank God, Hugh had been called out early to the hospital, not a usual occasion, but perhaps fate was with her.

Philippa was not at all sure why she was making this visit to the doctor – nor was she really sure why she was trying to make herself look so smart at nine thirty in the morning. Did she want an affair? She wasn't at all sure she could handle an affair if she got involved in one. She tweaked her hair into a more girlish appearance round her forehead and temples. She had been to the hairdresser the day before and had worn a net during the night. Her hair looked stiff and lacquered. She used a hairbrush and tried to make the style look less severe. She noticed that there were curves – she didn't want to say lines – at the corners of her lips that made her look older. Dissatisfied, she turned the corners of her mouth up in a slight smile, preparing for her entrance into the surgery; then, quite suddenly, she wished she wasn't going at all.

When she arrived at the health centre she felt better. The receptionist knew her slightly and greeted her warmly. 'Good morning, Mrs Ainsworth. You won't have long to wait. What a lovely colour your coat is. I love red.' The girl smiled; Philippa smiled back and went and sat down. Her short black skirt rode up slightly as she sat on the plastic chair. She saw an elderly man look at her legs. She pretended not to notice, crossed her legs and pulled down the skirt – she felt pleased, she had good legs, slim ankles, and the light stockings and new black patent leather shoes with the small flat bows on the instep looked pretty.

'Mrs Ainsworth, Room 4.' She almost jumped as her name was called – twenty to ten, she hadn't had to wait long. She began to feel her heart go faster as she pushed open the white door marked 'Room 4'.

Eric Barnes looked up as she entered, then stood and held out his hand. 'Mrs Ainsworth.' He shook her hand and his hand was warm and firm. 'Do sit down.' He gave her a little time to settle in her chair and put down her handbag. 'What seems to be the trouble?'

Philippa looked at him – this was the man with whom someone had said she was having an affair. For a moment she found speaking difficult. He was so different from Hugh; her husband was a bigger man, heavier in both appearance and manner. Did she love Hugh? As she sat there opposite the doctor she tried hard to make herself speak. Dr Barnes asked again, quietly and without impatience, 'What is troubling you, Mrs Ainsworth?'

'Oh nothing really, Dr Barnes, it's just these colds. I keep getting colds and I wondered if I had the flu jab do you think it would help?' She searched for a word. '. . . Ward them off, I mean?'

Dr Barnes relaxed back in his swivel chair and rotated slowly from side to side. 'I hardly think so, Mrs Ainsworth. It's in October or November you need –'

She interrupted him. 'Oh yes, yes, I know. I only thought . . .'

He drew his prescription pad towards him, then pressed a button on the computer beside him. 'I see you're registered with us, but you don't often come and see us.' He smiled and Philippa thought his smile was the most charming she had ever seen.

'No, no, I'm very healthy. It's just these colds.'

'Have you a cough?' Dr Barnes started writing on a pad in front of him.

'Oh no – well, only just after a cold for a little while.'

'Do you smoke, Mrs Ainsworth?'

She shook her head. 'Oh no, never.'

'And otherwise your health is good – no other problems?'

She nodded again. He got up, took a sphygmomanometer from the desk beside him. He was close to her now, bending over her, the stethoscope pressed into the vein in her arm. He pumped air into the apparatus and it tightened a little. A little whisper of air sounded as he watched the dial. 'A tiny rise in your blood pressure, nothing to be worried about.' As he moved away she was conscious of a slight smell of Tabasco – mixed in with the faint tobaccoey smell was an expensive aftershave. She wondered if he had noticed her perfume.

'Well, for the cold some vitamin C tablets might help.' He tapped the keys of his computer; the taps were curiously dry and lifeless, not like the familiar typewriter that Hugh used. 'There, take those, twice a day.'

She felt that any interest he might have felt on her entry had faded away. He handed her the prescription. 'Thank you.' She took the paper, folded it and put it into her handbag.

He turned nearer to the screen at the side of his desk. 'Oh, I must just confirm your date of birth, Mrs Ainsworth,' he said.

'Nineteen forty,' she said; if only he would make some remark, some reassuring remark like 'Well, you certainly don't look your age' – anything that would make her feel she was different, she interested him. She almost wished there was something wrong so that he would say, 'I'll see you again next week,' – or next month, or any time . . . But no, that smile again, then 'Come back if you need to, Mrs Ainsworth,' and she was dismissed.

Outside she screwed up the prescription and threw it in the gutter. She must hurry home – she had asked several people in for coffee. She regretted it now . . . perhaps she had thought that after her visit to the doctor, her supposed lover, she might have something to hint to them – just a hint. She had hoped that he would make some slight – very slight – pass so that she could say . . . but there had been nothing; no long intimate glance, no touch where perhaps no touch was needed, nothing! She looked at her watch, ten past ten. She would get biscuits at the shop in the village, she remembered that she had looked in the cupboard and seen that she was out of biscuits. She hurried to her car, got in and for a moment could not start the engine; there were tears in her eyes and it made her sight misty. She took out a handkerchief from her pocket and dabbed them clear. As she did so a whiff of the expensive perfume she had bought herself wafted round the car. Why had someone written that letter, why, why? Was it to hurt her, hurt Hugh? Could it be that in his surgery Eric Barnes couldn't give away the feelings he had for her? Hope came again;

64

perhaps . . . could she persuade her husband to give a small party, a drinks party? Ask Dr Barnes – Eric – and his wife, Nigel Fisk and his mother, Dorothy and Michaela, the Brigadier, perhaps, and his son Nigel, why not? They could just have wine – that wouldn't be too expensive. Perhaps half a bottle of whisky – she somehow couldn't see the Brigadier drinking wine.

Philippa drove home feeling a little better, after stopping at the village store for a packet of chocolate digestive biscuits. Once home she got her best coffee cups and saucers out of the kitchen cupboard, pulled in the trolley from the hall. The names of those she had asked ran through her mind – Carmen, Jane Fisk, Dorothy and Michaela, Mrs Thornton, Margaret Eales, so she needed seven cups and saucers. As she put them out she felt again enveloped by depression. Carmen knew about the letter, so probably the others would by now. Would they mention it? She thought again of Eric Barnes' very good-looking face and his warm firm hand. Yes, she was determined – she would make Hugh give that party and then she would see Eric Barnes again.

Dorothy and Michaela met Jane Fisk at the vicarage gate. It was Dorothy's first coffee morning since her removal to hospital; she had not wanted to come, but Michaela had persuaded her. Dorothy still appeared pale and nervous, but when Jane Fisk looked at her she did not feel any remorse. The whole village knew of Dorothy's 'illness' and while they were talking and speculating about that, Nigel's association with Jeremy and Nigel Dawson might, she hoped, have gone unnoticed. Channel talk elsewhere when you have a crisis near home, wasn't that a good political idea? Jane greeted Philippa Ainsworth with a wide smile.

The three ladies were ushered through into the sitting-room. The weather was sunny but still had a spring coolness about it. Through the french windows the neat, well-kept garden was boasting a few daffodils and one or two rather reluctant-looking bergenias – not, Michaela thought, as good a display as they had at Hawthorne Cottage. She remarked on this when their hostess disappeared into the kitchen.

Dorothy nodded and suddenly turned to Jane. 'I want to thank you, Mrs Fisk, for . . .' She tailed off and Jane broke in quickly, indeed almost brusquely.

'Nothing to thank me for, I just happened to be passing, that's all.'

'Nevertheless . . .' Dorothy tailed off again rather lamely as Philippa came back into the room.

'I've put the coffee on, but we'll give the others a few minutes, shall we?'

'Oh, is someone else coming?' Dorothy looked rather accusingly at Michaela as if she had said that only one or two would be there.

'Yes, Carmen; and I asked Mrs Thornton, she's . . . Well, I expect you know, she has had what my husband calls an "anxious operation", so I thought . . .'

She was interrupted by a ring at the door bell and Carmen and Mrs Thornton came in, followed by a newcomer to the village, Mrs Margaret Eales. There was a moment of silence and taking-off of coats and smiling greetings, then Carmen said, 'Glad to see you out and about again, Dorothy.'

Philippa, ever the tactful vicar's wife, hastily put in a remark to save Dorothy answering. 'And you, Mrs Thornton, you've been in the wars, too, I understand.'

It was not easy to quieten Carmen, though! 'And you, Philippa – I saw you coming out of the health centre this morning. Just a social visit, was it, or something wrong?'

'Social visit? Whatever can you mean, Carmen? When would I ever make a social visit to the health centre?' But it was obvious that the remark had not displeased her. She smiled at Carmen, who smiled back.

She knows about the letter, Jane thought, and she had already noted the smartness, the new look, of Philippa. No remorse needed about that letter, either; she had obviously raised the vicar's wife's morale, but she wondered about the vicar, what had the letter done to him? It was fun stirring, and she felt it would be even when Nigel had gone – life need never be boring.

Once they were all seated, sipping Philippa's excellent coffee, the conversation became as dull as usual – the comparison of prices at Tesco's and the general store in the village, the usual 'Well, of course, the big stores buy in bulk,' 'Even so, I think 10p on a tin of soup is rather a lot,' etc, etc.

Jane Fisk decided to throw in her own, she hoped, more interesting news. 'Well, after all these years I won't have to be buying so much food and thinking so much about meals, I'm

66

afraid.' In answer to their 'Whys' she explained: 'My son's leaving home. He has a girlfriend and they are setting up house together.'

She saw Philippa's very quick look of surprise directed at Carmen and that lady's similar expression. 'Really! When is he going? I didn't know he had a . . .' Margaret Eales, the newcomer, was the only one who looked uninterested.

'Oh yes, he's been going out with this girl for some time. You know how it is nowadays – they decide to set up house together. Marriage seems an old-fashioned idea these days and my son's old enough to know his own mind.'

Carmen finished her coffee and handed her cup to Philippa for a refill, then turned back to Jane. 'Have you met her, the girlfriend? I mean, how old is she, is she nice?'

With the exception of Margaret Eales, even including Dorothy, they all seemed to be hanging on her words.

'Oh, she's over thirty, I should think. Yes, I do like her. She seems a very down-to-earth, sensible young woman. They should get on well together.'

Jane Fisk was really enjoying the expressions of curiosity and surprise on their faces. The questions stopped for the moment, then Carmen, on her third biscuit: 'Is she pretty, your future daughter-in-law, Jane?'

Jane laughed. 'Future daughter-in-law, Carmen? I don't think of her as that. That for me means a marriage.' Quite suddenly Jane saw the girl in her mind's eye – not tall, not short, about five foot four perhaps. Slightly plump, a round un-made-up face, a pretty, generous mouth, blue dark-lashed eyes, hair cut short, light brown, shining, clean – the blue eyes and dark lashes made her look Irish. Perhaps the girl was Irish.

'Jane, more coffee?' Philippa touched her arm and Jane jumped.

'Oh yes, thank you. Your coffee's always delicious.'

Mrs Thornton moved her seat and came and sat beside her. Jane made an effort to drag her mind away from the imagined girl. 'How are you, Mrs Thornton? Quite better for your stay in hospital?'

Mrs Thornton answered in a low voice, 'Yes, thank you. Well, I'm to have radiotherapy at Southampton. I'll stay over there in the hostel – quite a nice place and I believe they're all very kind, but it's worrying, you know.'

Jane nodded. 'I'm sure; but they do wonderful things nowadays, don't they?' It was no use pretending that she didn't know what Mrs Thornton had had done.

'Oh yes, they do, but . . .' The rest was unsaid.

Philippa came back with more coffee. 'Will you mind living alone, Jane?' she asked.

Jane shook her head.

'When will Nigel leave and where will he live? Near the school?'

'I don't know.' Jane felt she really must stem the flow of her own imagination. 'How is the vicar, Philippa?'

'What – oh, Hugh? He's very well – a little worried about the dwindling of his congregation, though.' She looked almost accusingly at her guests. Mrs Thornton dropped her eyes and concentrated on the plate of biscuits, although she did not take one. She looked slightly embarrassed; she and Ted had taken to going to the little chapel . . . After that the conversation became general and Nigel was not mentioned again. Jane saw to that, because she was beginning to be rather afraid of the picture that was forming so firmly in her own mind. She would have to sort out, alone at home, what was truth and what was coming from that apparently very fertile imagination. It would be fun, though, making up the story – making it real – making them wait for the next episode!

Dorothy and Michaela walked home together. Dorothy's spirits seemed to have been improved by the visit. 'There you are, that proves it, doesn't it?' she said suddenly and looked quite animated.

'Proves what?'

'That beastly letter accusing us of being lesbians came from Carmen.'

Michaela was silent for a moment, trying to rationalise her friend's remark. Dorothy went on. 'Yes – just the sort of thing she would do, accusing us of being lesbians, then starting quite a lot of talk about poor Nigel being queer. I've heard it and you've heard it and obviously it was just malicious gossip. He's going to live with a girlfriend.'

Michaela nodded. 'Well, Dorothy, I did say when we got the letter that it was so stupid, so untrue, that we needn't take any notice of it.'

'It's Carmen, that's who sent it! She's the village witch, that woman!'

Michaela demurred slightly, then had to make one admission. 'I've got to say I did see one look pass between Carmen and

Philippa Ainsworth,' and she laughed. 'How ridiculous people can be.'

'It's no laughing matter, poison pen letters can do dreadful things to people – and don't I know it!'

Michaela refrained from taking Dorothy's arm or giving her a reassuring touch; she knew her friend would draw away as if she had been burnt, the letter still on her mind.

'I wonder how many more letters like ours have been sent out and who to – I could strangle Carmen!'

Michaela led the way up the little garden path. 'Oh come on, Dorothy, we don't know it was her!'

'I do!'

Michaela opened the door and Dorothy let out a stifled scream as she saw the long white envelope on the mat inside the door. 'Another one!' she wailed.

Michaela picked it up. 'It's from our accountant, Dorothy; for goodness sake get a grip on yourself.'

'No, it's all very well saying that.' Dorothy ran upstairs.

Michaela sighed and split open the envelope. 'It's only a bloody demand for us to pay some more tax,' she called, but Dorothy's bedroom door had banged and obviously she had not heard Michaela.

Michaela wandered through to the kitchen, thinking, I wonder if it could be Carmen ... She turned to the oven, put two large baking potatoes on the top shelf and banged the door shut with rather unnecessary violence. 'Bugger it!' she said. 'Could it be ... ?' She tried to visualise Carmen's face at the party – yes, it had looked rather shifty, but she always looked like that. Can't imagine her doing it somehow; gossip yes, but not ... She sighed. The potatoes would take about three-quarters of an hour. She called up the stairs, 'Want a sherry? I've put some spuds in the oven.' She didn't wait for a reply. If she doesn't want to come down she can damn well stay up there, she thought; but Dorothy did come down and she accepted the sherry Michaela had poured for her.

She looked thoughtful but not as miserable. She sipped the sherry. 'You know, Michaela, I've come to a conclusion and I feel better for it.' She took a larger gulp of the sherry, looked at her glass and went and refilled it.

'Conclusion?' Michaela held out her glass, too, for a top-up.

'Well, after all those totally malicious rumours spreading about

69

Nigel Fisk, why should I bother about the letter we got? Just as stupid and just as much of a lie.'

'Good on you!' Michaela took a risk, then stepped forward and gave Dorothy a peck on the cheek. She did not recoil or shrink back, as Michaela had been half afraid she still might; she gave Michaela a similar peck and they both laughed and finished their sherry.

Dorothy enjoyed her lunch, but Michaela could see that she was preoccupied, hardly answering her companion's remarks. 'Let's have a cup of tea, we've had enough coffee today.'

'OK.' Dorothy continued to gaze out of the window. Suddenly, as Michaela put the tray of tea on the table, she spoke. 'Right, Michaela – two can play at this game!' She put two lumps of sugar in her tea.

'What game, Dorothy?' She had never heard her friend sound so determined, so forceful.

'Poison pen letters – I'm going to send one. You've got a type-writer.'

'Oh, come on, who to? It's a horrid idea, I think.'

Dorothy shook her head. 'No, Michaela – I know you're cleverer than me and stronger minded, but I'm not going to let you put me off this time.' She poured herself more tea, picked up the cup and saucer and went through to Michaela's little office.

Michaela followed her. 'But who to and why?' she asked.

Dorothy drew the chair up to the typewriter table, opened a drawer, took out a piece of paper, fed it into the machine and wound it to the middle, pushing down the Capitals key.

'I said who to and why?' Michaela repeated.

Dorothy looked up at her. 'Carmen, who else? She's going to get a dose of her own medicine.'

Michaela shook her head and said no more. She left the little room and went back into the kitchen; as she washed up she thought that it was the first time that Dorothy, usually so persuadable, had got the bit between her teeth.

Tap, tap went the typewriter. After ten minutes Michaela heard the front door close and peeped out of the window – her usually docile companion was disappearing up the road in the direction of the post office.

Even her walk was different. Michaela could only shrug her shoulders. 'There goes our born-again poison pen letter-writer,' she said and wished in a way that she had stayed and seen what Dorothy had written.

8

Mabel and Ted were enjoying a cup of tea. 'Wonder whether Nigel Fisk has set up house with his girlfriend yet,' pondered Mabel.

Ted looked up at her over his half-glasses. 'That Nigel Fisk! I thought he was more of a mother's boy – far too much of a mother's boy to leave home. Hope he doesn't regret it.'

He moved his feet and the movement attracted Mabel's attention. 'Ted, you didn't go out to the gate in your carpet slippers, did you?'

He looked guilty and held up one foot. 'It's me toenail, I had to cut it and I cut me toe.' Mabel looked concerned. 'It's nothing – I just nicked it.'

'Ted, you know what the doctor said, you're a diabetic. It's dangerous. You can't see well enough to cut your own toenails.'

Ted's face set; he was an obstinate man and it showed. 'I know what you're going to say, Mabel, but I'm not going up to that hospital to have me feet done and sit with all those old biddies.'

'Old biddies! I suppose you'd call me an old biddy, too!'

Ted shook his head again. 'Course not.' He moved his slippered feet further back to get them out of sight.

'You needn't go to the hospital foot clinic, Ted – now we've sold the car we can afford a private chiropodist.'

'I don't want –' but Mabel could be as obstinate as her husband if she wanted to be.

'No, Ted, I mean it. You could get gangrene – that's what the doctor said. Take care of your feet, he's said that once or twice to you.'

She went into the hall, got out the Yellow Pages, found the page she wanted and ran her fingers down the names advertised. 'Here we are,' she muttered to herself. She dialled the number; it was an answering machine. Mabel hated leaving messages on machines but she determinedly left her particulars. For Ted's health and well-being she would do anything.

'They're going to ring back,' she said, returning to the cosy little room. She didn't mention that a woman had answered in case Ted might object. Perhaps he'll think of her as a nurse, she thought.

Ted's lower lip stuck out. 'Can't cut me own nails – diabetes – I'm cracking up.'

Mabel touched his arm as she passed his chair, but he shrugged her hand off. 'Come on, Ted, we're both getting old, that's really the truth of it.'

The telephone rang about two hours later and Mabel made an appointment for three o'clock the next day. She explained that Ted was diabetic. 'Well, we must take special care of his feet then, Mrs Thornton.' The voice was the same pleasant one she had heard on the answering machine. Ted received the news of the appointment with better grace than Mabel had expected, even suggesting that they had a whisky each before they went to bed – his way of saying he was sorry he had been so irritable.

He took a gulp of his whisky and smiled at her. 'Count your blessings – I know that's what you'd say, and you're a blessing, old girl,' he said. 'Especially if you'll get me a bit of bread and cheese. And don't tell anyone I'm having me feet done – please, Mabel.' Mabel promised him that she wouldn't tell a soul.

The next day Mabel supervised the washing of Ted's feet – the small cut on his big toe looked quite sore. At three o'clock the chiropodist's small red Mazda stopped outside Blackthorne Cottage. Mabel went out to the girl. 'Miss Wheeler?' she asked.

'Yes, but I can't park here, can I, Mrs Thornton? The road's too narrow. Shall I run down to that bit where it widens? Will it be OK there?'

'Yes, park outside the house with the tall chimney – Mrs Fisk's house.' She pointed down the High Street.

'Right. Won't be a minute.'

Mabel watched her approach with approval – neat grey suit, the skirt not too short, but short enough to reveal a well-shaped pair of legs, patent leather flatties, a white shirt fastened by a small gold brooch at her throat which made her look professional. Her hair, light brown, waved back from her face and stirred in the breeze, her make-up was discreet, not too much – Mabel was glad of that as Ted did not approve of heavy make-up. She didn't look all that young, thirty-five perhaps.

Ted was rather shy of meeting new people in his own house. He stood up as Mabel and the girl entered the room. 'Good afternoon,

Mr Thornton.' He looked slightly embarrassed, standing on the piece of clean towelling that his wife had placed under his well-washed feet, which were bare all ready for the chiropodist's attention. Miss Wheeler sat down and opened her case and took out a notebook. Mabel excused herself and left them to it.

She decided to clean out the refrigerator in the kitchen and set to. The slight pain in her arm and breast since her operation had almost completely gone now. She was due to see the radiotherapist next Friday; he would tell her if further treatment was necessary. She shrank a little from the idea of what he might say, but it was no good being like that, she thought, dismissing even the thought from her mind. She half filled the washing-up bowl with water for the job in hand. A day at a time, that was the way to cope with it – cope with anything, she thought. Opening the cupboard she got out a little carton of bicarbonate of soda and mixed some into the warm water in the bowl.

From the sitting-room she could hear the chiropodist and Ted talking and she heard Ted give his rather gruff chuckle. Thank goodness he was getting on with the girl, she thought. Ted had very definite likes and dislikes and the chiropodist would probably now have to come on a regular basis – no letting Ted try to cut his own nails, and his toes as well! That, Mabel was certain about – it was something she would not allow!

Jane Fisk was busy in her kitchen preparing a meal for Nigel. He had telephoned to say he would be coming home that evening to fetch some of his things. He had found a small cottage in Billingham and had rented it for six months. Jane felt rather baffled at her own acceptance of events. Her son's homosexuality seemed to have been pushed into the background by her wish, her anxiety, her determination that his post – or his future post, wherever it might be – should in no way be jeopardised by what was happening.

She walked through to the dining-room to lay the table. Through the window she noticed a red car parked opposite her house. This was a nuisance because when Nigel came he usually parked there; her own car took up the small driveway. Jane went to her front door, opened it and looked up the High Street. A neat female figure walked briskly towards her – nice-looking, dressed in a way Jane approved of and with short, but not too short, well-cut hair. She carried a small black suitcase and as she reached Jane, who was now standing at her gate, she smiled pleasantly.

'Good afternoon – Mrs Fisk, isn't it? I hope my car being there is not a bother. I've been to the Thorntons' and it's rather narrow in that part of the High Street.'

'Oh no, it's perfectly all right,' Jane heard herself saying through her abstraction. Here was the girl – the young woman who could, as far as appearance went at least and, by the look of it, age, represent Nigel's girlfriend. Right height, probably married though? Jane looked at the left hand holding the suitcase – no ring on the finger.

'I'm afraid I must impose on your kindness again next week.' The girl shook out the keys from a leather key-case, unlocked the car and placed the suitcase on the passenger seat, then turned again to Jane. 'I'm Amelia Wheeler, chiropodist.' She took a card out of her small handbag and handed it to Jane. 'Not advertising, just excusing the car being parked so near your house.' She laughed, showing white even teeth.

'A chiropodist! Are you from the hospital?' Jane asked.

The girl shook her head. 'No, I'm in private practice.'

Jane tapped the card on her thumbnail. 'Well, I've a little trouble with a corn at the moment. Could you help me?'

'Of course. Would you like to make an appointment?'

Jane opened the gate. 'Do come in and we could decide on a time.'

'Right.' The woman relocked the car and followed Jane into the house. 'What a pretty village this is. Do you know, I've not had a patient here before – not that I've been working on the Island very long.'

Jane fetched her handbag, in which she kept her diary. There was a click from the kitchen. Jane put the diary and pen on the table before her. 'Oh, that's the kettle. I was just going to have a cup of tea, would you join me?'

Amelia Wheeler smiled again. 'Yes, I'd love one – what a pretty room this is,' she said. 'Thank you.'

Jane left the room and when she returned with the tea and biscuits the girl was seated comfortably, relaxed, on the settee.

'You live here, did you say?'

The girl sipped her tea. 'No, I live in Newport – well, not in Newport, just outside. I've got a little flat, very little, but I love

74

sailing so . . .' She took a biscuit. 'May I? I didn't have time for lunch.'

'Of course. Shall I make you a sandwich?'

The girl laughed. 'No, it's very kind of you but no thanks, my lunch is in an all-night cooker, so it will be ready for me when I get home.' She finished another cup of tea. 'Now, your appointment, Mrs Fisk.' She took out a small book from her handbag. 'I've got my big appointment book in my car, but I can transfer it.'

Jane Fisk examined her diary. The girl broke in. 'I'm coming to the Thorntons' today week, how would that be for you?'

She looked up and Jane noticed that her eyes were grey. She shook her head. 'No, I can't manage that day.' She named another.

'Yes, that's all right for me. I've an appointment in Sandown so I could come straight on here. Eleven o'clock?'

'Yes.' Jane noted it down.

The girl looked at her watch. 'I must go.' She got up. 'Thanks for the tea and the parking place, Mrs Fisk.'

They walked towards the front door. Jane opened it and walked up to the gate with Amelia Wheeler, looking at her, taking her in, her personality. She liked what she saw.

Michaela passed by on the other side of the road. She skirted the bonnet of the red car and waved to Jane, who waved back – such luck, Jane thought. Even better, Philippa Ainsworth drove by. She slowed her car perceptibly as she passed Jane's gate, took in the two people who were standing there, waved as Michaela had done and passed. 'You know everybody, Mrs Fisk,' Amelia Wheeler said with a hint of amusement.

Jane watched the chiropodist cross the road and unlock her car, get in and with a final smile drive off. If only . . . Jane thought. A grey-eyed, light brown-haired girl – a woman – just right for her son. She shut the front door and hurried into the kitchen. Nigel's supper, she must get on. Satisfaction and a certain amount of excitement made her mouth curl in a smile. Michaela had seen her and, more important, Philippa Ainsworth had seen her. It was a good start to the deception that would, she hoped, save Nigel his reputation and, if all went well, his job. How would he take it, though? Would he play the same game as she was planning? At least the girl was coming to the village and her car would soon get known. Would the Thorntons tell, though, that she was a chiropodist and that she was coming to them? Well, she would have to take risks to keep in line with the lies and convolutions of her plot.

She must take it one day at a time between now and the end of July, or whenever Nigel and Jeremy were able to leave the Isle of Wight and sink into the anonymity of a large city – London, Birmingham, Manchester or wherever Nigel could get a post, either as headmaster or as deputy headmaster, or indeed any position in any school.

She heard her son's car. The oven was already on – she put in the two cutlets, turned up the potatoes. Probably he would say he hadn't time to stay and have a meal . . . probably, but Jane knew she could make him stay, eat and listen to her plan and, if she used enough force of will, she knew she could make him agree to it. She heard his key in the front door.

Carmen had not held a coffee morning for ages, ever since she had received what she thought of as 'the letter'. She had put it in the drawer in her bedroom, but even days after it had come she felt compelled to reread it, though she knew it by heart – short and to the point, brutal almost:

YOU HAVE A MALICIOUS AND WICKED TONGUE. YOU DON'T
MIND WHAT YOU SAY OR WHO YOU HURT.

The awful part of it was that Carmen knew she did talk about this and that and sometimes she did repeat bits of gossip she had heard in the village. She felt guilty about that, but malicious and wicked, that was a bit too much, wasn't it? Well, she had to admit that some of the things she had heard and repeated were sometimes – well, not malicious or wicked, but not exactly kind.

She suddenly decided she would have a coffee morning. If she didn't, her friends would begin to wonder why. Philippa Ainsworth knew about the letter. Carmen had just had to tell someone and, after all, Philippa had had one herself – at least the vicar, her husband, had – and anyway, how wrong the gossip you heard could be, like Philippa and Dr Barnes! She was sure that was wrong, well, she was almost sure – and then someone had said Nigel Fisk was . . . well, you know. Carmen disliked the work 'homosexual', so said 'queer' to herself, indeed she didn't much like that word either. She wanted to forget the letter upstairs under her underclothes. She picked up the telephone and started organising a little coffee party – to take her mind off things, as she put it.

After asking four people she put down the receiver and walked across her small hall, catching sight of herself in the large mirror over the table against the wall. She walked towards it and peered at herself. 'Malicious and wicked' – no, she wasn't! 'No gossip – well, no nasty gossip,' she said to the woman in the mirror. No gossip! What would they talk about, she wondered – what could they talk about? Clothes, shops, illness – no, they couldn't do that because she'd asked Mabel Thornton again. Oh dear! Perhaps one of her guests had sent the letter. Oh no, that couldn't be, because they all gossiped. She left the mirror. It gave you a nasty feeling, this. She was almost sure it couldn't be any of them – and yet, you didn't know! When these things went round the village it could be anyone – someone who didn't like her, and was getting back at her, perhaps. Carmen almost never swore, she thought it rather unladylike, but as she left the hall and went through to the kitchen she said, 'Damn the letter and damn whoever sent it.'

'No, Nigel, I want you to stay; I have something to tell you. I've cooked a meal and it's nearly ready.' This was Jane Fisk's answer to her son's predicted remark, 'No, Ma, I haven't time to stay for a meal.' As Jane pressed him a little more he gave way. 'I'm sure Jeremy will understand, Nigel.' He looked quickly at his mother's face as she made the remark, but he caught no trace of sarcasm or irony. 'Get us both a gin and tonic, would you, dear?' She went into the kitchen to check the cutlets, then joined Nigel in the sitting-room. He had mixed her drink just as she liked it. She smiled at him and patted the seat beside her, 'Sit down, dear, I want to tell you something.'

The plan she outlined seemed at first to leave Nigel dumb while the full ramifications of the – what could one call it – conspiracy unfolded before him: the girl, woman, her appearance, her car, his mother making use of her services just to get her noticed as a visitor, and letting everyone draw the conclusion that she was Nigel's girlfriend; the staggered visits she intended the girl to make, her repetition of the girl's name, Amelia Wheeler – he was sure she only did it so that it would be imprinted on his memory . . . She was supposed to be the one he was living with. He felt trapped by his mother's arrangements. She had already set the scene, in the village anyway.

'Ma, we can't do this.'

His mother waved away his objections with that familiar dismissing gesture of the hand. 'Nonsense, it will be perfectly all right. I'm only interested in covering your . . .' She paused. '. . . your activities until the end of term, when you can leave Shanklin. I must get your meal.' She left the room.

Nigel sat finishing his gin. His mother's description of the girl had amused him a little: 'Neat, slim, pretty – professional-looking.' That was the type of girl she had always wanted for him, someone neat, pretty and professional-looking. He sighed and thought of Jeremy waiting for him at Billingham – petulant, furious that he hadn't come straight home, selfish, ill-tempered at times; demanding, yet it was Jeremy he loved . . . Why? Why was he made like this? He knew, or at least guessed, what his life would be like with him: full of quarrels, then making up; loving, sulking – the pouting mouth that he longed to kiss . . . But no matter, even if Jeremy didn't let him kiss him, those blue eyes with their dark lashes could bring him almost to the point of begging for forgiveness, for something he had probably not done.

'Come and eat, Nigel.'

He sat down at the dining-room table and ate the meal his mother had prepared. 'Shall I tell Jeremy about this, Ma?' he asked at last, pushing his practically empty plate away.

'That's entirely up to you, dear. I know nothing about his feelings – will he think the deception a good idea or be jealous of it?'

Nigel looked at his mother with admiration. 'You're no fool, Ma.' He made the remark almost ruefully.

Jane looked back at him. 'I know,' she said without humour, then she went on, 'You may have to be seen with the girl, once at least, in the village. I shall need a little back-up – just visiting me is not enough.'

'But how?'

'Leave it to me, Nigel – leave it all to me.' Again Jane felt a faint thrill of excitement at the difficulties – some would say impossibilities – of the task she had set herself for her son's sake.

When Nigel left, Jane felt tired. It was only at that moment she realised how much she had had to pressurise not only Nigel but herself, to 'sell' the idea – the camouflage, the cover, to see him through the next few months.

The telephone rang. It was Carmen asking her for coffee. It was some time since Carmen had asked her and Jane was still smouldering from Philippa and Carmen's remarks about Nigel – but now, now that he was out of the closet, living the life they had suspected him of, she felt, strangely enough, more secure and more kindly disposed towards them both. It was perhaps a feeling that she could forgive them. Now Nigel would be protected. Anyway, she would be interested to see more of their reactions. She was sure Philippa would have registered the chiropodist, Amelia Wheeler, talking to her at the gate – maybe even Michaela had noticed her, too. She accepted the invitation, put the phone down and went to enter the coffee morning in her diary. As she did so she saw the entry for Amelia Wheeler's visit. She put the name 'Carmen' down. The two names meant a lot to her – Carmen and Amelia. Of course it was true what Carmen had said, or Philippa, Nigel was homosexual, but now they would have to retract their words, say he wasn't, he had a girl.

Jane cleared the table, ran hot water into a bowl, added washing-up liquid and thought further about the grey-eyed girl. She plunged Nigel's plate and cutlery into the hot soapy liquid. Poor Nigel, she thought; the plate was somehow symbolic of her son, drowning submerged by his feelings.

Nigel drove to what was now 'home'. As he drove he was thinking of Ma's meal. In spite of himself he had enjoyed the cutlets and being cooked for. Jeremy was no cook; he had shown that already in the few days they had been together. Nigel debated with himself as he drove along the curving lanes – should he tell Jeremy Ma's plot? He couldn't decide, not immediately – but if he didn't, suppose the outline of the conspiracy got to Jeremy? If Ma insisted that he must be seen with the girl and take her out, he must tell Jeremy. Perhaps it would make him laugh; perhaps it wouldn't. Nigel had a lot to learn about how Jeremy felt. Pouting and sulking, he was good at that, but afterwards he would be so sweet, so nice, so endearing.

When he arrived at Billingham the church clock was just striking seven. The little cottage they had rented looked inviting. The sitting-room light was on, illuminating the rather neglected front garden. Nigel felt his heart quicken as he thrust his key in the lock and entered the small hall.

'Hello there, where have you been?' Jeremy called over the noise of music from the television. He stood up as Nigel entered the door, gracefully swinging his long legs off the settee, and stretched his arms above his head. He lowered them and came over, kissing Nigel lightly on the cheek. 'You've been drinking without me?' he said as he smelt the gin on Nigel's breath; he said it half seriously, half teasing.

'Yes, I had to have a meal with Ma, she wouldn't take no, and I had a gin.'

'Lucky you. What do I get to eat?'

Nigel kissed him back just as lightly but on the lips. 'I'll make you something,' he said.

Jeremy threw himself back on to the settee. 'The springs have gone in this three-piece suite,' he said.

'Well, it's only for letting – I don't suppose they care. When we get our own place we'll have a new leather three-piece suite, with beautiful springs.'

'God forbid! These three-piece suites are the end,' Jeremy called after Nigel.

'OK, we'll have a two-piece suite.' Nigel felt comfortable, relaxed, even though he had decided that, after he had fed his lover, he would reveal to him Ma's plot.

Jeremy's reaction was unexpected. 'Good old Ma,' he said, smiling up at Nigel. They were both on the settee, Nigel sitting, Jeremy lying full length, his feet on the far arm of the sofa, his head on Nigel's lap. There was a hole in his sock, his big toe showing through it, and Nigel vaguely supposed he should do something about that.

'You don't mind?' Nigel asked, smoothing back Jeremy's hair. He felt so happy – it was as if he had never in his whole life known or experienced this blissful feeling of loving before – well, that was true, he hadn't because he had never chosen to; but had he been right? 'So I may have to take the woman out to a meal or something, that is if Ma puts the pressure on.'

'OK, love. Can I come along for the fodder?'

Nigel put his hand on Jeremy's shoulder and pulled him closer. 'That's not a good idea. I'll take a doggy bag.'

'Ta.' Jeremy settled his head more comfortably. 'July, you say, and we can be off, leave these rural surroundings and get to the bright lights.'

Nigel did then feel a slight shock of anxiety shoot through him.

He had given in his notice, would finish this term and the next, and then, as Jeremy said, the bright lights – but would there be a post for him and what sort of post? Deputy head if he was lucky, head if a miracle happened. Other than that, back to just being a teacher.

Jeremy's blue eyes looked up at him. 'It'll be all right, won't it? I mean, you'll get a . . . ?'

'Of course I will, no problem.'

'I'll do a bit of modelling up there.'

'But it might not be London, Jeremy,' Nigel said.

The blue eyes opened wider. 'Oh come on, Nige dear, London it's got to be,' he said and closed his eyes. Please God, thought Nigel, please God it can be London, if that's what he wants.

He went on stroking Jeremy's hair; suddenly the blue eyes opened again and the mouth curled in a smile. 'Let's go to bed, Nigel.' The long legs unwound like a graceful spider, he got up, took Nigel's hand and the two went up the narrow cottage stairs to the bedroom.

9

Carmen arranged sherry glasses and a decanter on her carefully polished, silver-plated salver. She intended to offer her guests a glass of sherry before they left. She had filled the decanter with Harvey's Bristol Cream. Perhaps because of the beastly poison pen letter, she was hoping they would go away with a sweet taste in their mouths, and she was determined that not a nasty word about anyone would pass her lips – nor, if she could help it, anyone else's. It crossed her mind again with something of a shock that she might well have included the writer of the letter among her visitors . . . She paused, the hand about to put the last sherry glass on the tray arrested by the thought. No, not one of them could she suspect of such a thing, and then there was the poor vicar – he'd had one about Philippa. She thrust the suspicions out of her mind as the front door bell rang. The hands of the kitchen clock stood at exactly half-past ten: someone was very punctual.

It was Mabel Thornton. Once in the hall, sensing from the

silence that she was the first to arrive, she began apologising profusely for coming early, for being the first one there. Carmen assured her that she was very pleased she had come early; it would give her time to ask how she had got on and how she felt after her operation. 'Of course, Mabel, I know about your problem. Is all well?' Mabel hated being asked about her lumpectomy, so she assured her quite falsely that everything was perfectly all right, no problems at all. 'And Mr Thornton, is he well?' Mabel Thornton was saved from going any further into her family's health by the front door bell ringing again. 'Please go through to the sitting-room, Mabel.' Mabel drifted through while Carmen ushered in Michaela and Dorothy. They divested themselves of coats and cardigan and joined Mabel.

Philippa Ainsworth arrived next. As she stood at Carmen's front door a car drew up, and her heart seemed to do a somersault – it was Eric Barnes. He got out of the car, came round to the passenger side and opened the door. Someone sitting in the car looked up at him; it was his wife, Sheila.

She smiled at Philippa. 'I'm a casualty.' She pointed at her ankle, which was bandaged. 'Tripped on a wet stone in the garden, silly me.'

Eric Barnes smiled at Philippa. 'Bored stiff at home so I said I'd bring her here to join the ladies.' He helped his wife out of the car. 'My day off,' he explained, taking his wife's arm as she limped up the path to Carmen's front door. Then he put his arm round her waist to help her up the two steps.

His wife gave him a quick peck on the cheek. 'See you at twelve, darling,' she said.

Eric Barnes nodded. Philippa felt a quick stab of envy as she rang the door bell. Eric Barnes went back to his car and got in. Philippa felt deflated; he had hardly noticed her, hardly glanced at her, just that curt 'My day off'. He would have said that to anyone.

'Do come in – oh dear, what have you done to yourself?' Philippa almost started as Carmen spoke; she had been watching the car drive away. They joined the others and after a small barrage of 'Oh poor Sheila', and 'Do let me help you', Sheila Barnes was made comfortable and they all settled down.

Jane Fisk arrived after about a quarter of an hour. She carefully hid the amusement she felt as she took in the scene: Philippa sitting next to Sheila Barnes. She wondered if there had been any reaction to her letter to Philippa's husband. She felt suddenly that she wanted to hurt Philippa – that remark about her son still rankled. Perhaps she'd send a letter to Sheila Barnes, it might make the situation a little more explosive.

The conversation meandered around various topics and suddenly Brigadier Dawson was mentioned by Mrs Thornton. 'He's so nice. When our car broke down he took Ted into Newport to the hospital. So nice of him.'

Carmen agreed. 'I think he's a sweet old gentleman – so gallant.'

'Gallant!' Philippa broke in. 'He was very gallant to that poor little cleaner of his!'

Dorothy asked, 'What happened, Philippa?'

'Well, the girl said – told her mother he'd interfered with her and she left – the cleaner, I mean. It was all over the village at the time, that was some six months ago. It was common knowledge.'

Mabel Thornton looked uncomfortable. 'Well, I can only speak as I find, Mrs Ainsworth.'

Carmen was more forceful. 'Philippa, don't say such things.'

'Well, it's true.'

Carmen's face flushed. 'It may be, but after that letter we don't . . .'

'What letter?' Dorothy's face was the picture of innocence.

'Oh, I didn't mean you to know. I didn't want to . . .' Carmen stopped and looked really upset. 'I had a letter, anonymous – I'll go and get it and you can all see it. I'm not the only gossip.' She left the room and they could all hear her running up the stairs.

There was a dead silence. Michaela fixed her eyes on Dorothy until she turned and looked at her. Her expression surprised Michaela; Dorothy looked so complacent, so pleased with herself. The thought went through Michaela's head that the letter they had got and that overdose had changed Dorothy. Mabel Thornton looked even more uncomfortable. Sheila Barnes looked bewildered and expectant. Jane Fisk was perhaps even more surprised than anyone else. She took a handkerchief from her handbag and brushed a few biscuit crumbs off the front of the green woollen jumper she was wearing.

Carmen came down the stairs more slowly than she had gone up them. She entered the room, the letter open in her hand. She handed it first to Mabel Thornton, who took it as if it was white hot, read it, closed her eyes and handed it to Michaela. It eventually ended up with Jane Fisk, who read it more slowly than anyone else. 'Well, well . . .' she said softly as she handed it back to Carmen, who put it down on the coffee table.

'I'll just get . . .' Carmen did not finish what she was going to say, but left the room and returned almost immediately with her offering of sherry. Mabel Thornton at first shook her head, but Carmen's 'Please do' made her change her mind.

'Well, I don't think you gossip – not all that much,' Philippa said. Her remark was greeted by a pregnant silence. She drank some of her sherry. 'Anyway, I was . . . It was probably wrong about the Brigadier.'

Jane Fisk got up, put down her glass with a little click on the table. 'Too late to say that now, Philippa,' she said. Then to Carmen, 'I must go, dear – things to do.'

'Of course.' Carmen did not accompany her to the door. Jane let herself out. She wanted to think – she hadn't sent that letter, so who had?

Jane had hardly reached Carmen's gate when she saw the vicar coming out of a similar gate about four houses down: Jim Bosworth's house. Jane had heard he was not well; she had met his wife in the post office just a couple of days ago. Phlebitis, his wife had said.

She could see by the expression on his face that Hugh Ainsworth was not best pleased with life. He stopped in front of Jane, conjuring up rather a false smile. 'Mrs Fisk.'

Jane smiled back at him. 'Visiting the sick vicar?'

'No, I'm not. I intended to but found I had been forestalled.' He paused. 'Our minister – in, of course, his usual attire, sandals, open-neck shirt, hair down to his shoulders.'

'Oh! I'm sure it must be rather discouraging for you, but he does seem popular, doesn't he, and if Mrs Bosworth or Mr Bosworth is getting spiritual comfort you must be pleased?'

The vicar's face hardened. 'It doesn't please me, Mrs Fisk. Jim Bosworth and his wife were my most faithful parishioners at one time.'

At that moment Dr Barnes' car drew up at Carmen's gate. He gave a brief toot on the hooter and then got out of the car. Carmen's front door opened almost immediately and she helped Sheila Barnes down the two front steps, where she grasped her husband's arm.

'Have you had an accident, Mrs Barnes – Sheila?' Ainsworth asked.

'Yes, but it's nothing, only a sprain. I slipped.' She turned to Jane. 'Oh, wasn't it awful, Mrs Fisk, that letter! I've never seen anything like it.'

'What letter?' her husband asked without a great deal of interest.

'Not another!' the vicar said. He was holding the door open for Sheila, helping to get her into the passenger seat.

She looked up at him. 'Well, she showed it to us – Carmen. It said she was a gossip and more.' She got into the car and the door closed after her, but she wound the window down to continue her story. Dr Barnes went round and got into the driver's seat. 'It was awful – awful things in it. I suppose that's what's called a poison pen letter – that's what they're called, isn't it? It was anonymous – no signature, of course.' Dr Barnes started the car and she wiggled her fingers in goodbye.

Hugh Ainsworth looked at Jane. 'Did you say *another* letter?' she asked.

He looked decidedly uncomfortable. 'Yes, yes. I was shown one by a parishioner which he had, she had, received.'

You liar, Jane thought, but she feigned surprise, mixed with dismay. 'Poison pen letters in this village – how unpleasant. Two is enough. I hope there'll be no more.'

'Indeed, so do I, Mrs Fisk. Did you get a chance to read this one – that Carmen has been sent?'

Jane nodded. 'Most certainly I did, vicar – most certainly I did.'

He fingered his collar, running his forefinger round the inside of it as if it were too tight for him. 'And what did you think of the contents?'

Jane opened her handbag to take out her front door key, then she gave him a long, level glance. 'Every word of it true, in my opinion, Mr Ainsworth. Carmen is a gossip.'

'But surely only –'

'No, not only what you were going to say, mere unimportant gossip that women indulge in – no, I myself at one of her little gatherings heard her and another guest talking about my son. I have acute hearing and the conversation was taking place between the two of them in the kitchen. I heard every word.'

'But was it of a scandalous nature, Mrs Fisk?' Ainsworth's eyes were fixed on her with both curiosity and anxiety.

'They accused my son of being homosexual and therefore unfit to be a headmaster. Vicar, do you call that scandalous?'

He looked genuinely shocked. 'Mrs Fisk, I hardly know what to say.'

Jane Fisk's mouth set in a hard line. The man was a liar and his wife had blackened her son's name. She would not spare him. 'I thought of going to my lawyer, vicar. After all, my son is thinking of becoming engaged and you can imagine the hurt and damage to his alliance and career which might result if such a remark got abroad.'

Hugh Ainsworth backed against the fence to let Mrs Thornton pass, saying, 'Good morning, Mrs Thornton.'

Jane let her get out of earshot, then went on: 'Do you think I should have taken further advice on such a delicate matter?'

Ainsworth loosened his collar again; he looked hot. His normally rather white face was flushed. 'Well, one feels that Carmen deserves the letter, but one hesitates to approve such missives.'

Pompous ass, Jane thought as she delivered her final volley. 'Well, vicar, the recipient of Carmen's gossip and the person who seemed to agree with her diagnosis of my son's lifestyle was your wife.' She did not wait to see the effect of her remark, but snapped her handbag shut, turned her back on him and started the walk to her house. As she crossed the road she saw out of the corner of her eye that Hugh Ainsworth was still standing by Carmen's fence, looking down the road at her retreating figure. She smiled to herself. Would he now suspect that the letter he had received about his wife had come from her? She doubted it, but she didn't really mind if he did suspect her.

As she put her key in her front door lock, turned it and entered the house her mind was still full of curiosity as to who in the village – and it must have been someone in the village – had sent that letter to Carmen.

Hugh Ainsworth arrived home before his wife. He was furious. His initial irritation regarding the 'poaching' of one of his parishioners by Patrick Beattie had been increased by Jane Fisk's story about his wife's remarks to Carmen about her son, Nigel. How could Philippa have let herself be drawn into such a scandalous conversation with another woman and allowed that gossip to be audible to others? As a vicar's wife surely she should be guarded about everything she said; but she wasn't, he knew the truth about her.

He knew Philippa hated being a vicar's wife, but even so . . . He went through to the kitchen and poured himself a glass of milk. He felt upset. He sat at the kitchen table sipping the milk, then he heard his wife's key in the front door. He knew she would probably come through to the kitchen. He didn't at that moment wish to see or talk to her, so he picked up the glass of milk, walked out of the back door and down to the bottom of the garden.

At the far end of the lawn a wooden fence divided the garden from a small rutted lane and then rolling hills. He stood looking at the scene – it did nothing to calm him. He drained his glass then threw it with all the force he could muster against the fence. The glass struck the wooden palings and fell unbroken on to the compost heap below. The fact that the glass remained unbroken increased Hugh's feeling of frustration more than ever. 'Shit,' he said. He turned and was surprised to see Philippa standing in the doorway watching him. He picked up the tumbler and walked back towards the house. As he walked his fury mounted. He realised that his hand was holding the glass so tightly that if he wasn't careful he would crack the tumbler and cut himself. He let go a little.

In the short walk back up the path to where his wife stood he felt that everything was crowding in on him – his diminishing congregation, his dull sermons, the anonymous letter, Patrick Beattie and his tinpot chapel, the peculiar clothes worn by him, his long untidy hair. His own gossiping, cold, uncooperative wife standing there in the sunlight watching him. As he approached she called out, 'Pizza do for your lunch, dear?'

'No, it bloody well won't!' He stopped about two feet away from her; he had never felt like this in his life.

'Well, what would you like then?' Philippa looked startled.

'I'd like some more bloody support, not constant undermining.' He was aware that he was shouting.

His wife backed into the kitchen and he followed her. Philippa had never seen her husband in such a passion of rage. 'I do support you – I do,' she wailed.

'Some support, flirting with your doctor, quarrelling with the church cleaners, never having my meals ready!'

Philippa was getting as enraged as her husband. 'You've got it wrong. I've never flirted with Dr Barnes, you know that –'

He interrupted her. 'Yes, I suppose it's ridiculous, ludicrous even – what notice would he ever take of you anyway?'

That remark seemed to be the last straw for Philippa. Everything she had wanted to say for weeks, months, perhaps years, came tumbling out. 'Do you consider yourself a success, Hugh? Your church is nearly empty, your sermons are so boring that people fall asleep. That young man, Pat, he understands the religion of today; he understands people – soon he'll have stolen all your parishioners.' Her voice rose. 'They should pull down your church and make it into a car-park.'

'You bitch!' Hugh Ainsworth struck his wife across the face. Maybe he only intended a hard slap, but the signet ring on his finger cut a circular wound under her eye. She reeled back against the table – a tiny trickle of blood came from the cut.

Hugh, alarmed at his own violence, stepped closer to her. Perhaps if she had wept, perhaps if she had said nothing, he might have taken her in his arms and the row would have ended, but alas she spoke: 'No one likes you in the village. The Bishop thinks of you as – what is the word they use now – unproductive, that's it, isn't it?' Her mouth twisted in a sneer. 'You'll never get any higher in the Church than vicar of this village – I hate it, hate it, and I hate you!'

Hugh's face went very white. He could feel the blood draining from his head and he felt faint. Every word she said was true. The Bishop – good-looking, urbane, unyielding – had made it clear that there was not likely to be any promotion: 'Some people are born for higher things in the Ministry, Hugh, some are not. You're doing sterling work here.' The words sang through Hugh's head. He had never hit a woman before in his life, but her words 'I hate you' seemed to loosen something in him. This time he hit her, not with his flat hand, but with a clenched fist, and the joy as his knuckles made contact with the side of her head was almost like an orgasm. She swayed, but remained upright – just put out her hand and steadied herself on the wooden kitchen table. Her face was expressionless. He turned, left the kitchen, banged the front door and made his way to the church. The village street was deserted, the post office had closed for lunch. He opened the big wooden door and went inside.

The church, his church, smelled of candle grease and wax polish, a familiar smell. He stepped into the first pew; he looked at the pulpit. 'Your sermons are so boring that people fall asleep.' Philippa's words of just a few minutes ago came back to him as if she were standing beside him saying them again. He sank forward on to his knees, covering his face with his hands, but not to pray. A hymn book from the ledge in front of him fell to the floor with a little bang, startling him. 'Failure, failure,' he said into his hands. What had made him hit her like that? He flinched at the thought.

Why had he chosen the Church? No one in his family had ever done so, but even at school he had been determined. Why, for God's sake? He had never been good with people, never made friends – not many, anyway – never joined groups. Why a clergyman? Well, every word Philippa had said was true. His 'calling' had been a failure, a miserable, dismal failure. He had nothing but contempt for himself. He knew now that he was beginning to know himself better. Perhaps it was all for the good. He and Philippa must talk things over and try to decide what to do. Talk about future plans, what they could do together, how they could get out of this mess they had got into. The trouble was, he had no skills – what could he do? Philippa had worked in a market garden and understood when and how to plant things – trees and shrubs. She had more skills than he had. He must go home and say how sorry he was, make it up and start again. He looked up at the small stained glass window, but he hardly saw it. Barnes – Dr Eric Barnes – was that letter true? He stood for a moment looking at the altar – what a con it all was. When he hit his wife he had 'seen red', like a piece of glass in the little window. He knew exactly what that expression meant now; he had seen red, not his wife's face, just that glaring colour.

He left the church feeling exhausted as if he had done a hard day's work. He went through the front door and called his wife's name; there was no reply. He called again, this time standing at the foot of the stairs. Still no reply. Then he went into the kitchen. Philippa lay on the floor, her legs slightly bent, her feet under a fallen chair. There was no more blood, only now almost dry congealed blood around her eye. Hugh knelt down beside her. 'Philippa,' he said. He lifted her head. Underneath was a small triangle of wood. Her head must have struck a corner of the kitchen table and broken the piece off as she fell. There was a dent in her temple. Her neck as he raised her head bent at an abnormal angle. She was dead.

Hugh could not get up – he tried but his legs felt weak. Who had she shown the letter to? Who had she told? Lately she had looked prettier; her clothes, her make-up and the perfume.

At last he struggled to his feet. The police, a doctor. He staggered to the phone and dialled the doctor's surgery.

'Can I help you?' The receptionist's voice.

'Dr Barnes, may I speak to Dr Barnes?'

'Sorry, it's Dr Barnes' day off today – and then he's going away on a course for a month. What name is it, please?'

Gently he put the receiver down. He went back into the kitchen; he looked down at Philippa. Suddenly his mind seemed to clear: if he dialled the police what could he say? What would they say? Only one thing could be said: 'You have murdered your wife.' They would put him in prison – he couldn't stand that, not prison. Dispose of the body. He felt as if he were in a play, an Agatha Christie play. He could see the headlines in the papers: VICAR KILLS WIFE – MURDER AT THE VICARAGE. Well, his marriage, his career, his life weren't worth it – weren't worth for ever suffering. He looked down at Philippa and suddenly he hated her.

Hugh sat down at the kitchen table; he still felt curiously weak, but was beginning to come out, he felt, of a long black tunnel into the light. He went and locked the back door and drew down the kitchen blind. Barnes was going away for a month; and he had the letter still in his desk drawer. She had brought it back – whoever she had shown it to, she had brought it back. It would be a godsend; the village gossips, they would cover her absence. 'Dr Barnes and Philippa Ainsworth gone off together – well, you saw or heard of that letter. No smoke without fire.' Perfect! There was a place, too, to put her – a little copse – well, almost a wood – near the village. No one, not even children or many dog-walkers, would go through it because quite recently a young girl had been attacked there. Some months ago, but it was still avoided. Perfect, too – his car had a large boot. How often he had wanted, wished he could afford to change it for a modern hatchback. Now he was glad he hadn't. Fate was with him, he only had to wait for tonight and the darkness!

When darkness came his feelings changed a little. Loading his wife's body into the car was a dreadful task. He shed bitter tears as he did it. 'Her poor face; her poor face,' he kept saying to himself after the car boot was locked and the car garaged. He realised then that darkness was not enough – he must drive to the wood at about one or two in the morning. He must stay here until then.

Back in the house, still shaking and crying, ashamed and afraid, he felt terribly alone and wished Philippa was alive and here with him, but it was no good wishing that! He realised he had not eaten all day. 'Pizza do for your lunch, dear?' He heard the words again and remembered the torrent of abuse with which he had answered. He couldn't remember her face nor how she had reacted at the time – perhaps he had turned away, but he couldn't remember.

He opened the refrigerator door – eggs, bacon, butter, orange juice, milk. He felt sick as he looked at it. The milk glass was still on the table. He remembered it falling on to the compost heap . . . He took out the bottle of milk, poured some into the glass and drank it. He had only to wait that little while until he could be sure there would be no stragglers driving or walking down the street, coming from the pub or a party, then he would do it!

At twenty past one in the morning Hugh pulled back the tangled half-brown, half-green brambles over her grave. It looked as if no one had been there at all. He pulled up some grass and wiped the spade, then replaced it in the boot, closed the lid and drove home.

Once there he went straight to his desk and opened the drawer. There was the letter safe and sound – more precious than before. Once a stupid and anonymous insult to him, now proof, or at least rumour, of his wife's infidelity. For the next month he was safe – after that he didn't want to think about it. Once bathed and in bed he began to relax. Before he fell asleep he looked only once at the twin bed beside his before turning his back on it and drifting into a dreamless sleep.

10

'Come on, boys,' Brigadier Dawson called to his two fat black labradors. With some reluctance they arose from where they had been lying by the fire on a comfortable rug; one gave a huge yawn. 'Come on, you lazy buggers,' Frank Dawson said. They followed him out into the panelled hall. He took two leashes off a hook on the wall by the side of the door and snapped them on to the dogs' collars.

The old man looked the part – bristling moustache, well-cut if ancient tweed jacket (pockets out of shape from holding tobacco pouch, matches, pipe), baggy trousers, hand-made shoes. He put on his equally ancient deerstalker and opened the front door. The dogs obediently sat at his side as he stood trying to light his pipe. The match flared high once or twice then the tobacco ignited, surrounding him with a pleasant-smelling smoke. He picked up the dogs' leads and walked down between the fairly well-cut lawns, through rather impressive wrought-iron gates – one of which squeaked as he opened it.

His gardener, who was wheeling a barrow-load of manure, touched his cap to him. 'Morning, sir. Nice day,' he said.

'Gate still squeaks like a bloody stuck pig here,' the Brigadier answered. 'If I've said oil that one once I've said it a dozen times, Gutteridge.'

'Yes sir, you sure have, sir. That's right enough. I'll do it when I have the time, sir.'

Frank Dawson knew he couldn't say much, so he just grunted. He was well aware that three gardeners had been employed to keep these grounds in order when his father had been alive, but since . . . There wasn't the money now.

The smoke swirled around his head as he went a short way down the village street then up a small lane into the woods. He always brought the dogs this way for their walk. The animals loved it – rooting around, chasing imaginary rabbits, doing their jobs without anybody noticing; it was an ideal place. As he turned into the woods he heard someone call his name. 'Brigadier Dawson!' He turned: it was Hugh Ainsworth. Even Frank Dawson, usually completely unobservant, thought he looked ill; wasn't sure if the man had even shaved. As he himself wore a neatly trimmed beard he was quite critical of other men's chins. Bugger, what does he want, he thought to himself; he had no love for the Church or clergy.

Hugh Ainsworth crossed the path and joined him in a little turning. 'Just off for your constitutional, sir?'

'Yes, yes, Ainsworth – must keep the old legs working, you know.' He stopped dead so that Ainsworth would continue down the village street to wherever he was going.

'Just been to see poor Bosworth – not at all well.'

Frank Dawson made some non-committal remark and turned to go.

'May I walk along with you, sir? Don't get enough exercise myself these days.'

The Brigadier puffed a cloud of smoke at him and nodded. 'Right, if you must.'

'People avoid these woods now, since that girl was attacked,' Ainsworth said. He put a hand up to his chin and rubbed it. Frank noticed that the hand was shaking. Got a drinking vicar here, have we? he thought.

The dogs, pleased to be let off the leads and out in spite of their initial reluctance, ran along the path in front of the two men. Hugh called them back once or twice.

'Don't do that, padre, they want to get some exercise, too. They won't get lost. They like to be able to scamper about.'

'It's the brambles, sir. I thought they'd better not get tangled in the brambles. Their eyes, they'd better not get scratched. I believe there are adders, too.'

The Brigadier stopped. One of the dogs started barking excitedly. 'Adders! Adders! They come out in the summer, in the sunshine, Ainsworth. Anyway, I don't think there are any adders here; and the brambles, why are you worrying about those – what's the matter with you, vicar? You unhinged or something?'

Hugh Ainsworth turned away. Both men stood for a moment in the cold dappled sunlight. The Brigadier's pipe went out; he got out his matches and the flame flashed high twice then diminished and flashed high again. They walked about a quarter of the way into the small forest. 'Quest! Bruce!' Frank Dawson called the dogs and they came bounding out from the undergrowth towards him.

'I thought they'd found something.' Hugh's voice was husky.

Frank Dawson turned and faced him squarely and waved his stick at the dogs, who set off at a run up the path again. 'Look, Ainsworth, something the matter, man? You look shot to pieces. Anything I can do to help you in any way?'

'My wife has left me.' The words were blurted out, just the five words.

'Good God, that's bad. Where did she go?' Dawson banged the ground with his stick. 'Taken off with some other chap, has she?'

'I can't say any more.' Hugh looked as if he was going to cry.

'Well, don't blub about it. Can't be helped. Women do go off sometimes.' Dawson coughed and stamped on.

Hugh walked behind him. 'I don't like these woods – depressing,' he said suddenly.

'Yes, well, they would be. When did she take off – your wife?'

'The day before yesterday – that's not all. We . . . I had an anonymous letter saying she was having an affair.'

'Anonymous letter! Poison pen stuff? Oh, I had one of those – put it on the fire. Sick bastard wrote it. Don't give it another thought.'

'Yes, but she did go,' Hugh replied.

'That's true. Well, obviously the bastard that wrote it knew more than you did about your good lady, eh?'

Both dogs started barking furiously. Quest was digging, front paws busy throwing earth out of a hole. It was nowhere near where Philippa was buried, but Ainsworth felt . . . just supposing . . . just supposing?

The Brigadier waved his stick at them again as they passed. 'No brains, dogs. They like a dig, though.' The two animals gave up and passed them on the path, Quest still barking.

The two men reached the end of the wood, turned and started back.

'You look all in – come in and have a whisky. Do you good. Pull you together. No telling with women, is there?'

They entered the hall and Frank Dawson let the dogs off the leashes. One lapped at a bowl of water, splashing liquid over the polished pine, floor; the other stood waiting then did the same – splashing just as much on the wooden floor. Hugh looked around him as he followed the Brigadier into the large sitting-room opposite the front door. One wall was completely lined with books, some in tidy rows of red and gold with spines shining, some brown and gold. A pair of library steps leant against the shelves. The whole room breathed with well-kept, well-tended age. The old leather chairs had one or two holes in them and a little puff of white stuff came out of one of the holes. The floor was polished and here and there a rug was thrown down almost at random – some of the rugs were worn, some newer, but scattered here and there they gave a touch of luxury to the room.

Hugh knew that he would never, never own a house like this; he never had and he never would. The sense of time, leisure, money, was protective somehow. If he and Philippa had lived like this and he had not been a clergyman but something else – a farmer or a writer, yes, an author – then things would not have been as they were now: Philippa under the rotting leaves in the wood, he alone, disliked, useless. He suddenly felt the room going black, a whistling in his ears. God, he was not going to faint, was he? Frank Dawson took his arm; he could just hear him saying, 'Sit down old man, I'll get you some brandy.' Hugh sank on to the leather chair, gripped the fat small arms and came back to himself. The fiery spirit went down his throat and warmed him, heartened him, made him feel better, and the faintness receded.

After a minute or two he realised that his host was seated in the chair opposite him. He must have been talking to him, but Hugh had not heard the beginning of what he was saying. '. . . you'll get over it, old man. More difficult for you, tied up in this religious nonsense, I can see that, of course . . .'

'Yes sir,' Hugh agreed automatically and got to his feet. 'I must get back.'

'OK then. Feeling better?'

The Brigadier accompanied him to the door, the dogs following him, their claws making a clicking sound on the pine floor. They shook hands. 'Thank you, you've been most kind.' The Brigadier stroked his moustache and beard self-consciously and in some embarrassment. The door closed on him and his dogs. Hugh walked down the long drive. The gardener touched his cap to him. The big gate squeaked as he closed it.

Hugh Ainsworth walked home. He must, he thought, get some brandy. Then the thought of the wood came back to him – and Philippa; Philippa, if only she were home now, waiting for him, if only she were . . .

11

To say that Shelbourne's jumble sale at the village hall was a disaster could almost be called an understatement! It rained and when it rained outside such was the state of the village hall's roof that it rained inside almost as much.

'Oh look, it's gone all over my blouse!' a tea-drinker, seated at one of the few small tables, exclaimed. She was referring to her tea. A large plop of water from above had fallen into her cup and the resultant splash had stained the front of her white blouse. She dabbed at it with a tissue and grabbed her cup and saucer and retreated, looking upward and receiving another plop in her eye.

Michaela and Dorothy, manning the jumper and T-shirt stall, were similarly affected by leaks from above. 'How much money in the float, Dorothy?' Michaela asked her co-worker, her face creased with laughter under her rainhat.

Dorothy did not even smile back. 'It's disgusting, this, Michaela, everything getting wet. Look at this!' She held up a T-shirt; printed on it were the words 'I should like to sleep with you'. She turned it round and on the back it said, 'Why not?' The letters were beginning to run in the dampness. 'The letters will soon be washed off.'

Dorothy had obviously not taken in the message. 'Just as well, I should think.' Her friend gave one of her deep, rather attractive guffaws. She looked round the hall. In spite of the rain and the leaking roof there were a lot of people there. The raffle-lady, in a dry corner, was signalling for help. The place smelt of wet macs.

Carmen and Sheila Barnes were in charge of the skirt and slacks stall and had been firmly wedged against the wall behind them by their trestle table being pushed by a fat lady flourishing a fifty-pence piece.

'That grey pleated skirt hanging on the wall, I want it.'

She pushed harder and Carmen struggled for space. 'It's only size 10,' she gasped.

'Never mind, I can let it out,' persisted the fat one, whose bust and waist size suggested 18 at least.

Carmen handed the skirt over and the large lady departed in triumph. 'It looks like new,' she was saying to the small woman beside her, who had missed the skirt by inches and was much nearer its size.

The scarf stall lady had sold out. 'Made four pounds twenty on my stall,' she boasted as she made for the little kitchenette for a cup of tea. As she passed Dorothy and Michaela she said, 'I'll bring you both a cup, dears. I think we deserve it, don't you?'

At that moment there was a small explosion from the kitchen and a disconsolate face appeared at the small serving hatch. 'The kettle's blown up. It's the rain in the plug, I expect. It's danger-ous.'

The rest of the jumble sale was much the same and illustrated, according to Michaela, why they must work to get the place repaired. The jumble sale had been her idea, just as a start, and they had made forty-five pounds – not much, she admitted, but it was a start. Next Michaela was determined to go to greater lengths – a wine and cheese party. She hoped to hold it at the Brigadier's house. The approach to him, she felt, was going to be difficult and he would probably bellow at her and say, 'Absolute-ly no,' or, 'Not having herds of people in my house, treading all over my floors,' but Michaela was determined to hand-pick the guests and make it an evening occasion. She hated these dreary coffee mornings that did nothing but spread gossip and wanted to try something a little more up-market.

Dorothy did not take to the charity scene at all. 'It's so tiring, Michaela, and I don't like the village people anyway. Carmen's a gossip – well, aren't they all – and those letters! Think of those letters!'

'Never mind, if we can get people more mixed together, more motivated, working for the hall roof, you'll see what a difference it will make.'

Dorothy sniffed. 'I know what you're aiming at, community spirit and all that. Well, it won't work here – I can tell you that, not after the way I've been treated.'

Michaela had tried. 'Oh, come on, Dorothy, that letter was hor-rid, I know that, but after all it included me as well.'

Dorothy would not be convinced. Michaela knew how obstinate she could be when she wanted to, so she decided to say nothing about the proposal she was going to make to the Brigadier.

Amelia Wheeler parked her car opposite Jane Fisk's house. This was her second visit to Mrs Fisk and she was a little at a loss. People who wanted the chiropodist really needed treatment and care for their feet, but Mrs Fisk, for her age, had little wrong with hers. The nails were well cut, no nail ingrowing, no hard skin on the soles of her feet – oh yes, there was a minute corn on the inside of her small toe, that was what she had pointed out to Amelia on her first visit. It hardly needed treatment at all, but Jane Fisk had insisted on it, so here she was back again.

Jane opened the door as if she had been waiting in the hall. She gave Amelia a welcoming smile. 'How nice to see you again,' she said. Amelia felt that her effusiveness was not in character, but she replied with the same enthusiasm. She was a kind girl and she felt that perhaps Mrs Fisk was lonely: she had told her that her son had recently moved out. The now almost invisible corn was treated and Amelia repacked her bag, went to the bathroom to wash her hands and returned to the sitting-room to say what she felt would be a final goodbye and receive her fee. She could hear Mrs Fisk in the kitchen.

When she came in she was bearing the same tea tray that she had before, with some rather nice-looking biscuits on a plate in the middle of it. Amelia did not mind staying for tea as it was her last case of the day – five o'clock. The tea was welcome. 'You are kind to me, Mrs Fisk,' she said.

Jane had just poured out their first cup when there was the sound of a key in the front door and Nigel walked in.

'Someone's parked where I usually . . .' He stopped as he saw Amelia. 'Oh sorry, didn't know you had a visitor, Ma.'

Jane got up. 'This is Amelia Wheeler; she's a chiropodist.'

Amelia held out her hand. 'How do you do, Mr Fisk.'

Nigel looked surprised and, Jane noticed, a little awkward. 'I'll get another cup, dear,' she said and she left the room.

Amelia turned to Nigel; her grey eyes were frank, friendly. 'Mrs Fisk tells me you used to live here with her?'

'Yes, I did.' Nigel sat down in the chair opposite her. There was a silence. Jane Fisk returned with the extra cup and saucer. Nigel got up. 'No, Ma, sorry, I'm in a bit of a rush. Just want to get the camcorder, then I'm off.'

'Don't be rude, dear. Just have a cup of tea with us.'

Nigel, rather to Amelia's amusement, sat down again and took the proffered teacup. The conversation limped around a little, then Amelia got up. 'I must go, Mrs Fisk. Thank you so much for the lovely tea and delicious biscuits.'

Jane saw her to the door. When she came back in Nigel had left the sitting-room and the tea she had poured out and gone upstairs to get the camcorder. He came downstairs almost immediately carrying it. 'Sorry to rush, Ma.'

Jane hid her feeling of resentment. 'You could have been a little more polite to Amelia,' she said.

Nigel was about to reply when the whirr of a car-starter

sounded outside – but the engine did not fire. Whirr, whirr, went the starter.

Jane went to the front door. 'It's Amelia's car, it won't start.'

Nigel came and stood behind her, looking at the red car opposite. 'Ring the garage, Ma,' he suggested, picking up the camcorder.

'Can't you just help her, Nigel? Can't you just see if you can make it go? For goodness sake, Jeremy will wait a few minutes, won't he?'

It was the first time she had mentioned Jeremy's name, in that tone. Nigel looked at her sharply, left the house, and crossed the road to the red Mazda.

Amelia Wheeler smiled up at him through the glass of the car window. He opened the door. 'Having trouble?' he asked. He knew his voice sounded sharp – he spoke in the same way to his colleagues at school, male or female; never any difference; in the classroom as well, boys or girls, the same manner, the same attitude to both; guarded – guarded. He tried to relax, then went round to the other side of the car and got into the passenger seat.

At that very moment Carmen's car drew by. Jane could hardly believe her luck! Nigel sitting beside the girl in the car! She was sure Carmen had seen them. Fate, Jane felt, was on her side; on Nigel's side. Her lies would save him, save his job, and when at last he went away no one would be any the wiser.

Amelia tried the starter again – nothing. 'I shouldn't do that too much, you'll run the battery down.' Nigel tried to make his voice softer, more normal. Her perfume was pleasant, fresh, like herself. So many women chose the wrong perfume, he was aware of that; and men the wrong aftershave – he was even more aware of that.

'Perhaps I'd better walk up and get the garage man?'

Nigel almost jumped at the sound of her voice. 'No, no, just a second, let me try something.' He got out of the car and found the battery. One terminal was slightly loose. He tightened it. 'Now try,' he called.

The engine started at once. Amelia wound down the window as he came forward beside the driver's door. 'Oh, how clever of you. Thank you so much.'

He noticed that her teeth were very white and even and there was a small, very small, gold stud in her ear. 'Just the terminal a bit loose, not very clever really.' Nigel suddenly laughed; he felt pleased with what he had done. 'Are you coming to see my mother again?' he asked.

'Well, she has no further appointment with me, not with her toes, anyway.'

'I hope you do come and see her. I feel I've left her in the lurch somehow and I'm afraid she might be lonely.'

Amelia shook back her brown hair. 'I'll see then. I've got another patient in the village, maybe . . .'

Nigel went round and slammed the passenger door shut for her. 'Goodbye.'

She drove out, her head turning from side to side to make sure the road was clear both ways, her hair moving softly as she did so. Then she was gone.

Nigel crossed the road and joined Jane. 'Just the battery terminal loose, Ma.'

'Pretty girl, isn't she?' Jane asked. She was aware that she was looking at him too long and too hard.

'Hardly a girl, Ma,' Nigel replied. 'Hope she calls on you again, though – she's nice.' He picked up the camcorder, gave Jane a swift peck on the cheek – unusual – and left.

Jane shut the door, heard him drive off and went into the sitting-room to collect the tea things. Carmen! Carmen of all people! To motor by just at the perfect moment! What a support for her story! Jane was well content with her afternoon.

Nigel Fisk drove home, to his new home. He wanted to get rid of the feeling of guilt about his mother living alone. That girl Amelia had seemed to be friendly with Ma. Of course there were all the old girls in the village, but he could not help feeling that his mother's interests and intellectual capabilities were rather superior to theirs – that is, the few he had met. The vicar and his wife were a drag. That girl, Amelia – Nigel could still smell her perfume, see that smile and the tiny gold stud in her ear. He smiled to himself. Nice girl, he hoped his mother would see more of her.

As he passed the Bensons' house he saw Robert swinging on their gate. The garden behind him looked full of junk. Outside stood a rather broken-down-looking car, a blue car with a white door and a brown bonnet – a put-together car, a bits-and-pieces car. On the lawn behind the boy an old moped leaned at a drunken angle. Two tea chests stood near the door and an old carpet, brown and soaked with rain, spilled out of the top of one. Robert was stroking a ginger cat on the gatepost; he waved as Nigel passed. His hair was cut short now; he looked better, healthier. Maybe the letter had worked. Perhaps it had done some good. Nigel remembered the boy's warm body. Since Jeremy, though, he no longer felt that terrible longing. He drove faster.

As he approached his house and was about to park he saw a white sports car draw away and speed off. It was Nigel Dawson. He was surprised: he had not known that Jeremy had told Nigel One, as he called Dawson, where they lived; secrecy until July had been their idea. Or so he thought . . . He entered the house.

Jeremy was upstairs and had obviously seen Nigel's car arrive. 'You just missed Nigel One,' he called and came down the stairs. He was smoking a cigarette and looked slightly defiant. 'I've done nothing about getting supper. I thought we might go out?'

'All right, we'll have a pub supper in the village – that should be safe enough.' Nigel went upstairs. 'I'll just change.'

When he came down Jeremy was on the telephone. Nigel went through to their little living-room – he did not like to appear to be listening. The telephone was in the hall. After a few moments Jeremy came in. He crossed the room, put his arms round Nigel's shoulders and danced him round the room. 'A job for Jeremy – only a catalogue, but four days' work.'

Nigel was pleased for him; his boredom was already apparent and the time had to be got through somehow until July. 'Have you ever modelled before, Jeremy?'

'Oh yes. Had a few. Some porno, when bread was short.' He laughed at Nigel's expression. 'Oh, don't worry, I didn't get raped or anything, darling. The photographer was into women – I mean, into – not interested in little me.'

Nigel hated it when Jeremy talked like this. The relationship to him seemed to be so precious and that kind of conversation cheapened it. 'What was young Dawson doing here? I didn't know you'd told him where we were living. Was that wise?'

Jeremy mocked him. 'Don't talk like that, Nigel Two – you sound like a schoolmaster.'

'Well I am a schoolmaster, if you remember, Jeremy.'

Jeremy leaned over the electric fire and peered at his face in the mirror. 'Look, Nigel dear, I'm putting up with living in Boresville just for you.'

'Yes, I realise that. It must be dull for you.'

Jeremy wheeled round. 'Never mind, relief's coming up – I can go to London and pose.' He stood, making a gesture with his hands. 'I shall need some money.'

'Money?'

Jeremy looked at him, his blue eyes wide. 'Yes, dear, money – the folding stuff. Bread, loot, dosh – you know, the stuff that keeps body and soul together.'

'All right, I'll see to it,' Nigel said.

The two went out to the car and got in. 'How much will you need, do you think?' Nigel asked.

'Oh, two hundred. I can stay with a friend.'

Nigel was aware of a stab of jealousy. 'Who?' he asked abruptly.

'Oh, you needn't worry, sweetie pie, I'll stay with Daphne. Daphne's a girl, but an all right dame. We've known each other for years, so stop worrying.'

They motored on in silence and hardly spoke until they were standing at the bar of the Boar's Head in Billingham and had drinks in front of them. They both scanned the menu written on a blackboard on the wall in chalk and chose scampi and chips. Then Nigel ventured again. 'What was Nigel One doing there when I got home? You didn't answer me when I asked you.'

Jeremy pouted. 'Visiting an old friend – what do you think he was doing there? Having sex with your little Jeremy?'

Nigel ignored the remark and they ate their meal, had a couple of drinks and drove home. That night there was a coldness between them that neither did anything to bridge.

Early the next morning, before school, Nigel drove Jeremy to the station. Once he was settled in his seat, Jeremy stared through the window at Nigel, who was standing waiting for the train to move. Nigel wished he could go. They had said goodbye. Jeremy had pecked him on the cheek. Now they were separated by the glass window and he felt sad. As Nigel had handed up the suitcase Jeremy had straightened his back and looked down at him, his blue eyes full of suspicion. 'I can smell perfume on you – a woman's perfume.'

Nigel thought of the girl with the small gold stud in her ear.

'Nonsense, Jeremy,' he had said. 'It's your aftershave you can smell.'

'Bollocks, dearest, that's a bitch's smell,' and he had got into the train, swinging his hips like a girl.

Now as the train began to move slowly forward he pursed his lips in a mock kiss or two, then raised a hand and slid from Nigel's view as the train gathered speed. Nigel walked out of the station. The car-park was nearly full. He felt tears pricking his eyes and he had a strange premonition that he would never see his lover again. 'Ass – stupid ass,' he said aloud and a woman getting into a car next to his looked at him in surprise.

He suspected that Jeremy would have left the bathroom in the usual state, wet towels on the floor and no top on the toothpaste or aftershave; pyjamas dropped by the side of the bed; slippers, socks. Nigel looked at his watch; it was time to go back and tidy up after him. He would hate going home to find that mess, but knew that in truth he needed to touch these things, the objects so recently used. This time when he arrived back at their house it seemed very quiet, but as to the usual disarray that he had expected he was wrong. No pyjamas lay on the bedroom floor, no socks, no slippers. He went into the bathroom – the wet towel on the floor, yes, but Jeremy's toothpaste and aftershave were gone. Well, Nigel reasoned, he would take these things, he'd need them. He opened the bathroom cupboard; it was almost empty. His electric shaver, a newer one than Jeremy's, was gone, the aspirins, the little store of Brut aftershave belonging to Nigel, all were gone – dental floss, everything. Nigel closed the cupboard door and saw his face in the mirror on its door – tragic!

A quick look round revealed other things. Nigel's little bedside clock, an expensive one Ma had given him for Christmas, was gone. He looked in the wardrobe: several of his ties . . . oh God, why, why?

He looked at his watch again, time to go. He knew as he locked the front door of the house he had rented just because of Jeremy that the relationship might well be over. He felt that, but dismissed it almost as a superstition. The friend Jeremy had spoken of who would put him up for the week . . . He would let Nigel have the address and telephone number. But of course, he did not intend to. The telephone call, had it been true, had he got a job up there or was there someone . . . ? The address and the telephone number and the letter he knew would not

come. He blamed himself; he had not been able to see the untrust-
worthiness there. It was his fault, his stupidity. Jeremy was just
Jeremy.

Standing at the lectern on the dais at assembly, outwardly calm
but inwardly weeping, he decided he would tell Ma. Thank God
she had shielded him from everyone else. This morning he would
telephone and try and rescind his notice. Was that a good idea?
Yes, he thought so. He couldn't live without a job. He couldn't
think at the moment what to say. 'Due to family reasons there was
no longer any necessity to . . .'

He felt the PE teacher nudge his arm. 'Got an announcement
about football practice, headmaster – OK?'

Nigel pulled himself back into the present. 'Sorry, of course.' He
moved away from the lectern.

The PE master, young, chunky, adored by the whole school,
gave him a quick, rather leery grin. 'Far away with the girlfriend,
headmaster?' It was only a whisper, only a sentence, but in a way
it was a comfort, although it brought to Nigel even more confusion of mind to remember a smile, white even teeth and a tiny
gold stud as an ear-ring.

The post of headmaster had not yet been advertised. Yes, they
would see what they could do. Nigel, when he at last put the
phone down, had been speaking to the chairman of the governors.
The man had called him 'old man'. 'Yes, old man, I understand.
I'll do what I can. The resignation can't have gone far down the
line. Don't worry.'

That day was like a mini-nightmare to Nigel. He felt sick, excused himself from the staff lunch and went for a walk. As he
walked the need to confide in someone, to cry on someone's
shoulder if you like, became stronger and stronger. Jeremy, his
first and last love. What a way for a forty-year-old headmaster
to be thinking, to be behaving! Where could he have gone wrong
. . . ? He would tell his mother – she would hardly be able to
conceal her delight. There was no one to tell who would understand how he felt. As he headed back into the school gates he
suddenly knew who he would tell – the other Nigel, Nigel One.
The very title brought back Jeremy's blue dark-lashed eyes. That
night in the Dragon when he had first met him – it seemed years
ago but it was only weeks. 'And in a little time, with so much
feeling . . . can the soul be torn to ribbons.' Who had said that? He
couldn't remember, but he felt it was true.

He telephoned: 'Sure, come and have a drink. On my own here. Pa will be out, shooting anything that moves. Actually he's going out shooting poachers. Fair game in the dark.' He laughed; Nigel remembered the laugh from the pub. He was putting his trust in someone who might let him down, but it didn't matter – he had to tell someone. He looked forward to that evening, half with fear yet half with longing.

Michaela approached the Manor with confidence. This was slightly marred as she gave the long iron bell-pull a tug and it came off in her hand. The bell had rung inside the house before the fracture occurred and she was left standing with the foot-long black iron staff in her hand. She held on to it and waited. There was the sound of firm footsteps across a wooden floor, the barking of two dogs – then she heard a large and impressive rusty mortice lock turning and the door opened. The Brigadier stood there, rather to Michaela's surprise – she had expected a servant of some kind to open the door.

The Brigadier surveyed his visitor, took in the piece of ironwork in her hand and stood back. 'Miss . . . Brook, Hawthorne Cottage?' It was obvious that he was hazarding a guess.

Michaela spoke. 'I've come to ask a great favour of you, Brigadier.'

'Come in, come in.'

As she stepped into the large hall the two dogs came forward, not barking now, but tails wagging. Michaela bent and with her free hand patted Quest's head, then she turned back to the Brigadier. 'Would you like your bell back?' She handed him the tall wand.

He blinked. 'Oh yes, thanks. Does that. Better knock when you . . .' He leant the large iron piece against an umbrella stand packed with walking sticks, umbrellas and a couple of ancient shooting sticks.

It was obvious to Michaela that Frank Dawson was not used to droppers-in. He dithered a little. 'Er, er, come through,' he said. In the same room in which Hugh Ainsworth had nearly fainted, Michaela looked round in admiration; as the Brigadier made no effort to sit down himself and did not offer her a chair, she walked over to the bookcase wall of the room. She looked with interest at the contents. Winston Churchill's *The Second World War*, well read, Sassoon's *Memoirs of a Fox-hunting Man*, then, surprisingly, a row of Jane Austen, including *Lady Susan* and *The Watsons*, beautifully bound in red leather, their spines gold-lettered. Butler's *Lives of the Saints* took up nearly half a shelf. The glass panels of the door needed cleaning.

'What a wonderful collection of Butler's *Lives of the Saints*. I am not a Catholic, but I always had a softspot for St Jude, patron saint of lost causes.' Michaela smiled up at the Brigadier; she was five foot eight, but his six foot two, at least, made her look up at him. 'Jane Austen, too, a lovely set.'

He began to look less awkward. 'Do sit down. Tell you what, no one to make coffee at the moment, how about some Madeira and a biscuit?'

'Delicious!' Michaela nodded her head in approval.

He was absent for a few minutes then came back with two glasses. He handed her one and sat down on the chair opposite. 'The Austens were my wife's,' he said, almost abruptly, as if to excuse them; then 'Can't find any biscuits.'

Michaela sipped the Madeira, sweet and dark. 'Bual, isn't it?' she asked.

'That's right. A woman's drink, I think, but acceptable after dinner for dessert.'

As they were drinking it at eleven in the morning she let that pass. However, he saw the point and laughed. The laughter broke the tension between them. His rather bushy brows drew together over his surprisingly blue eyes. 'A favour then. What is it? What do you want, Miss Brook, some money for something? That's what it usually is, eh?'

'Rather more I'm afraid, Brigadier.' Michaela crossed her legs and noticed that he looked at them, with a shade of approval – she did not mind. Her sixty-odd years had not changed her slim ankles and she always splurged out on shoes. Her neat brogues went well with the tweed skirt above. She felt a little flirtatious. Anyway, she wanted to soften him up a little.

'It's the village hall roof – leaks like a sieve,' she started.

'I'm no good at roofs,' the Brigadier broke in. Michaela really laughed then, and threw back her head. He started again. 'Oh, you want a contribution, eh?'

'Not really, it's more than that even.' Then Michaela outlined her scheme. 'A wine and cheese party, about six o'clock. Wine – white only – assorted cheeses. Tickets three pounds; by invitation.'

The Brigadier let her finish, then answered with a flat, 'No, not having herds of people in here. Haven't got the glasses.' More excuses poured out. Michaela waited, savouring the Madeira. He ground to a halt, muttering.

'Brigadier, you are the squire of the village, after all. There seems to be no community spirit and, you may know, a lot of gossip and unpleasant poison pen letters are going about.'

'So . . . ?' He finished his Madeira and filled their glasses again. 'Squire, eh, is that what they call me? Buggardier was the name for me, I thought.' He took a cigar from the box by his side. 'Mind if I . . . smoke?'

Michaela shook her head. 'Not at all.'

He went on, 'Matter of fact I had a letter – bloody cheek.' He paused to light the cigar. 'Son's a poof, you know. You've probably seen him – looks like one, too.' He puffed at the cigar. 'Sent his friend packing because of that bloody letter. Excuse me.'

Michaela wondered whether she should tell him about their letter, but decided not to. There was silence for a moment or two; the pleasant-smelling cigar smoke drifted round Frank Dawson. The fire in the hall crackled. Quest got up from the rug and clicked into the room. 'Logs falling out, boy?' The Brigadier got up. 'Squire, eh? Well, come through and I'll show you the room we could have your cocktail party in.'

'Wine and cheese party, Brigadier,' Michaela gently corrected.

Through the hall into the drawing-room, one of the most beautiful rooms Michaela had ever seen, culminating in french windows opening on to the spring garden, which had been allowed to run wild and yet had kept its charm. White jonquils and yellow daffodils grew in clumps of colour; here and there a late crocus popped out of the lawn and the daisies had been allowed to flourish. Tall trees framed the garden, but did not exclude the sunlight. Primroses, already trying to bud, showed yellow tips. The room itself was like the rest of the house. Michaela had seen pine floors, rugs scattered. A large settee and four equally big club chairs were scattered around the room, two by the fireplace, large and empty A sofa table, charming in its proportions, stood in its proper place behind and close to the big settee.

'This is beautiful.' Michaela stopped in the doorway, entranced.

The Brigadier glanced at her, then looked away. 'Not used much now, since my wife . . . Do you think it would do for the, ah, cocktail – I mean, wine and cheese do?'

'They should feel privileged to be allowed in such a room and such a house – and they will, I'm sure.' Michaela went towards the fireplace and looked up. Over it hung a portrait; a brown-eyed woman looked down at her, her shining hair coiled, her hands, white and long, relaxed in her lap. A golden spaniel sat at her feet gazing up at her. 'Your wife?'

'Yes.' The Brigadier turned away.

Michaela put a tentative hand on his tweed-clad arm. 'You must miss her so much; and Nigel, your son, must miss her, too.'

'Yes, I do. Perhaps he does, too, I don't really know.'

'I'm sure he does.'

The Brigadier looked at her again and walked over to the french windows and threw them open. 'This garden was once . . .' He stopped, tapped his foot on the floor, pulled at his cigar. 'You a country woman?' he asked.

She shook her head. 'I was a farmer's daughter in Yorkshire, but . . . Then I left and landed in a town. Regretted it in some ways. I was teaching. I wanted the country again, that's why I came to this village.'

'Bad choice. Used to be good, now it's full of back-biting old women – all of them. No decent families.' Michaela let the remark pass. 'All right, you can have the party thing, the charity thing, but don't expect me to come.' It was said in a very curt way, but Michaela saw him look up as he passed at the brown eyes in the portrait and forgave his curtness.

When she left, the date and the number of invitations, the food, the wine had all been decided on. As they stood at the door with his dogs, their tails wagging now, the Brigadier suddenly said, 'I'll supply the wine – two dozen bottles?'

'That's very generous, Brigadier,' Michaela said, but she said it to thin air because the door had closed on him and the dogs.

As she opened the gate to leave, a white sports car stood there. Michaela recognised the young man getting out as the son of the house. 'Oh thanks,' he said as Michaela opened the other gate for the car to come through.

'I'll shut them after, shall I?'

He smiled at her affably, got back into his car and drove through the gate. She closed the gates after him; one squeaked. Michaela, feeling satisfied, saw the latch was in place and left.

12

Nigel heard nothing from Jeremy, no letter, no telephone call, nothing. Yet at the end of the week he felt sure at times that he would return, that he, Nigel, had jumped too quickly to the conclusion that Jeremy would be gone for good. At night, when he couldn't sleep, he found himself trying to justify the disappearance of the bedside clock, the razor and all the other things that Jeremy had taken. He tortured himself as he alternated between two conclusions: his lover was a thief and he had seen the last of him; or he had just borrowed the things and would return. One night he dreamt a horrible dream from which he woke sweating. Jeremy had returned and had stood in the door of the bedroom naked, ready to cross the room and jump into bed and embrace him, but just as he had held out his arms another pair of arms, strong, sunburned and hairy, had encircled Jeremy's waist and dragged him back; Jeremy had struggled, trying to break away from the encircling arms, but could not. Lying awake afterwards Nigel could not dismiss the thought from his mind that Jeremy was being coerced, kept away from him – perhaps by money or threats or . . . The next day he had felt ill and hung-over, but in the evening he had still waited for the telephone to ring. It didn't.

At the end of the week, at about seven in the evening, he had a visitor. When he saw the white sports car drive up he almost decided not to answer the door, but the sitting-room light was on and he decided that it would be foolish and might look as if he was hiding – afraid.

At the front door the other Nigel stood, tall, rather angular, handsome. 'Jeremy here?' he asked.

'No.' Nigel Two's answer was abrupt.

'Didn't think he would be. Had a card from him.' He hesitated, then: 'May I come in?'

Nigel stood back. 'If you want to.'

'Look, old chap, I'm not here to gloat, just to give you the gen.' Dawson smelled of tobacco and fresh air. 'Will you have a drink?' Nigel asked him.

'Got any whisky?'

Nigel poured out two measures and put a glass on the table in front of Dawson.

'Great. Thanks.'

His reluctant host took in the well-cut slacks, expensive pullover, hand-made shoes. 'He sent me a card, through you?'

'Yup. I suppose he meant me to give it to you.' He pulled the card from his trouser pocket and handed it to Nigel Two:

Nigel One. Dearest. Poor Nigel Two, Boresville. Can't stand it any longer. Have taken off. Till July was just too much. Love always – well nearly always. Jeremy.

Nigel read it, then looked across the room at the other Nigel. There was a strange feeling of bonding between them, not voiced just felt. Nothing sensual, just . . .

'Typical of the lad. Couldn't see him just staying here, staying put to wait for you, especially in these surroundings. He likes the bright lights, Jeremy.'

Nigel Two threw the card down. He felt he didn't want to touch it. 'Boresville', that's how Jeremy had thought of him. Probably the boy was right, he was a bore.

Dawson took the card and tore it into four pieces. 'Don't get overwrought, old boy, about Jeremy. There's plenty more where that came from.' He saw how his companion flinched. 'OK, OK, so you were fond of him – so was I.'

Dawson sat there with his legs crossed, a cigarette dangling from his hand. Nigel noticed there was a heavy gold signet ring on the third finger of his left hand. There was something he had not squared up to in his own mind. He had a confession to make, Nigel Two, and he made it.

'I never should have been a schoolmaster, I'd never . . . ' He stopped.

Dawson nodded. 'I could tell that in the pub, you were a beginner.' He laughed, but not unpleasantly.

Nigel went on, 'That's it. Now he's gone – it's funny, Dawson, the biggest feeling is relief. Is that how you felt?'

Dawson shook his head. 'No, mate, I didn't feel anything much. I'm sort of broken in, you know?'

Nigel poured more whisky into each glass. 'Why do you wear that ring?' He blurted out the question. Nigel One seemed so cool, so unruffled by anything. There was no attraction between them; it was just another man – it was comfortable. Nigel One and Nigel Two, what the hell was it all about?

Dawson put the cigarette in his mouth and his eyes narrowed and blinked against the smoke as it curled up. He touched the heavy ring and twisted it round and round on his finger. 'Wedding ring. I was, and am, married. Got a boy, six. Nice brat for a brat. I see them often. Wife, Bunny, wants me to move back with her. Dad does, too. May do, I'm not sure – I'm not sure I'm a marrying animal. Still it was great at first.'

He left, leaving Nigel feeling that he had not lived at all. His sensuality had always been hidden, just in his mind; dominating his every action, every thought. He tried again to think, when had he first become convinced of his homosexuality? The girl, the young pert little schoolgirl of long ago – he remembered only too well his feelings for her. At sixteen, muddled with shame, excitement, fear – twenty-five years ago. Things were different now. The young seemed to have fewer problems – fewer problems with sex anyway, but maybe that was the pill. Perhaps it had given them more problems – how did he know?

He began to wonder whether he was fit to cope with a school. Had he ever been fit to cope with the young? One thing he had learned today, or this week, was that he knew little or nothing about himself and little or nothing about anyone else – that, he had the humour to admit, was a step forward. At least maybe his humour remained. He had felt better for Dawson's visit.

He thought of the boy Robert Benson and his feelings about him. Jeremy had taken the place of that feeling, satisfied it. He didn't know if that was permanent. Why then this feeling of relief, of escape? He couldn't work it out.

A few days later his resignation was rescinded – they said they were glad he was staying – and then a note came in the post to confirm that he could keep his job. A card arrived from Jeremy in an envelope – at least he had that much discretion:

Sorry Lover. Couldn't bear the country life. You
were a doll – but not for me – I'm a shit really. J.

He also received an invitation to a wine and cheese party at the Brigadier's. That he rated unimportant – but he rated wrongly.

111

Carmen received her invitation with some trepidation. Every typed envelope that came through her door she opened as if it might be a letter bomb – but a wine and cheese party and at the Manor! What would she wear? Oh, she realised it was only for the village hall roof, but fancy the Brigadier doing such a thing! She pulled herself up with a jerk; just supposing the letter-writer was there – well, probably would be if all the village came. She'd have to be very careful what she said. She'd talk to Philippa; surely she would be back by then. Dr Barnes had returned, he came back a week ago – more than that – but no Philippa. She'd gone to stay with her sister in Northampton, that's what the vicar had said. Perhaps it was true, but that letter! Was there something going on between Philippa and Dr Barnes? Of course, they wouldn't – couldn't – return together, could they? And the vicar looked so ill; just like a man whose wife had left him. She stopped the thought there and spoke aloud: 'Now, Carmen!' She was getting into the habit of censoring her own thoughts and words. 'Of course she's with her sister in Northampton – don't even think of any other explanation . . .' She cracked open her breakfast egg as if she was beheading someone. 'Not a word; be extra careful,' she said aloud.

'What, Mrs Delano?' the milkman asked. 'Extra pint, is it?' The back door was open, the mornings were getting warmer and the sun was pleasant.

Carmen jumped and nearly spilled her coffee. 'No – no, thank you.'

'I thought you said extra,' the milkman said, looking at her rather accusingly.

'No, I was just thinking about . . .' she said.

He departed and she continued her breakfast, the invitation propped up against the toast rack. Many printed invitations did not come her way. She would stick it in the frame of the mirror over the mantelpiece in her sitting-room.

At the Thorntons' the little printed card was received with some pleasure and excitement by Mabel, but with suspicion by her husband, Ted.

'Six pounds, that'll be – just for some wine that I don't like and cheese that gives me heartburn! Not likely!'

'Oh, Ted, it's lovely to be asked to the Manor. I'd love to see inside and it's good of the Brigadier, you must admit, to take an interest in the village hall – I mean . . .'

'You go, you'll enjoy it.' Ted took refuge, as usual, behind his paper.

'Do you know, Ted, it's my birthday – it'll happen on my birthday – and the ticket will do for a birthday present. But I won't go if you won't.'

Ted lowered the paper and looked across at his wife; she was taking the treatment well, but she didn't look all that bright, he thought – a bit pale. He hid his anxiety; because they knew each other so well he knew that she was hiding her own. They tried not to worry each other. 'All right then, I'll take you, but it's not a birthday present. I've already got you something else.'

Her face lit up like a girl's. 'Oh what, Ted?'

He shook his head. 'Not telling,' he said.

Ted never forgot birthdays or anniversaries, though sometimes his presents were a shade too practical. Last Christmas he had given Mabel three new enamel saucepans, although they were pretty, flowers all around them. Mabel hoped it wasn't an electric kettle this time as her old one was a bit dodgy. Still, the wine and cheese party would be nice. Like Carmen she immediately thought, What shall I wear? Then she decided on her blue summer dress, new last year – long sleeves. If she wore a spencer under it no one would know. It might be cold at the Manor, but that would make it warm enough. It might show where her bust was a bit different – she hoped not. She'd pad her bra if it did.

'Who will be there, Ted? Most of the village, I suppose. I wonder if Mrs Ainsworth will be back. I'll have to press your suit.' She rambled on, happy to have something to look forward to.

Ted answered none of her questions, but closed the discussion with: 'Well, I hope it's worth six quid, that's all.'

Jane Fisk was pleased to get the invitation. It gave her an idea. Nigel had been to supper twice this week. He had not mentioned Jeremy except to say that he was going to London to do a modelling job; nothing more. He had been quiet, watched television with her, had supper, then left. He had changed – said nothing about his resignation. He had mentioned earlier that he had resigned, but after that he had said nothing about it. Nothing about an application for a new job anywhere else. Usually he told her everything, now nothing.

The wine and cheese party . . . She hoped Jeremy would not come – he might be away. She was determined to ask Amelia Wheeler. After all, Nigel had met her and would speak to her – and she could add a little to her plot to still the rumours about her son till he had gone. He knew the form, she had explained it all to him; he would have to act as she said, otherwise it was risky. She would have to insist that Nigel stayed with Amelia, stayed by her side, talked to her. Please God she wouldn't see anyone that she wanted to flirt with – young Dawson, perhaps. The old frisson of excitement came back. The party itself might be rather a bore; people meeting in more formal surroundings, greeting each other when probably they had already met in the village that morning – still . . . She put the invitation on the mantelpiece, took the chiropodist's card out of her handbag and dialled Amelia's number. The answering machine . . . She put the message on: 'Would you like to come? If you feel shy, Nigel and I will introduce you to people.' She put the telephone down, then wondered whether she should have added that last bit. Well, it was too late now.

Now there was just Nigel to cope with, and that was easy. The thought of it being so easy made her pause; the little fair-haired schoolgirl of long ago came back to her, with her cross, pouting lips and her narrowed eyes, her frown, the expression, all brought on by her, Nigel's mother. 'Go away and leave my son alone.' And here she was, planning his life again, only this time thrusting – well, helping – him into the arms of a man; or at least plotting so that he could go unobserved into the arms of that man. How much was it her fault?

Hugh Ainsworth walked about his house and did his parish duties in a daze. His sermon on Sunday he'd taken from a book of sermons on his bookshelf. He hardly noticed or cared whether the reaction of his small congregation was good or bad. The rows of vacant pews meant little or nothing to him except perhaps to illustrate how right Philippa was, or rather had been. He was a failure as a clergyman and also as a man, though nothing really mattered to him now.

The one small positive thing he had done after burying his wife had been to glue into place the corner of the kitchen table; it had fitted perfectly, the crack not even showing. This small act had given him pleasure, something he had done successfully. It didn't matter to anyone else, but to him the small piece of wood fitting into place and forming again the square of the table was satisfaction, a triumph even.

Dr Barnes came back looking happy and relaxed. The story now circulated by Hugh was that his wife was visiting her sister in Northamptonshire. Perhaps they, the village gossips, thought she was staying in some hideaway supplied by her lover, Eric Barnes – those who had seen the letter, that is. Hugh didn't give a damn what they thought. He missed Philippa, not as a wife or companion but as a person close to him who understood nothing of his feelings and understood only his failures – that had been a comfort, after all. None of his flock could tell him to his face what a bore he was, they just voted with their feet and went in greater numbers to the little ramshackle chapel, while Beattie preached and apparently charmed . . . Oh well, it didn't matter any more. Left with hardly anyone in the church and deserted almost by his verger, he felt that his life was more restful. He sat at his breakfast table – he had cooked himself bacon and eggs, though he didn't want food much or relish it. He must, he felt, eat as normally as he could, not allow himself to get thinner and thinner, waste away as if his life was falling apart. Wives did, after all, go and stay with their sisters. He would perhaps embellish the story a little, add another lie or two, say perhaps that Philippa's sister had just lost her husband or that one of her children had been killed in a car crash. His imagination ranged all these possibilities; they were endless. His feelings of guilt about his wife disappeared, giving way to a strange blank feeling, almost as if he was living outside the man in the clerical collar.

As he breakfasted the postman dropped letters through the front door. Hugh got up, collected them and came back to the kitchen.

One was a reminder that his TV licence was due, another a circular from a catalogue addressed to Philippa, the third a white typed envelope – another bloody anonymous letter, he thought, but without the slightest anxiety; after all nothing mattered now, whatever anyone wrote about Philippa or her actions was irrelevant. He slit open the envelope. 'Wine and Cheese at six o'clock in aid of the village hall – tickets three pounds – at the Manor' (a slight surprise, the Brigadier did nothing for the village or the

115

church usually – well, just a donation now and again perhaps, but even that was unreliable). Hugh sighed. He would go, of course; it would look strange if he didn't, and he did not want anything to look different, odd.

The Brigadier and the Manor brought to his mind the two dogs running and scratching and digging. Every day the old man took them walking and if one day they dug a little deeper, scratched a little more – well, what would they find? Strangely he felt no dread; if they found Philippa or if anyone else found her that would be the end of him – and would that really matter? He could not bring himself to believe that it was of importance at all.

Why not confess, then – go to trial and prison? Why tell lies about the sister in Northampton? He pondered that and came up with an answer that surprised him: he liked being alone, having no one to accuse him of anything. Most of all, he realised he might have hated her, hated his wife, and never known it. His congregation, too, his church, the Bishop, his job – he loathed them all! One day he might take off, disappear into the blue yonder, but before he went he would preach a sermon that they would all remember . . . He would practise that, he would write it; he looked forward to doing it.

The opportunity came that evening. A drizzle of rain began to fall; at six the sky was overcast, making the evening dark. After a quick supper Hugh made his way through the wet grass to the cemetery, avoiding the path through the lychgate; he didn't want to be seen going into the church. Once there he switched on the small light over the pulpit. The subdued glow made the church look bigger, more imposing, and the pale light from the windows hardly illuminated it at all. Hugh stood in the pulpit, his hands resting on the edge. 'This is not going to be one of my usual sermons, it's going to be the truth about this goddamned village and the people in it.' He went on, preaching to the empty pews, the embroidered hassocks, the cold stone altar, the brass cross, the candlesticks, the tall wax candles. He poured out his frustrations and anger, his grief and his guilt, his loneliness. The empty church echoed a little.

The door creaked, he had forgotten to lock it. The local bobby put his head round the door. 'Oh sorry, Reverend, I saw the light. I thought them vandals had got in again – not you, like . . .' He reached for a word. '. . . not practising, like.'

Hugh came slowly down the steps of the pulpit, light-headed

but feeling, too, a necessity to justify his behaviour. 'Yes, just trying my Sunday sermon out; rehearsing, officer.'

'Yes, Reverend, but don't forget to lock up, will you?'

Hugh shook his head. 'I won't,' he said.

When the policeman had gone he turned the big key in the lock, walked down the aisle, turned right at the altar – did not even look towards it – out through the sacristy door, locking that, through the wet grass, down the path and out on to the road. Back in the vicarage he poured himself a stiff whisky. Did he feel better for letting out that stream of words? He was not sure, but then felt he would never be sure of anything again.

At the post office almost everyone who came in to post a letter, cash a pension, or buy groceries spoke of their invitation. The comments varied: 'Three pounds – it's a lot of money just for –' to be interrupted by: 'Well, it is for the hall, it's useless at the moment.' 'I don't know whether I'll go or not. I don't like wine, I wonder if there'll be soft drinks?' 'I hate cheese, it gives me a migraine.'

The postmistress enjoyed the influx of queries and speculations. She had been invited with her husband, but had met with a flat and immovable refusal. 'Wild bloody horses wouldn't drag me there. I'll pay for your ticket, though. You won't mind going on your own, will you?' The postmistress didn't mind at all; she knew that if her husband came with her he would hate it and be tugging at her arm as soon as they got there, saying, 'Come on, let's go.' Knowing everyone in the village, she would enjoy herself. She'd never known the Brigadier do anything like this before. No one, in her memory, had ever been asked to the Manor, either for a charity or for a sightseeing trip, so all were curious. It promised to be a real occasion.

13

Pat Beattie was expecting his wife and baby home from Italy. He had found an empty cottage next to the disabled Bill Ritter. He liked the old man and often went in to talk to him. This morning he was in the cottage drinking tea and telling Bill about his wife's return. He was

going up to London and his excitement and pleasure were evident.

'I can't wait to get her back, but I just couldn't go with her. She
understood, though.'

'Well, the cottage next door isn't much.' Bill Ritter didn't let the
conversation stop him working on his cardboard signs. In spite of
his age and disability his hand was steady and the sign-writing
perfection.

'We'll manage. I've already done a bit of decorating and a bit of
plumbing. The kitchen's workable. I've done two bedrooms pale
blue. It's going to look nice and I'm going to put a frieze round
Baby's room – Snow White and the Seven Dwarfs.'

'I can see you've done something pale blue.' Bill Ritter pointed
to Pat's trousers, which were spattered with the coloured paint.

Pat laughed, then became more serious. 'Do you think I should
be more . . . you know – more ministerish, Bill?' he asked. His
brown eyes looked at his companion with some anxiety. 'I mean,
Hugh Ainsworth looks so . . . well, so much the part – so respect-
able, so right. He's a nice man, too. I reckon if only he'd let me get
near him and chat, you know . . .'

'Well, here's your chance.' Bill pointed at the finished but still
wet letters on the sign. 'You going to this? I'm going. They're
fetching me.'

'Yes, I suppose I should. Maria won't be back till two days later,
but I'll go.'

'Well, you can have a chinwag with the vicar then, perhaps.'

'Maybe.' Pat sighed again. 'There's a lot to do here, Bill, in the
village. I wish my chapel was well built, not the hash-up it is. Still,
I suppose God doesn't mind a bit of plastic. After all, in a way he
invented it.'

Bill laughed. 'More people come to your plastic place than go to
the church now, Pat.'

'Yes, true. I suppose Ainsworth resents that, but if only we could
get together, both use his church – me one Sunday or . . . Oh, I
don't know what people want religion-wise these days.'

'Well, I don't hold with sermonising and collars on backward –
I don't hold with any of it. It only causes wars and fights and
arguments. Take the Crusades.'

Pat got up. 'Gotta go. See you at the party, Bill.'

'Yes – and put some clean trousers on.' Bill's parting shot just
reached Pat's ears as he walked down the little rutted lane.

Michaela arrived early at the Manor. She had suggested to Dorothy that it might be a good idea to come with her; they could both then see that everything was ready for the first and maybe early arrivals. She did not want to involve Frank Dawson with the village ladies on his own. Dorothy refused – rather coldly, Michaela thought. 'I'll come with everyone else,' she had said. Michaela wondered if she was jealous and could not quite understand why. She had been careful to discuss all the arrangements for the party with her friend and she felt that she had really tried to make Dorothy part of the whole affair, but throughout she had not obtained much response. Michaela was disappointed in Dorothy's attitude; she felt the relationship had deteriorated since that beastly letter had arrived. She would cheerfully, she felt, have wrung the neck of the person who had sent it. But why was Dorothy so changed? The overdose, that had been a shock of course, but since then she had been irritable, aloof, difficult. Their friendly relationship was fading away. Sometimes Michaela was even tempted to ask Dorothy if she would like to split up – sell the house and make other arrangements – but she could not bring herself to do so. Warm-hearted and affectionate herself, she could not easily tolerate coldness and remoteness in someone she lived with. She had made a great effort. 'Oh, come on, Dorothy, do come with me. Tell you the truth, I am a bit nervous about the whole shindig and I really coaxed Frank to have the do.' 'Exactly!' Dorothy had replied rather tersely. 'It's nothing whatever to do with me; it's your party – and "Frank" is it, now?' The last remark was a little more revealing to Michaela – it must be jealousy. 'Yes, Frank it is now, Dorothy; Frank it is. We have become friends, planning all this, and his son I call Nigel. It's no longer Brigadier and Mr Dawson.' Dorothy had sniffed and gone out for a walk on her own.

Now, as Michaela walked through the gates, up the drive and in through the open front door of the Manor, she did indeed feel a sense of friendly familiarity. Frank Dawson came out of the drawing-room. He was dressed for the occasion: he had on a patterned worsted suit, which was beautifully cut and showed off his tall spare figure to advantage.

'Oh Frank, you do look nice.'

He smoothed the sides of his moustache, as he always did when embarrassed, and tried to hide the pleased smile. 'Thought I'd better look decent, now I'm the squire.' His eyes twinkled.

'You've always been the squire, Dad.' Michaela was pleased to see Nigel walk in. 'Anything I can do to help before I go and fetch old Bill Ritter?' he asked.

'Nothing. Everything looks so good.'

Michaela looked round the big room with appreciation. A log fire blazed in the fireplace and in the hall too. The day had started sunny, but now in the evening it had grown cooler, and it would have been quite chilly without the fire.

'We'll have a job washing glasses,' Michaela said. 'We'll have to do some as we go along.' They had borrowed three dozen from the pub.

'No, we won't,' Nigel broke in. 'Dad's got Mrs Hunt in the kitchen – she's washing up and clearing up afterwards – and we're paying her. I'm going to supply her with wine and cheese. Shall we take the covers off the cheese now?'

Michaela nodded. 'Thank you so much, Brigadier, I didn't expect a paid help.'

'Neither did I expect you to go back to "Brigadier", instead of "Frank",' he said, watching Nigel going round the cheeses, unwrapping them from their plastic covers. Michaela had yesterday done one or two flower arrangements for the drawing-room and hall.

'Sorry,' Michaela smiled, 'I forgot. It's that new suit – it makes you look . . .' She giggled like a girl.

'Old-fashioned?' Frank Dawson suggested.

'No . . . handsome.'

Michaela drifted round the room distributing the plates of cut-up cheeses. The wine table had a white cloth on it and rows of uncorked bottles, their outsides slightly misted from their chilling in the refrigerator.

Young Dawson went to the front door, which Michaela had closed behind her. He opened it with a flourish. 'I now declare this knees-up open,' he said, throwing it wide back to the wall. He was about to go down the steps; in the distance the iron gate squeaked.

'Damn man hasn't oiled that gate – leave them open, Nigey.'

His son turned round. 'Long time since you called me that, Dad.' He smiled.

The first guests could be seen walking up the gravel drive as the white MG started up to go and fetch Bill Ritter and his wheelchair.

*

It's not often, Michaela thought, you start something that doesn't get overtaken by some large or even small mistake, but as she looked round the beautiful room, full now with people smiling at each other, drinking wine, eating her carefully cut up cheese, she was pleased. Mrs Hunt, the Brigadier's 'live-out' housekeeper, liberally supplied with glasses of wine by Nigel Dawson, walked about discreetly, putting down clean glasses and taking away dirty ones. Michaela hoped that Nigel was not supplying her too liberally with wine, but she certainly kept the used glasses washed and returned as some visitors left and others came in. The Brigadier sat at the door, taking money from those with invitations and explaining tactfully to those who had not received them that it had not been possible to send too many because of the expense, but they had hoped that Bill Ritter's signs would attract people to the affair – which had obviously been the case. So the non-invitation holders were quite happy. 'Never seen Dad so bland and charming for years, Michaela,' Nigel said, proffering her a glass of wine. Two fat ladies announced that they were from Leeds but had thought they might come to look over such a pretty house.

Michaela watched Jane Fisk drive away Nigel Dawson from the young brown-haired woman she had brought, and when her son Nigel arrived he stood beside the brown-haired one and his mother and never mingled. Must be the girlfriend Jane had talked about; nice-looking girl, quite the youngest person in the room.

The appearance of Hugh Ainsworth, the vicar, when he arrived shocked Michaela – and other people, too. His loss of weight, his pallid face, the hand which shook as he accepted his glass of wine from the table. When she had a minute she mentioned him to Frank, who nodded, understandingly Michaela thought.

'Poor chap, life's a bit complicated at the moment – needs a bit of support. Thought the ladies in the church would rally round a bit more than they have, though.' He looked across at where Pat Beattie, the minister, was holding court with quite a little crowd, as the Brigadier put it, of 'ladies'.

Michaela went and stood by Hugh Ainsworth. He made an effort. 'Very successful venture, Miss Brook,' he said.

'Sure, thought it would be. Glad you could come, vicar.' She thought she would question him, although she wondered if she was right in doing so. 'Is Mrs Ainsworth due back soon?'

121

He looked at her almost vacantly. 'What? Oh no, not yet. Family business. It takes time – you know how these things go when a crisis arises.'

'Yes, of course.' Michaela felt even sorrier for him; he looked so ill and sounded so . . . She couldn't really find the word – muddled, confused.

The Thorntons, she noticed, seemed to know Nigel Fisk's girlfriend and went and chatted to her. Michaela felt she had seen the girl somewhere before. Dr and Mrs Barnes arrived at that moment; Sheila Barnes was walking without a limp, so her ankle must be better.

Michaela felt smug – it was all going so well. Dorothy left before anyone else; she had not mingled much or appeared to enjoy meeting new people. Oh well, there was nothing she could do about it. She would be sorry, but if Dorothy wished to ruin their relationship they would have to part. Hawthorne Cottage had been ideal for them, but since that beastly letter and Dorothy's overdose nothing had been the same. She sadly watched Dorothy leave; they had always got on so well, or so Michaela had thought. Well, relationships change.

Carmen Delano broke into her thoughts. 'What a lovely party. Oh, I have enjoyed it – and the Brigadier . . . he's not a bit like I thought. And his son Nigel, what a nice boy – though we all know he's . . .' She stopped abruptly and her cheeks flushed. 'Oh, no, I didn't mean that. I meant . . . By the way, Michaela, I want to introduce you to . . .' She took Michaela by the arm. 'He's quite a famous author – television and all that – and she's very elegant. They've rented that lovely house down by the sea, near the golf course. They're thinking of buying it. They've been there two or three months, I think.' She rattled on and Michaela allowed herself to be led across the still-crowded room. 'A fire!' So nice to see a fire, isn't it?' Carmen murmured.

By the french windows stood a man and a woman. Michaela was immediately struck by the 'elegance', as Carmen had described it, of the woman's pale green linen suit, the beautifully cut silky hair and her perfume which came softly to Michaela.

Carmen introduced them. 'Mr and Mrs Turner.'

Michaela got a warm, firm handshake from the man. Slightly plump and bearded, he looked pleasant enough. The woman did not shake hands; she looked with a curiously cold level stare at Michaela. 'It's actually Bill Turner and my name is Agnes Turner.' Her lips did then curve in a small tight smile. 'Surnames seem completely out now, don't they?' and her smile widened a little more.

'Yes indeed. My name's Michaela. Christian names are in, as you say; everybody uses them, even in hospital the doctors and nurses are all Sally or June or David now.'

The woman in the green suit stiffened slightly, then relaxed again. 'Yes, I've always thought that a sorry state of affairs.' As she said this her husband looked at her with a face of humour.

'Are you in Highbury House at the moment? Carmen tells me . . .'

Bill Turner answered with enthusiasm. 'Yes, we love it – been there . . .' He looked at his wife. '. . . nearly three months now, isn't it, darling? Haven't been around this side of the Island much, though. We only came from Ryde. Didn't know this little village, so thought this would be a good way to break the ice.'

'Yes, I'm glad you came. You must come and have a meal with us, my friend and me, some time. We live here on the Green, Hawthorne Cottage.' Michaela was feeling hospitable to all the world.

At that moment Agnes' smile grew a little warmer. She turned to her husband. 'We'd like that, wouldn't we, darling? I want to get involved. I'm not too used to village activities.'

Her husband took his wife's hand with an affectionate gesture. 'I'm an author. I write murder mysteries. Hack them out in fairly large numbers.' He looked at his wife again. He was obviously very much in love with her. 'Agnes helps me quite a bit. Don't think I'll get any stimulation for murder plots in this little village, though.'

Michaela laughed. 'Don't be too sure,' she said. 'Gossip abounds and one does sometimes feel like strangling someone.'

The conversation became general before Michaela excused herself and left the two newcomers to Carmen's tender mercies while she went to hand out more wine to the now diminishing numbers. Indeed, Frank Dawson had given up his 'seat of custom', as he called it, and was chatting away to Bill Ritter, who looked as if he was enjoying himself hugely.

By eight o'clock everyone had left. Mrs Hunt had been paid and, Michaela noticed, rather weaved her way out. 'Lucky she's not driving!' said Nigel. 'I offered to take her home, but I happen to know she's got a couple of nearly full bottles in that bag, so I thought I'd better leave well alone.'

'She's earned them.' The Brigadier stretched his long legs out in front of the fire. They were all there, Michaela, Frank, Nigel and the two dogs, munching away at ham sandwiches that Mrs Hunt had made for them in lieu of dinner.

'That dame in green, with the bearded bloke – do you know, she drove off in a Porsche – new one, too – no less!' Nigel said, taking a long draught of beer.

'Well, he's a writer,' Michaela said.

'She was driving. I'd love a Porsche.' Nigel looked wistfully into the fire.

'Well, you're not likely to get one unless you take that job your father-in-law offered you, Nigey.' Michaela was surprised by the remark; 'ambidextrous', she thought – well, it takes all sorts!

After the nine o'clock news the party broke up, a hundred and fifty-six pounds nearer mending the village hall. 'Not bad, hundred and fifty-six,' said the Brigadier.

'That amount is thanks to you for supplying the wine free – that was a most generous gesture.'

He waved away the remark with what to Michaela was now a familiar dismissive gesture. He accompanied her to the door as young Dawson went to get the car to take her home. Once there, as Michaela turned to say goodnight, he stroked the sides of his moustache, and she wondered what he was going to say.

'Would you care to come out for a meal one evening, say next week? We could go to Gatcombe Hotel. It's rather nice – or was.'

Michaela beamed. 'I'd love to.'

'Say Tuesday?' he said.

'Yes, thank you. I'll look forward to that.'

'I'll call for you, at seven then?'

'Yes, that'll be lovely.' She held out her hand and he clasped it warmly.

'So . . . well, I, I . . . I'll look forward to it, too – ah, here's the boy.'

Nigel drew up in the MG and Michaela got in. 'Sporty car,' she said. They drove off. She looked back. Frank Dawson was still standing in his doorway, lit by the hall light behind him. He looked so right standing there, the two dogs beside him – but he looked lonely, Michaela thought.

Jane Fisk and her son Nigel walked home together. She was pleased that Nigel had taken Amelia to her car and that the two had remained talking for a few minutes before the red Mazda drove off.

Jane was determined to say nothing, ask nothing, about the girl or Jeremy or Nigel's resignation from the school. Indeed she was fearful of saying anything at all that might influence her son, for she was now haunted by the fact that she had influenced him in his adolescent years. She was doing her best to conceal something now in his make-up which could perhaps be laid at her door.

'I'm quite hungry, Ma, are you?'

She nodded and smiled at him. 'I'll make us a meal – a snack. Wine makes you hungry, I think.' She was delighted that he wanted to stay and eat with her. Jeremy must still be away, but she was not going to ask.

'And thirsty, too.' Nigel came through to the kitchen with her and took a bottle of mineral water out of the fridge. 'Want some?' he asked.

Jane shook her head. 'Scrambled eggs do?' she asked.

'Great,' he said. As he passed her he put a hand on her arm and squeezed it. She looked up from beating the eggs. 'Thanks, Ma,' he said, then he left the kitchen and went through to the sitting-room.

Jane was pleased but puzzled; what was that little gesture for? Thanks for the help with her cloaking his homosexuality – thanks for the meal – thanks for Amelia? She couldn't imagine; perhaps it was thanks for the party – thanks for using Amelia as a cover. She wasn't sure.

After their meal she found out.

'I want to talk to you, Ma.' Nigel lit a cigarette; he had never smoked – she had never before seen a cigarette in her son's hand. She still said nothing – made no comment, just sat quietly. 'Jeremy's not coming back, Ma. He left, taking a few things *en route* – my new clock, the one you gave me, my razor – oh trivial things; but I had a card, too, saying goodbye.'

There was a long pause, a long silence. Perhaps, Jane thought, he was waiting for his mother to say something, anything, but probably 'I told you so'. She didn't, so he went on: 'I was devastated, Ma, I really thought I . . . but I don't want to embarrass you with the sordid details.'

Jane shook her head. 'I'm sorry, Nigel, that it turned out to be . . . that you got hurt – I hate that.'

'That's what's strange, Ma, but it's as if something went with him. I felt such relief after a while – I couldn't understand my own feelings. I don't, even now; I don't understand them any more.'

Jane still made no comment, but put out a hand and covered his.

'Ma – I'm forty years old; I should know what I am, for God's sake, by now, but I don't. This evening, that girl Amelia, I felt comfortable with her.'

'Well, that's good, isn't it?' Jane suggested.

He nodded and sighed and drew on his cigarette. 'Well, you had to cover for me, Ma – thanks for that. I've still got my job, by the way. I'm still what you wanted me to be, a headmaster.' Jane tried to find bitterness in the remark, but couldn't. 'Perhaps I'm nothing, Ma, neither one thing nor the other. Anyway, I've asked Amelia out for a meal next week – I think she'll be safe with me; well, that's what I think now.' He smiled suddenly and got up. 'I must go, Ma.'

'Do you want to move back here, Nigel, with me?'

'Not yet, Ma.'

They walked towards the door.

'Nigel . . .' He turned. 'Do you remember that fair-haired girl at your school? You were keen on her. I wasn't.'

'Sandie Sherman?' He looked at her curiously.

'Yes. You liked her, didn't you?'

'Liked her! I was mad about her, Ma – couldn't get enough of her, but I was straight then.' He left the room. She heard the front door close, then the car door slam, the engine rev up and the tyres crunch on the gravel. He was gone.

Jane sat for a long time gazing into space. Whose fault? Hers? Nature's? She didn't know enough about sex; she wished she knew more – all the experience she had had had been horrible. Nigel had been the result. Did that make a difference? What was the use of trying to work it out? She got up, collected the plates and cutlery, put them in the sink and turned on the hot tap.

He had remembered her name, Sandie Sherman. He had been mad about her, that's what he had said. She plunged her hands into the too-hot water as if to punish herself.

14

The wine and cheese party had been a great occasion as far as most of the village was concerned and days later they were still talking about it. Carmen felt that she had resisted gossip pretty well; there was that one slip when she said – or nearly said – that Nigel Dawson was a . . . well, she had bitten it back. Thinking about it, there had been very little gossip, so far as she had heard anyway. The Turners were nice and had made quite an impression on her; rather posh, Carmen thought.

The Thorntons, too, were pleased – even Ted had enjoyed it. 'Didn't like that wine, though – acid stuff.' Mabel had watched him carefully with cheese and the wine. He was only allowed so much on his diabetic diet, but it had all gone well. Her blue dress had looked nice, she thought – but it was chilly in spite of her long spencer and the log fire. Fires don't warm the whole room, she thought. Still, one or two people had told her how pretty the dress looked and how smart she was. The Brigadier had been nice to her and Ted – and young Nigel Dawson; she had always thought that young man was rather stand-offish, but he hadn't been at all. Everything had gone off so well and Ted and she had felt so comfortable there. They had been a bit nervous at first, but everyone had been so . . . well, it had been lovely.

Bill Ritter had been perhaps the most delighted person of all, as he had been able to exercise his old skill, sign-writing. The Brigadier had told him that his signs had brought no end of people to the party who hadn't received invitations, which had saved writing and posting. Young Nigel, too – Bill was very surprised by him, putting his wheelchair on the back of his precious car, being jolly and telling him about his wife and little boy. He had known Nigel had married and thought they had parted, but the way he had talked it didn't seem like that. He had always thought Nigel was a pansy but just when you thought you knew someone – you found you didn't. The other Nigel, Nigel Fisk – his girl was pretty; he was a lucky chap. The fires, the lovely room – to be inside the Manor was great. He would have liked to have seen the dogs; he had heard them barking, but supposed they were better kept out of that crowded room. Added to all this enjoyment the Brigadier had sent him a lovely box of cheeses – special ones, not just the cut-up bits from the party, but wrapped ones in a lovely box, as a thank-you for writing the signs. The whole thing had been really great and thinking about it would last him for a long time. That Michaela lady had called on him, too, to thank him and ask if he would do signs for other things she was dreaming up; she was a pleasant lady. Since the party he had felt his loneliness disappearing a bit. He had friends now for whom he could do something, not rely on them doing things for him.

Michaela hoped that her friendship with Frank would grow and prosper. If such a friendship had been formed by Dorothy, Michaela would have been delighted for her. 'Ho, ho, it takes all sorts,' she muttered to herself. How many times had she thought or said that? Hundreds – but all sorts sometimes took a lot of taking. She liked Frank, and she hoped that Dorothy would not prove to be a stumbling block in that friendship.

For a while everyone who came into the post office had something to say to the postmistress about the party: 'Wasn't it great?' 'Wasn't it nice?' It was pleasant and it really made the village draw together for a bit.

Sheila and Eric Barnes sat drinking their pre-dinner drink. The little clock on the mantelpiece chimed seven times – the pretty bell-like tone always pleased Sheila.

'What's for dinner?' Eric asked, folding the sheets of *The Times* over and to the sports pages.

'Beef casserole.'

'With wine?'

'Of course. I marinated the beef for a couple of hours or more – just the way you like it.'

Her husband nodded slowly, wrapped in the football news.

The room in which they were relaxing was comfortable; a shade chintzy, perhaps. The curtains matched the cretonne of the three- piece suite, roses climbing all over the material – Sheila's choice. Dr Eric Barnes left such things very much to his wife: as long as he was comfortable he was not particular. If you asked him what was the pattern on his sitting-room furniture he would probably have been unable to tell you. A good and conscientious doctor, he gave most of his mind to his practice and the little that was left to sport.

'Eric, do you think the vicar's wife has left him? He looks so ill and depressed.'

'Er – what? Oh, how should I know?'

'Well, I only thought . . .'

Sheila went out into the kitchen to check on the casserole and put two plates in the warmer. She came back still talking. 'Edie Jevons – you know, in the post office – she was saying to Carmen Delano –'

Her husband rolled up his eyes. 'Carmen Delano! Well, what you have heard from her must be gospel truth.'

'Yes, well . . . that's what I thought.' Sheila rattled on. 'She was telling Carmen that Philippa Ainsworth can't be staying with her sister because she told Edie she was an only child.' Eric Barnes, behind the pages of his paper, rattled them a shade irritably.

Eric lowered the paper. 'Perhaps she *has* left him – gone off with another man. The Bishop, perhaps.' He laughed, then became slightly more serious: 'Funny, when she came to see me a little while ago she was very made-up – blue eyeshadow, hair done rather . . . well, different. Nice perfume, too. Rather unusual for her, I thought, she's usually a bit of a frump.'

'Well, there you are! Poor man, she's run off.' His wife was triumphant. She got up and soon called her husband into the dining-room.

'Smells good,' he said as he lifted the lid of the casserole.

'Poor man! Wonder who's cooking his meal.'

'Whose meal? Oh, Ainsworth! Don't know – his problem, not ours. He's a dull dog anyway.'

'You on call, Eric?'

He shook his head. 'No, Banbury is.'

'Well, there's a good play on.' Sheila helped her husband to more food.

'I want to see the football.'

'OK. I'll go upstairs to watch the play.' She looked across the table; Eric was eating his second helping with enjoyment. She again felt a stab of pity for their pale-faced, miserable vicar. At the party at the Manor he had spoken to hardly anyone. 'We're very lucky, Eric,' she said.

He looked up. 'Yes, yes, certainly we are.' He spoke the words, but he looked puzzled – she could tell he had already forgotten the conversation about the vicar and was looking forward with pleasure to watching the football. Men! she thought. They really don't understand anything!

In the days that followed the party, Dorothy became more and more introspective and depressed. Michaela's efficiency and drive and her easy manner with other members of the village community made Dorothy aware of her own disabilities in communication and her inability to make friends. The little children she had found easy to talk to, but the banter in the staff room – the rather risqué intimate remarks of the men and women teachers, the teasing about where she had been the night before (it had usually been spent watching television) – she could never take. As she tried to put a brave face on it, she discouraged communication with them even more; they would leave her out of their chatter and go to the pub at lunchtimes, something she hated – the smell of beer and of smoke, the sound of everyone talking at once, the whole atmosphere was distasteful to her.

On holiday with Michaela, she felt differently. With just the two of them, their holidays had been a delight. Michaela had made most of the arrangements and had done most of the talking to other members of the tour. But Dorothy had loved it, had loved exploring the various places they had visited. Their tastes seemed similar – cathedrals, mountains. But now . . . At first Dorothy had felt comfortable. They had arrived in the village knowing no one. Fixing up the cottage and garden had been fun, just the two of them – Michaela dealing with the tradesmen, the electrician, the carpenter who put in more cupboards. The move itself – it had all been cheerful, outgoing; anyone would do anything for Michaela. She, Dorothy, had made the endless cups of coffee and when at last everything in the cottage had fallen into place they had driven round the Island together exploring, finding places to have a meal. Then things began to change. Michaela made friends, was asked out. Dorothy went with her, but more and more it was becoming obvious that Michaela was the lively one, the one who brightened up the party, contributed to the coffee mornings. Dorothy was now convinced that she was only asked to tag along because of Michaela – they couldn't very well leave her out.

The letter, too, had been a terrible shock – one she could not forget, could not get over, would never forget. If people thought *that*, then how well she fitted the description, tagging along behind her 'friend'; nothing to say, no animation. The overdose – she wished it had worked. 'It was just a cry for help,' the psychiatrist had said. What rubbish – she hadn't wanted help, just oblivion. They couldn't, or maybe wouldn't, see that.

These village activities – the jumble sale, the wine and cheese party, the Brigadier's obvious liking for her friend (she had hated that party, couldn't think of a thing to say to people) . . . Oh, Michaela tried to involve her, but she didn't want to be involved, she just wanted their holiday-type relationship, with no other people breaking in. That feeling worried her most of all – did it mean she *was* what the letter had said? She had never felt the need of affection from Michaela, just companionship. Sometimes they had kissed when meeting after a term or two apart, but she had never felt . . . never, never! Why then was she not able to shake off the accusation in that terrible letter, like Michaela had? Was it guilt? Was there in her a buried feeling that she *was* like that – more fond of women than men? No, no, no!

Michaela could not, would not, understand her thoughts. She knew, of course, about homosexuality, but had merely laughed at the letter, been surprised at Dorothy's reaction to it. Suddenly Dorothy felt she had to tell someone, someone who would listen but was disinterested, not involved in the relationship – but where would she find someone like that, who would listen? None of the women, that was certain. Then she thought of the vicar, Hugh Ainsworth – he looked as miserable himself. She could not imagine him laughing the matter off, as Michaela had done and might do again if she confided in her.

On the Monday after the party she telephoned the vicar. She knew that Michaela was going out to dinner with the Brigadier – or Frank, as she now called him – on Tuesday. 'Tuesday, about seven,' she had said. She rang the vicar. 'May I come and see you at about seven on Tuesday?' she asked. 'Yes, that will be . . .' Hugh Ainsworth sounded surprised at her request to come and see him – reluctant almost – but he agreed. She would confide in him, confess her feelings, how mixed-up she felt – all of it. She could talk to a vicar – after all, that was what they were there for, to help and comfort their parishioners. Though Michaela and she hardly ever went to church still . . . She almost longed to get there and spill out all her confusion, let him sort things out for her.

Before she went to the vicar and before Michaela's dinner date they went to Tesco's. Michaela enjoyed the big store; she was an enthusiastic buyer of foreign foods. 'Let's try this, let's try that.' She loves life and I don't, Dorothy thought, trailing behind her. She didn't want to make life miserable for both of them, but her depression was becoming so deep, so bottomless, she could see no light. It was like walking in a black tunnel with no light at the end. Try as she would – and she did try – to 'snap out of it', she simply couldn't. Now she put all her faith in her visit to Hugh Ainsworth; there was no one else.

'Do you like the Brigadier, Michaela?' she had asked. Michaela had bought a new dress for her dinner date with him.

'Of course I do – he's a dear fellow. Oh, you're asking that because I've bought a new dress for the occasion?' She grinned. 'Well, if you looked in my wardrobe you'd find mostly slacks and tweeds. Hardly dinner gear, eh?'

Dorothy had agreed, but turned away from Michaela as she showed the shoes she had bought to go with her dress.

'Would you rather I didn't go, Dorothy?' she asked, rather out of curiosity as she had no intention of letting Frank Dawson down.

Dorothy turned on her like a tigress. 'Refuse! Because of me? No, indeed, I wouldn't have that for all the world.'

She had left and run upstairs and Michaela had heard her bedroom door slam. What have I said wrong now? she had thought, left to herself downstairs; but for all Dorothy's outbursts of temper she was still looking forward to her dinner with Frank.

Frank Dawson drove up to the Hawthorne Cottage gate. He got out of his aged Rover and opened the door for Michaela. He looked even smarter than he had at the wine and cheese party, in a beautifully tailored, but this time dark, suit.

'Hope I don't smell of mothballs,' he said as he started the car.

Michaela made a great show of sniffing, but shook her head. 'Not a trace,' she said, laughing. She had put on a light flowery perfume that she had bought for a young teacher friend for her birthday; she suspected that it was too young for her, but her usual perfume didn't somehow seem suitable. She had decided to open the present and get something else for the young teacher; now she wished she hadn't, but was pleased when Frank

132

said, 'That's a charming scent you're wearing, so light and pleasant.'

They drove out of the village towards Bonchurch. He drove well and the old car was comfortable. Michaela thought briefly of her friend; she had noticed as she came out that Dorothy was dressed in a suit and the new blouse she had bought at the same time that Michaela had bought her dress. Going out? she had thought, but had not voiced the words in case Dorothy had shown resentment at being asked – one never knew with her these days.

'You're very quiet,' Frank said.

'Just enjoying the drive,' she answered – and it was indeed enjoyable: the grass on the sides of the road was spotted with wild flowers.

'One good thing the council does,' Frank said.

After half an hour's drive they pulled up at a low, thatched, pleasant-looking hotel. As they drew up they heard music coming from inside. 'Oh no!' Frank said, locking the car.

'Yes, music – but it's nice music,' Michaela said. They crossed the courtyard and together went into the red-carpeted hall.

Dorothy knocked on the door of the vicar's house a little late for her seven o'clock appointment. She had waited for Michaela and the Brigadier to leave before she went out. Hugh Ainsworth opened the door. He blocked the entrance for a moment then seemed to recollect himself, stood back and said, 'Oh, do come in, Miss . . .' He had obviously forgotten her name.

'Dorothy, Dorothy Worth.'

'Yes, yes, of course. You wanted . . .' He appeared so distracted, so ill that Dorothy wished she had not come. However, she could not back out now.

Ainsworth led her through into a small room; there was a desk, a chair on each side of it, and shelves of books covering one wall. The whole house did not in any way bring to mind the word 'vicarage' but, Dorothy thought, this was no fault of the clergyman nor of the Church. Probably the old vicarage had been so decrepit that restoration would have cost too much: vandals had smashed some of the windows and the garden was overgrown with weeds, so the poor man had had to take this small house and like it and try to live it down.

Dorothy sat down. The room was gloomy: the change to

summertime had started, but the evening light was shut out by a venetian blind, which was drawn down. The open slats made the gloom slightly green. Dorothy felt that the whole scene had an underwater quality, which jangled her already taut nerves.

The vicar turned on the desk light, which gave out a more comfortable warm feel to the room. He repeated, 'You wanted to see me, Miss, er . . . ?' Her name had gone again; this time Dorothy did not bother to supply it, she was too anxious to unburden herself. The sight of the man sitting opposite her, his dark suit, the whiteness of his clerical collar, his serious face, his white hands resting on the blotter in front of him, made the situation easier for her to start. The rehearsed opening speech was almost begun, but before she could utter a word she burst into a flood of tears.

Hugh Ainsworth's relaxed pose changed. He sat upright in his chair, then got up, crossed the room, came back and placed a box of tissues in front of her. 'Please try and control yourself. What is it? Whatever is the matter?'

Dorothy wiped her eyes, thankful for the tissues. 'I'm so depressed, so unhappy, vicar.' She at last managed to speak and the words began to tumble out. 'People think I'm a lesbian, but I'm not. That's why I took an overdose – perhaps you didn't know about that?'

He nodded. 'Yes, I heard about it. I was going to call on you, but . . .'

'I wish it had worked, I wish I wasn't here now.'

'But surely, if it's not true what people say, it's just something to be ignored.'

'It's these beastly gossips, what they say, they'd say anything, anything.'

Hugh Ainsworth lowered his head. 'Yes, you're quite right, there is evil about in the village, but there is little one can do to track down the gossipers, to stop them.'

'I cannot forgive them, I cannot forgive the suggestion.' Dorothy's tears had dried now, her anger and hurt were uppermost. 'I've done something about it.'

'What?' Hugh Ainsworth asked the question without much interest.

'I shouldn't have done it – I know how wrong it is, but people read and take letters more seriously than being told, talked to.'

'What did you do – write letters?'

'I wrote to . . . well, I won't tell you who, but I know who the gossips are. I wrote anonymously –'

Hugh broke in: 'An anonymous letter? A poison pen letter?'

Dorothy nodded. 'That's what they call them, don't they.'

Hugh fixed his eyes on her – they looked wild. 'Tell me, what did this letter – how did you . . . ?'

'Like the others, just typed on plain paper. I didn't sign it, of course, it was anonymous.'

Very quietly, he stabbed the pointed end of his letter-opener gently into the blotter, then let the opener slide down his finger and thumb and hit the other end of the blotter, reversing and reversing, his hand trembling ever so slightly. 'Was it . . . This letter of yours – was it typed in capitals in the middle of the sheet?' he asked, his voice slightly husky.

'Yes, just like the other one.' Dorothy was going on to tell him about the letter she had received, but he gave her no chance. He stood up so abruptly that the letter-opener clattered to the floor.

'Get out! Get out, Miss . . .' He still couldn't find her name. 'Get out of my house! You will never, never know how much harm you have done!'

Dorothy was transfixed by his expression – he looked as if he could kill her. She tried to speak, but he shouted her down.

'Get out, get out.' He strode across the room, across the little hall and threw open his front door. 'Never come to my church. Never come back here, ever, ever!'

Dorothy thought he was going to strike her. She turned and fled. The words he shouted after her made no sense to her at all. 'So you wrote it – you wrote it. It was a lie, a lie.' He slammed the door, but she could still hear him as she rushed down the path – 'It was a lie, a lie. You wrote a lie.'

Dorothy began to run; luckily there was no one about to see her. She felt herself begin to sob, which made it difficult for her to breathe. She tore up the path of her own cottage, fumbling with the key. Once inside she leant against the door to get her breath back, her mind racing. What was the matter with him? Had she gone to a madman for advice – a madman to tell her troubles to? She could still hear him in her mind, shouting, 'You wrote it, you wrote a lie.' Yet she had said the village was full of gossip; and he had agreed. What did he mean, what did he mean? She had done so much harm writing that letter, but what?

When she had calmed down she made herself a hot drink. She

couldn't stand any more – she must go upstairs, take the only two sleeping tablets that Michaela doled out to her nightly. She knew they were on her bedside table. To sleep, get away from her problems; she couldn't stand them any more. Her imagination leapt ahead. Michaela would marry Frank Dawson, she, Dorothy, would be alone. Maybe she should accept the fact that she was a lesbian – a lesbian with no companion to love, a lesbian who wanted nothing else but companionship, not sex, just companionship and caring. She was a poison pen letter-writer, too. It was right what people thought about her – she was nothing.

She swallowed the two pills, undressed and got into bed. She knew it was only about eight o'clock, but that didn't matter. She finished her hot milk and began to feel the pills working, feeling again the darkness and depression enveloping her. Sleep came at last. Much later, hours later, she heard a car draw up and the front door close. The small luminous clock by her bed said twenty past eleven. She was sleepy. She heard the car draw away, then later Michaela coming very quietly up the stairs, heard the familiar creak the third stair from the top always made when stepped on, heard Michaela's door close, again very quietly. Well, that was that. Dorothy felt no sense of companionship because Michaela was home – nothing, nothing. She covered her head with the duvet and lay there, feeling the tears running silently down her cheeks. Eventually she drifted off to sleep.

Hugh Ainsworth sat in his study for hours after Dorothy had gone. He could not get his mind around the fact that that small, old-maidish woman could ultimately get him to kill his wife – not intentionally, of course, but the letter, the build-up of circumstances, the blow he had struck, had all stemmed from that letter. He had got it out of the drawer and it lay on the desk in front of him. But why had she picked Barnes? He had heard that all women fell in love with their doctors – and their vicars, too, though by God he hadn't noticed any love or admiration coming his way from any of his women parishioners. It was Pat Beattie who they all fell for – that so-called 'minister' with his open-necked shirt, his sandals and his long hair. He had noticed at the party, that awful wine and cheese party, that Pat Beattie had been surrounded by people all the time.

He got up and filled a glass of milk. The sight of the white liquid brought back to him his rage and hurt in that terrible moment . . . his wife's face distorted with contempt for him. That beastly woman Dorothy something, she had given herself away. Why had she come to him to confess her sins? Did she expect him to give her absolution – to say, 'I forgive you for being a lesbian, for writing poison pen letters, one of which made me hit my wife and which led to her death by my hand. If I hadn't struck her she wouldn't have fallen to her death'? He walked up and down the kitchen. It was dark now. He drank the milk and realised suddenly that he had been chanting, 'What shall I do? What shall I do?' But he was alone and no one was there to hear him or answer him.

15

Amelia Wheeler was perhaps the most pleasantly surprised about the wine and cheese party. New to the Island, she had not expected to be greeted by many people – perhaps the Thortons. But Mrs Fisk had made her so welcome and had introduced her to so many people that it had been quite jolly, though most had been older than herself. Nigel, Mrs Fisk's son, had been attentive and Amelia smiled to herself. Perhaps gently egged on by his mother, he had been a tiny bit flirtatious. She liked him. The other Nigel, the Brigadier's son, had been friendly, too. Again, to Amelia's slight amusement, he had been almost shooed away by Jane Fisk. Amelia was under no illusions about Nigel Fisk; she judged him to be totally dominated by his mother, but she was fair enough to give her, Jane, some of the credit for her son's successful career from the little she had heard about Jane Fisk's background from her own lips. However, she could also see that there was love between mother and son – they were genuinely fond of each other in spite of the mother's rather bossy manner.

When Nigel Fisk had asked her to have dinner with him she had been surprised, but had accepted. Amelia was divorced. Her marriage had failed in large part because of her husband's obsessive gambling and his complete inability to work. He had found jobs – or, more frequently, she had found them for him – but after a few months, weeks or even in one case days, he would leave because of what he considered to be injustice from his colleagues or the boss's unfair attitude to him. They had stayed together for eight years, largely thanks to Amelia's determination to make the marriage work, but at last both, Amelia in particular, had realised it was a useless effort. As there were no children of the marriage she felt no guilt in starting divorce proceedings. Now after two years of freedom and in spite of several advances from men friends, she was still unattached. She liked men, though, and Nigel Fisk's diffident approach was rather charming. Over-confident men were too reminiscent of her husband's approach. But dinner with Nigel Fisk . . . well, he obviously, perhaps a trace too obviously, did not expect to apply the storm tactics. She had the feeling that perhaps it was his mother who had not pushed but gently tapped him towards asking her out to dinner. She might be wrong – it might be his idea altogether. Still . . . he had seemed willing enough to go along with the idea even if it was his mother's, and he had seemed pleased when she had accepted. She did wonder where he would take her – the Island hotels were still a mystery to her. Her white dress would do, with emerald green necklace and ear-rings to match. She smiled to herself. She hadn't any experience of teachers; he had been conservatively dressed at the party, but perhaps he would turn up in a khaki shirt and sandals for the dinner date – although somehow she didn't think so. For some reason she felt slightly anxious about doing the right thing – an unusual state of mind for Amelia.

Nigel called for her a few minutes early and she wasn't quite ready. She sat him down in her little sitting-room and went to finish making up her face.

'Sorry to be not quite ready.' She smiled at him.

'I'm a little early, I think,' he said almost hastily, shyly.

She gave him the evening paper and disappeared. After a few minutes she emerged from the bedroom, fastening a gold and green bracelet on her wrist. 'Ready?' she said.

In the car Nigel was acutely conscious of having her so near to him, by his side – her perfume, the stir of her hair as she wound down the window. He realised almost with dismay that this was the first time that he had had a woman beside him in his car. Oh, he had taken Miss Temple, the head of maths, home one night and had to listen all the way to a diatribe on 'teaching today', but never before in his whole life had a woman sat beside him with whom he was going to spend the evening and wine and dine. He knew that the dismay he felt was because he was afraid that he would show this lively woman that after all he was a bore. He thought for a second of Jeremy, but without regret. After all, he had loved him too . . .

'Penny for them?' Amelia touched his arm.

He realised that he had been silent for some time. 'Hoping I won't bore you to screams.'

'Why should you?' She did not smile as she asked the question, but looked at him seriously, waiting for his answer.

'Well, I don't think headmasters are noted for being interesting and good company.'

She turned the bracelet round and round on her wrist, but did not take her eyes off him. 'I've never been out with a headmaster and I bet you have never dated a chiropodist before.'

The remark made him burst out laughing and she joined in. Nigel felt his mood lighten, his spirits lift. 'You're right,' he said, still laughing. The car increased its speed a little. 'I'm thinking of getting a new car,' he said, which wasn't exactly true, but the normality of the remark struck him – he had said it because he wanted to impress this pretty woman beside him. Suddenly he remembered Sandie of long ago, a fair-haired schoolgirl. 'I can fight anybody and win,' he had said to her and her admiring eyes, her snub nose, her over-lipsticked mouth – he could almost see her again, see those lips moving as she said, 'I know you could beat anyone, Nigel.' This was just the same.

After she had looked at the luminous hands of her bedside clock, Dorothy lay in the near darkness, gazing at the ceiling. In her imagination and by some trick of light she still saw the hands, twenty past eleven – no figures or numerals seemed to be included in her mind's eye, just the hands. Twenty past eleven. They glowed there on the grey expanse of the ceiling. They didn't move as she watched them; time did not seem to pass at all. Twenty past eleven. Was she going mad? She had felt mad, making that terrified dash away from the vicar's insane yelling, stumbling up her own path. The sleep had not helped, it hadn't calmed her; she was still trembling and feeling terribly cold. Nothing would induce her, though, to get up and fill a hot water bottle, though she longed for it. She might meet Michaela going to the bathroom and have to explain to her why she had gone to bed so early and had not waited up for her, to hear what kind of evening she had had. Or would Michaela have expected that? Dorothy didn't know. Her thoughts felt muddled, without sense or reason.

She dozed – or did she doze? She wasn't sure, but when she opened her eyes the hands of the clock on the ceiling had disappeared and the square of her window was a tiny bit paler. Or was that, too, in her mind and not really so? She turned and looked at the real clock; ten past four, it was morning. She must have slept, but then that twenty past eleven on the ceiling above her had not been real time. She had lain there watching it for perhaps an hour, two hours – her confusion grew. The events of the evening seemed to be flying round the room like bats, in and out of her mind, disconnected. Michaela and the Brigadier, her own dash across the Green – had it happened? She turned her head a little; her suit was lying on a chair instead of being neatly put away on a hanger in her wardrobe. The confession, the letter about her lesbianism, the accusation that Hugh Ainsworth had shouted at her, his banning her from his church, even from his very presence! He had looked deranged, too. Perhaps they all were, Michaela, Carmen, the Brigadier. Perhaps she was a lesbian! Oh yes, other people saw these things. Even if you felt you were normal others thought you were not – and they knew the truth, they were the observers. It was all too much.

Dorothy had hoped for a pleasant, quiet retirement free from any commitment – no parties, no gossip. She had had enough of gossip, there had been too much of that in the staff room – and now here it was all over again, and she was more involved than she had ever been at work. Nothing would make her tell Michaela of her dreadful scene with the vicar, or even that she had been foolish enough to seek his advice. That was something she would keep secret for ever – but could she bear it? Could she bear to think of that scene alone? She had to, there was no one to tell. She would keep it in her head for ever!

The village clock struck a husky five. They had not liked that clock at first; unused to it, she and Michaela had wakened when it struck, but now they had got used to it and it no longer woke them. Tonight, though, or rather this morning, Dorothy counted the chimes. The window was definitely lighter – it wasn't her imagination. She sat bolt upright in her bed. She must go. There was no place for her here – the dream of a happy retirement with her friend was all destroyed. She knew what she must do next.

Dorothy threw back the duvet. She was still cold, shivering. The cottage was silent. She dressed very slowly in the same suit and blouse that she had worn to go to see Hugh Ainsworth. This time she felt it didn't matter what she wore – this time was different. When she was fully dressed, which only took minutes, Dorothy sat down at her dressing-table. Even after her bad, disturbed night her grey hair was pretty, the curls natural. She looked at herself: her face was not wrinkled yet; her expression was almost child-like; her eyes, wide and grey, stared back at her. Her lips looked blue, perhaps because she was so cold. She had a headache, too. She put on a little lipstick to hide the blueness. She wore a ring on her right hand, which she had not taken off last night – her mother's engagement ring. Now she took it off and laid it on the dressing-table for Michaela. Michaela liked jewellery; she didn't. She took the lipstick and applied more. Even so, her lips still had a bluish tinge; she didn't want that. She covered it with more red. Michaela! Michaela! How would she take what she was going to do? From the small, pretty bonheur-du-jour she took a sheet of headed notepaper and an envelope. She wrote:

I love you too much to stay. The letter was right. I am only capable of loving a woman and that woman is you. Don't grieve. Be happy. Dorothy.

She sealed the envelope and put it under the ring. Now she was ready. One look round the room and she crept out of the door, looking for a few seconds at Michaela's closed door. Then, care-fully avoiding the creaking third stair, she went down and out of the front door, closing it behind her. As the door closed she felt a terrible pang of sadness and her headache began to thump, not like the black depression that enveloped her but a sharp pain – perhaps a more normal pain, the pain of departure?

When she reached the beach the dawn had drawn pink lines across the sky; the clouds above and below looked black, but the pink promised a sunny morning. She walked along the beach; the tide was coming in and each wave edged a little further up the sand, nearing her shoes. She watched each wave choosing its place to stop and then recede. Her thoughts turned to herself and what she was going to do. She was a fair swimmer, but could never manage far; she hoped it wouldn't take too long – that she would not have to swim too far out into the sea away from the shore before she let herself go. Sink . . . Is that what you did? Just sink? The gulls had

found something edible in the water and were diving and screaming. She looked down at the pebbles at her feet. She remembered
herself and Michaela in Italy picking up a few shells from the beach
to bring back home, just the two of them. She looked up at the gulls,
trying to keep the tears out of her eyes. Michaela! Michaela!

She walked a little further. The morning seemed to be misting
over, the sea looked far away, yet the sun was still reflected on the
water. The pain in her head grew worse. She put her hand up and
rubbed the back of her neck. Still, it didn't matter, she often had
headaches! She stopped and suddenly felt the sea, the beach, the
grass verge above the sea wall, even the gulls, the world, whirling
round her . . . Then blankness . . .

She fell gently, gracefully, to the sand. Her open eyes stared
straight at the morning sun; but it didn't trouble her, neither
would it ever again.

The soft, frilled edges of the waves gently touched the fanned-
out pleats of her skirt, making the material look almost black.

16

Michaela woke at about seven – early for her. She lay, hands
behind her head, thinking of last night and the Brigadier. That
name was so right for him, but Frank was even more suitable for
he was just that, frank, open. He had told her about his wife and
the wonderful life they had had together. He had said little of his
son, an only child, but had shown, apologising for doing so at the
same time, a picture of Nigel and his wife and their little boy, who
looked about five. She was a pretty woman, and the little boy was
rather handsome. He had put the photograph back in his wallet.
'Silly young fool, my son, giving up that nice woman – a mere boy
when they married, but they were happy. My grandson, too . . . '
He stopped. 'Now that creep Jeremy has gone I think that there's
some hope for him. He may go back to his wife. Her father, a nice
fella, was in the army like me and left and started a firm. He's
done well – wants to give Nigel a job, but he doesn't know
whether to take it or not. He says it might make him feel trapped.'
He stopped, stirred his coffee vigorously. 'Sorry – sorry to go on
like this,' he said at last.

Michaela pressed him. 'Please tell me, it must be quite a worry to you?'

'Worry?' He drank. 'Yes, it was – it is. Young ass. Personally I think this poof business is just a bit of a fashion.'

So many of his remarks showed Michaela that he could confide in her with the ease of talking to a friend, a close friend, and that pleased her.

Now she looked at her watch on the bedside table. Ten past seven. She got up, put on her dressing-gown and padded downstairs. No stirring from Dorothy's room. Well, she had been getting up rather later recently, perhaps depression made you feel there was no point bothering. Her whole attitude seemed to be drifting that way; perhaps it was the two sleeping pills which Michaela had been instructed to dole out to her, before locking the bottle away. This had been the cause of resentment from Dorothy, who said she was humiliated by the doctor's thinking her incapable of having the pills in her own charge. They had arrived at an uneasy truce regarding the conflict. Michaela – always optimistic – hoped the matter had resolved itself but sometimes when she doled out the two sleeping pills she was not so sure.

Now for a change she made the early morning tea, opened the curtains in the sitting-room and dining-room, put up the kitchen blind, then poured a cup of tea and added the milk – Dorothy insisted on milk last. Upstairs she gave a gentle tap on Dorothy's door – no reply. So she tried again, slightly louder this time – again no reply. She opened the door. The room was empty, the curtains still drawn, but the bed was neatly made. Had she gone for a walk? That was it, of course, it was a lovely morning. Why then did she feel so apprehensive? She looked round the room; on the dressing-table lay a note, her name 'Michaela' scribbled across the envelope rather shakily. On the white surface of the envelope lay Dorothy's ring. Michaela felt a lurch of panic, went over and put the ring aside, opened the note and read it.

Jane Fisk felt restless and bored and isolated. She knew that she should be pleased that her scheme had worked so well – that Nigel had rescinded his notice and there would be no worry about him getting another post, which she knew only too well might have been more difficult than he had told her. Jeremy had gone, or at least Nigel was sure he had gone – she was not so convinced.

However, seeing Amelia and her son together at the wine and cheese party had done her good. She had heard nothing from Nigel since; he had not telephoned or called in for supper. This disturbed her a little and underlined her loneliness – and she was lonely. Getting a meal for herself was a chore, and when she was eating it she didn't enjoy it. Watching television was not the same – no one to talk to, to grumble about the programmes or praise them.

She had turned the room around a little, put an armchair in front of the screen in place of the settee on which she and Nigel had sat together, drinking their after-supper coffee. Whenever they had felt like it they had had a gin and tonic together before the meal. Standing back a little from her life with Nigel she could look at it more objectively. Had it been happy for him or too restricting? He had never said so, never complained, but had it been so good, so happy and comfortable for him? Half of her thought so, but then would he have gone away so readily? Would Jeremy have been able to seduce him away from her so easily?

Jane was an early riser and after breakfast, just toast and coffee, she didn't feel like doing any of the housework. Since Nigel had left, the cleaner was hardly necessary and Jane really preferred to do the work herself, but this morning she did not feel like it. She decided she would walk along the beach – she didn't get enough exercise these days. The morning was sunny and the tide, according to her little book of tides and sailings, would be going out now, enough room on the beach for walking. Nine twenty. She slipped on an anorak and a headscarf and out she went.

She met nobody she knew as she walked up the street then turned right into the smaller road leading down to the beach. It was slightly windy down by the sea; her headscarf blew off and she grabbed it, put it over her head again and tied the knot more firmly under her chin. The sand was still wet as the wavelets receded and they made a rustling sound. She stood watching the small dancing pebbles running out in the tide and coming back again, making a sound like people clapping. Her feet crunched on the shingle. She was deep in thought and walked with her eyes on the wet sand.

When at last she raised her eyes she saw something lying on the beach about a hundred yards ahead. Jane was short-sighted and disliked wearing her glasses, so it was not until she was nearer that she realised it was a body. The back was towards her, the suit skirt fanned out and wet at the edge; the upper part of the body was dry. It was Dorothy. Jane skirted the feet, the tiny receding waves wetting her shoes as she did so, causing her to move with distaste nearer the feet. Once she was on the other side of the body Dorothy's open eyes were gazing at her, though it was only too obvious they saw nothing. The grey abundant hair, still dry and curling as it had in life, stirred a little in the wind. A tiny crab came out with its queer sideways gait from under the neck. Only the size of a fifty pence piece, it scuttled away down to the sea.

The sight of this tiny creature, the movement, seemed to galvanise Jane back into life. Before it had emerged she had stood gazing down at the ashen face. The nose and chin seemed more prominent and pointed than in life. She looked around; there was no handbag, no scarf – nothing. The legs, blue-stained from the lack of circulating blood, were livid and stockingless, so unlike Dorothy's usual rather prim style of dress. The thought flashed through her mind – suicide – but this time it was for real. No dramatic dash to the hospital, no stomach wash-out, no attempt at resuscitation would ever bring back life – she was dead. Jane felt repelled by what she saw. She felt no pity or remorse. She did not want to get involved in this woman's death; calling someone, the police, an ambulance – what good would that do? Jane had stood there for longer than she had thought, the wavelets had receded a foot or two. She drew back and walked on, her footsteps becoming more rapid. There was a way up from the beach, a little hill of sand and grass, then a lane. She had only a short walk up that lane, round into the street, back into her own home and safety. Why safety? Jane didn't know, but she felt unsafe here, vulnerable, near Dorothy's body. That link between herself and the dead woman . . . The letter, the help she had given to Michaela. She didn't care. As she neared home she still didn't care. They had all, the gossips, prattled about her son. Dorothy and Michaela were probably no better than the rest.

She met Carmen on the way to her house. 'Have you had an invitation – the Turners – for next Saturday? So nice of them, isn't it? Mine came this morning. It's a kind of house-warming, I expect. I hear they're buying the house – they say they're rich. He's a writer – writes detective stories, so they say. I believe she's . . .' Jane watched Carmen's mouth spilling out words. She left her standing there without answering and heard Carmen exclaim as she left her, 'Well, really! I was only telling her . . .'

Jane got in and shut her door. It was a quarter to eleven. She made herself some coffee and added a dash – a big dash – of brandy; she felt she needed it. Well, let someone else find the body! The brandy and the hot coffee warmed and comforted her. She sat down at the kitchen table, her hands folded round the cup, and said aloud, 'Let someone else find her.'

Hugh Ainsworth was up and dressed early. He couldn't think why – after all, nobody needed him. According to Philippa nobody liked him, nobody would summon him – an unloved, unadmired, indeed disliked, vicar of this parish . . . He went into the kitchen and found himself just standing there, then recollected why he had come and switched on the electric kettle. It was empty but he didn't bother to switch it off; he filled the small plastic jug standing on the window ledge above the taps with cold water and emptied it into the kettle. The heated element gave a sharp explosive hiss. He sat down at the kitchen table, his head in his hands. He had had a wretched night; he had dozed off towards dawn only to be wakened by a sharp rat-a-tat. He rose heavily to his feet and opened the door – the postman. 'Catalogue for you, sir.' He handed Hugh a large heavy parcel, enclosed in a case which pictured the head and shoulders of a girl – pretty, perfect, blooming. 'They're heavy. Got six in the bag – that's why postmen get bad backs, I reckon.' He grimaced at Hugh, who didn't answer him but took the large parcel and several letters and shut the door – although not soon enough to muffle the postman's comment: 'Who's rattled 'is cage?'

Back in the kitchen Hugh stared at the girl on the cover – her perfect face, perfect skin, seemed from another world. The label was small and down in the corner of the parcel so as not to inhibit the beauty of the picture. 'Mrs Philippa Ainsworth, The Vicarage, Shelbourne, Isle of Wight.' He dropped it on to the table. One letter also was addressed to his wife; it was from her mother, who hated telephones and always wrote letters and cards. He couldn't think what to do about it. He opened it and read it. It was about the roof of the flat where she lived. It was to be repaired and the cost divided between the six tenants – this might well be beyond Philippa's mother's means. He played with the idea of sending her a cheque with a note saying that Philippa would be writing shortly – no, that wouldn't do, she wouldn't take that. He wouldn't send her anything, but she would smell a rat. In spite of her age and disabilities she was quick-witted.

For breakfast he drank black coffee and ate biscuits – there was not much else. He looked in the freezer – not much there, just some packet meals. It made him feel sick even thinking of eating them. He pocketed a couple of the biscuits and decided to go out. He couldn't bear staying in the house and he couldn't bear being out. The kitchen, the whole house, the whole world, felt like a box. He walked out of the back door – he didn't want to meet anyone, see anyone. He reached the sands without encountering a soul. He ate the biscuits from his pocket. The tide was going out. He watched the waves for a while, then he saw it – a body lying feet towards the sea. He drew nearer and recognised Dorothy.

He stood transfixed, gazing down into the open sightless eyes. He remembered their last meeting, her confession, his yelling, forbidding her his church – now he supposed he would have to bury her. He couldn't stand it! He couldn't stand it! He would leave her where she was. Because of her his wife was under the brambles in the wood, rotting. He stood back, then saw other footprints on the damp sand, skirting the feet, going on towards the grass and sand at the top of the shingle and disappearing. Someone had been here, had seen the body and had walked away. He was going to do the same. As he followed the footprints he thought of the Priest and the Levite and wondered who the Samaritan would be – the good Samaritan. She didn't deserve a Samaritan – she didn't deserve anything! He got safely home, opened the freezer and took out a lasagne. He suddenly felt better. He slammed the freezer door shut then turned on the oven, put in the little plastic dish and slammed that door. As he did so it crossed his mind that he was the Priest, but who had been the Levite?

The Samaritan at last arrived. Robert Benson had a new bike, a super job – his father had given it to him for his birthday. He no longer looked like an angel – he now resembled the other boys. His hair – at last his mother had let him have it cut. She had not gone with him to the barber so he certainly had had it cut – no kidding! His pink scalp showed through the stubble which remained. He had wanted a haystack cut – the top left on like a brush and jelled up – but the Newport barber said he hadn't enough money so he'd settled for a shaver. His mother had gone bananas when he arrived home, but she had given up ranting eventually. After all, she couldn't put the hair back on. His father had only laughed, said he looked more like a man now and not a sissy for a change, and then he'd got the bike for his birthday. 'Nice one, Robert,' his father had said when he had first seen the haircut. Things had been better from that day on. Perhaps because of his haircut he had felt tough and not minded or worried about his father bullying him – had stood up for himself, and so the bullying had stopped.

Robert felt that Mr Fisk – otherwise known in the school as 'Old Fiskie' – was responsible for all of it. The bike, his father's changed attitude, his mother giving him money for a haircut, was all due to that letter. And who had written it? Robert reckoned Old Fiskie himself. He had snivelled to him a bit, told him about getting no breakfast, just a Mars bar or crisps, no money for the school lunch, though he wasn't on the free list. It was great! Life was better. He pedalled furiously along the path by the beach. It was lunchtime and he was on his way home. He didn't normally bring his bike to school – too risky, the other kids would get at it – but today was a half-day so he had risked it. His rucksack of books bumped up and down on his back. He looked towards the sea – then he saw her! He laid the bike down on the grass and ran down the little hill.

It was one of the old ladies from Hawthorne Cottage. He had never seen death before except on telly. It was the eyes that got him. Perhaps she wasn't dead; perhaps he should give her mouth-to-mouth but he couldn't, he couldn't do that. He touched her face gently; it was cold, like ice. The eyes stared back at him. Television pictures and real life were pretty alike, he thought – they looked the same. They were good, those actors, but of course they weren't really dead. This one was. He got up from the squatting position beside her. 'Christ!' he said. He dashed up the grassy bank away from the beach, grabbed his bike and made for the house-cum-police station in the middle of the High Street. He would tell the fuzz. Fear and a sense of importance fought with each other in his mind – importance won. He parked the bike by the steps of the police station and walked in to break the news.

The one policeman Shelbourne boasted was seated at a small desk to the left of the door. One wall of the room was completely covered by notices. The station served as a dwelling house as well and kitchen noises came through the closed door facing the open street door. The small garden outside was well kept, the tiny lawn mown and edged. The beds round it were full of wallflowers, which were rather past their best now. Some rather incongruous yellow chrysanthemums bloomed in the middle of the wallflowers, obviously a present and put into the garden so as not to be wasted – because they had been forced in a nursery they had bloomed rather out of their usual context. One corner where the sun did not penetrate was lighted up with small white flowers where garlic had invaded. The street outside was quiet again; the morning traffic (which was pretty sparse) had gone – it was lunchtime. Further up the street the general store-cum-post office was firmly closed and the notice read, 'Closed 1–2.30 p.m.' It was a restful scene about to be shattered by the lad standing in the doorway peering at the policeman.

The man finished filling in the form on which he was writing and looked up. 'Yes? Lost your bike already? Had it stolen or something?'

'How did you know I'd got a bike?'

'Seen you once or twice going through the village – too fast and on the path sometimes. I thought of arresting you – dangerous riding!'

Robert smiled dutifully, recognising that this was a joke, the sort of stupid jokes that grown-ups made all the time. 'No, it's not lost or stolen, it's outside there.'

The policeman threw down his pen on to the table and proceeded to put whatever he had been filling into a large brown envelope. He stuck out a red tongue, licked the envelope and put it on the desk, thumping it with his hand. Robert watched him, waiting for his complete attention – waited as Old Fiskie at school always told them to do. 'Wait for eyeball-to-eyeball contact.'

At last he got it. 'There's a stiff on the beach.'

He waited. For a moment the man looked surprised then incredulous. 'I bet there is! Dead fish, is it, eh? I've been had that way before.'

'No.' Robert shook his head. 'No, not a fish – a lady. She lives at Hawthorne Cottage. I've seen her coming out of there. I often . . .' Robert was going to say that he often rode by her house, but thought after the policeman's remark about arresting him he'd better shut up.

'All right then . . .' The remark seemed to sink into the policeman's head. 'You sure? Let's go and look.' He put on a jacket and cap, opened the inner door and called out, probably to his wife, 'Won't be long, dear.'

A threatful voice came back: 'No, don't be long – lunch is ready. It'll all spoil.'

At the beach the constable saw with some horror that Robert was right. He told him to stay on the bank and not to come down with him. He slid down the little sandy path, almost falling (to Robert's secret delight). That was the end of the interesting part for him – he wasn't allowed near the body. The ambulance and more police were summoned and soon the bank above where the lady lay was full of flashing red and blue lights. She was put on a stretcher, carried up the beach and loaded into the ambulance. The doors banged and they were off. The police stayed – what Robert called 'pottering around'. He'd had enough. There was no one watching, so he leapt on to his bike; the lady gone and the ambulance driven away – the scene was boring. He heard someone call out – probably the policeman: 'Come back here, Robert. You found the body, so come back here. The police will . . .' Robert took no notice; standing on the pedals he took off down the road. He'd done his bit, he reckoned, told the fuzz. He hadn't liked looking at that lady all that much; her face looked . . . kind of . . . But still, it was like it was on the telly. Now the picture was fading from his young mind – anyway, he was hungry and wanted his lunch, so he pedalled faster.

17

Michaela could not stop going over and over the past few weeks. She could not get the guilt out of her mind. She had been so wrong, even over the arrival of that beastly letter. She had not understood Dorothy's reaction, nor had she made much attempt to reassure her. She should have made her talk more about why she had taken those aspirins. She should have thought more about their changing relationship, or at least not put it down to Dorothy's 'nerves', to over-reaction. She had never for one moment guessed that the letter was true, that Dorothy had been, she supposed the only word to use was 'in love with her'. God, why hadn't she taken more care? Watched more closely her friend's moods and depression? And what would she have done if she had known? She couldn't think.

Again, she relived the inquest. All of them sitting there quietly – the quiet voice of the coroner asking his questions – the boy Robert, subdued, eyes downcast, not looking at the man sitting behind the desk at the top of the room. And after his questions and deliberations, that same quiet, calm, controlled tone giving the verdict: 'Death from natural causes.' That had not helped nor comforted Michaela at all. As she had the letter written by Dorothy before she had set out for the beach, she knew it had not been in Dorothy's mind that she would die by natural causes – she had written a suicide letter. Michaela had shown it to no one, but it was a burden which weighed as heavy as lead round her heart. The fact was that she had not felt the same towards Dorothy, never could, never would.

Michaela would have loved dearly to show it to someone, to talk about it, to express her own lack of understanding. She could not tell Frank – some instinct in her knew that he would be put off by it, would find the whole thing unnatural and disagreeable. Men hated that kind of thing, couldn't understand or tolerate lesbians, didn't want to understand – especially Frank, who probably had worry enough with his son's way of life.

The funeral, though . . . Frank had been very sweet and support-ive. She remembered his hand over hers; she felt she could not have gone through it without him. The vicar, too – that had been a great surprise. His little sermon or speech had been really out-standing. She and Dorothy had not attended his church often and when they had his sermons had been . . . well, pretty average and sleep-inducing. But at Dorothy's cremation his address had been quite different. At the thought of it Michaela could feel tears pricking behind her eyes. She could remember clearly some of the things that Hugh Ainsworth, standing in the pulpit at the crema-torium, had said. He had looked white and ill. When he entered the pulpit he had stood silently for a minute before he spoke. Michaela had noticed, even in her own grief, that his eyes looked red as if he had been weeping – though she thought that was hardly likely. He had not known Dorothy well, he knew nothing of her now – nor of her intention to take her own life. Though, of course, he had heard of the overdose, he knew nothing of the sad letter Michaela had kept. Yet he had spoken of her death with such compassion, such feeling. He spoke of that death and of her walk in the beautiful surroundings of sea and shore – that death which, according to the experts, had been quick and probably without apprehension or pain. Many people had come to the crematorium, friends and acquaintances, to pay their last respects to Dorothy. One or two Michaela had heard commenting on Hugh Ainsworth's little dissertation. 'Didn't think our vicar could speak like that of anyone,' 'Well, it makes me see him in a new light, I can tell you,' 'He's a better bloke than I thought, never had much time for him really,' 'No, I like Pat better, lower church an' all, but today the vicar did OK.'

Michaela, sitting once again recalling it all, could only think, Poor Dorothy, poor Dorothy. She had got to tell someone, show someone that letter, talk about her own mistakes and misunderstandings – but who? Michaela was not used to this feeling in herself; it was new to her, self-doubt, the wish to rely on someone else – she had always been and felt confident, self-confident. Well, now that seemed to be shattered!

Hugh Ainsworth had shown himself in a new light . . . She suddenly decided she couldn't bear this alone any longer, she would go and see him, thank him for his lovely words about Dorothy and, if she felt he was receptive enough to take such revelation, she would show him the letter. Michaela was surprised at her own decision, in a way, but also she was hopeful that talking about her friend to the vicar – if, when she arrived there, she decided to do so – might free her from this dreadful feeling of remorse and guilt – free her, too, from the sleepless nights which she had been suffering since Dorothy's death. Would talking about it make it better? It was a childish belief, she knew, but she felt she did need help to come to terms with losing Dorothy – perhaps partly through her own stupidity and lack of perception.

In case her courage deserted her Michaela went straight to the phone. When Hugh Ainsworth answered Michaela felt that his voice was strained and odd, but he agreed to see her the following morning. It was obvious he had no idea what she wanted; once he had agreed he put the phone down immediately and Michaela stood, still holding the receiver in her hand, wondering whether she had done the right thing. Would she feel better? Well, she had made the appointment now and she would keep it – after all, she felt rather sadly, she couldn't feel worse about her friend's death.

Nigel had thought and thought and agonised whether or not to tell Amelia what his life had been like and admit his short relationship with Jeremy. He had even thought of talking it over with Nigel One, but he had gone up to London. A slight, a very slight, suspicion had crossed Nigel's mind that maybe he and Jeremy had got together again. What did comfort him, however, was the thought that he didn't care in the least.

As their friendship had deepened over the weeks he had realised that he was falling more and more in love with this pretty, confident and undemanding woman. Though she had at first been reticent about her marriage, as they grew to know each other better she had become more open and she had told him. After a somewhat shaky start it had been unhappy to a degree which, as she told him about it, he could see had thrown her often into despair. They never had enough money, thanks to her husband's determination to bet it away; she tried to laugh this off by saying that Nick, her husband, had been such an obsessive gambler that he would, and had, bet on two flies walking up a window pane. She had heard stories about such people, but never dreamt that she would actually marry such a one. Mostly on his bets he had been unlucky or perhaps not a good student of form.

She did not speak bitterly of him, indeed she tried to deal lightly with his inability to keep a job, made a joke about her husband's mother, who came to live with them almost directly after their marriage and, Nigel gathered, was, if not as dominating as his own mother, certainly much more difficult than she had ever been – always on her son's side saying that Amelia was wrong and Nick was right. A wish for children, too, at the beginning of her marriage, her love of them, his dislike of them – then the other woman who had eventually broken up the marriage. 'I really should thank her, Nigel. I hated her at the time, but after our divorce she married him and so inherited his obsession with gambling – not to mention his mother, who went to live with them, too!' She had smiled at him then and had said, 'That's all there is to tell, darling. Now tell me about yourself.'

He had kissed her; they had made love afterwards. Lying by his side, she had asked him again: 'You never talk much about yourself, Nigel, whilst I have babbled out everything – was I right to tell you?'

Nigel had put off the telling by saying, 'Of course you were right; I've loved hearing about it and am sorry you were so unhappy, but I'm just a boring middle-aged teacher – not much excitement in my life.' He was, however, afraid – more than afraid, terrified – to confess to her his past, almost priest-like existence and then his one break-out into what he now felt was not his true self; in retrospect it had been a desperate move to get the love he had missed out on all his life. But how would she take it? How would she feel about such . . . an abnormality? Oh, he knew that in these days women like Amelia had gay friends, were tolerant, did not . . . But a lover who had been gay or had called himself gay, who for one brief moment had had a homosexual lover – how would she take that? Was his silence making her suspicious? He didn't think so because she was so open, so un-afraid with him, a wonderful lover . . . She said he was too, but the old fear returned.

Then one day, taking a forest walk as they often did, walking along hand in hand, the sun filtering through branches, the leaves and twigs from last autumn crackling under their shoes, he had told her everything. Amelia listened; not once did she interrupt him, not once did she let go of his hand. As he talked she looked up at him, then up at the sunlit sky. Nigel glanced at her now and again, to try and assess her reaction – but he couldn't. The only hope he had was in her hand, which still clutched his. Even when his story, his confession, was over she still did not take her hand away, but suddenly stopped and faced him. He was silent, look-ing at her upturned face, waiting for her to speak.

'Nigel, dearest, all you have told me . . . I believe you would not have been able to tell me all this if you didn't love me. Am I right?'

'Yes, you are right, my darling,' was all Nigel could say.

Amelia moved closer to him. 'I love you, Nigel. Whatever you've been or however you felt before I met you, I still love you. Whatever I was before, I hope you still love me.'

'But you . . .' Nigel started to say, but she put two fingers on his lips, then took away her hand and replaced it with her lips.

In that moment Nigel was free. As he took her in his arms he knew that he was free of all the old sexual fears; whether they had been caused by his mother or through his own fault, they no longer mattered. Whether they had been true or imagined, forced on him or . . .

'Will you marry me, Amelia?'

'Of course I will.'

The birds sang, the sun shone more brightly and the sky was piercingly blue.

As Michaela approached the vicarage she saw that the front door was open. The hall curtains were drawn. She rapped loudly on the door; she had tried the bell twice, but it had made no sound. There was a neglected air about the place; the front garden, which was usually well tended, was weedy and the gravel path leading up to the open front door was scuffed, with grass pushing up through the stones.

Michaela ventured a little further into the hall. 'Vicar?' she called. No reply. Then, 'Mr Ainsworth – are you there?'

A sound came from the kitchen so she went through the hall-way. In the kitchen stood the vicar; he was leaning over the sink vigorously rubbing some white material which Michaela took to be a shirt. She coughed. He looked up, his eyebrows raised in surprise.

Michaela smiled apologetically. 'You said about eleven,' she began.

'Oh yes, Miss, er . . .'

'Michaela, from Hawthorne Cottage. We met at the wine and cheese party at the Brigadier's. If you remember?'

'Yes, oh yes, of course. I was just . . .' He dropped the shirt into the sink. He dried his hands on a tea towel and threw it down on the draining board.

Michaela tried to avoid looking round the kitchen; it was pretty chaotic – a burnt saucepan half-full of water stood on the work surface with a frying pan, still greasy with pieces of egg white still sticking to it. Dirty plates and cutlery littered the draining board. Poor man, was Michaela's first thought.

He had no jacket on, but as they went through the hall he picked one up from a chair and slipped it on, and they made their way through into a smaller room, which Michaela judged to be his study. In there he sat down and motioned Michaela to the chair opposite. This room was tidier, but a thin film of dust covered the furniture. The blind was drawn down, so the room was dark; Hugh Ainsworth hurriedly got up, crossed the room and threw back the curtains and put up the blind. 'Sorry about that,' he said and came and sat down again. Michaela thought how ill he looked, haggard and white. She started to speak as it was obvious he was not going to commence.

'I've come to thank you for that very sympathetic address you gave at my friend's funeral. It was so nice, so well expressed, but particularly as you knew her so little and had hardly met her. I'm afraid, as you know, we are not churchgoers.'

The whole remark seemed to embarrass him. 'Yes, yes, I hardly knew her, but one feels . . .' He fiddled with something on his desk. 'Her death was so untoward, so sudden.' He stroked back his hair and then put his hand on his forehead as if he had a headache.

Kind-hearted Michaela could not resist the question, 'How is your wife's sister, vicar?'

He looked at her, his brows drawn together in a puzzled frown. 'My wife's sister? Oh yes, much the same, I'm afraid.' He laughed nervously. 'These problems take time to work out – you know, family problems . . .'

'You're having to look after yourself, then?'

'Yes, Mrs Hardy, our help, is *hors de combat* at the moment, so just now I'm coping – well, trying to, Miss, er . . .'

'Michaela, please – I prefer it. Is there anything I can do to help?'

'No, no thank you.'

He waved his hand as if he were dismissing her, but Michaela was persistent. 'I've got a washing machine, I could –'

'No, no, I wouldn't dream of imposing on your kindness. Mrs Hardy will be back shortly, I'm sure.'

'Well, I hope Philippa will be returning soon also.'

Michaela was about to leave and almost got up, then the thought of taking back home the letter which Dorothy had written and which was in her handbag without confiding in anyone was too much. She sat down again.

'May I tell you something, vicar? You mentioned that Dorothy's death was unexpected, but actually . . . Well, this may shock you as much as it did me.' She took out Dorothy's letter and handed it to him.

He read it and then looked up at her. 'Why? Do you know why she decided to end it?' His voice shook.

Michaela was surprised at the effect it had had on him, but she nodded. 'I feel it's all my fault. We had this anonymous letter saying she – we were lesbians. We weren't. I just laughed it off, but if you remember, Dorothy took an overdose.'

Hugh Ainsworth nodded and looked stricken. 'You had one, too?' He handed the letter back to her.

'Poor Dorothy, if only I had realised what the letter had meant to her! I dismissed it too lightly. I destroyed it . . . but in the end I believe that when she went down to the beach she intended to take her own life – perhaps drown herself.' To Michaela's shame she felt tears welling into her eyes.

Hugh Ainsworth stood up, came round and put his hand tentatively on her shoulder. 'It may not be all your fault,' he said. 'This village is full of gossip and no doubt poison pen letters are not usually limited to one. When the person starts writing them, I have heard . . . they go on.'

'But who would write such letters, vicar? Someone sick . . . or revengeful?'

'Guilt is terrible, isn't it?'

Michaela dried her eyes and looked up at him; he had said it in such a heartfelt manner, gazing out of the window.

'A feeling of guilt is not easily overcome.' He turned and took her hand; the gesture was friendly, but his hand was like ice. 'Yes, I suppose a feeling of guilt is one of the greatest punishments handed out to us.' He seemed to become preoccupied, almost as if he had forgotten her, and went to stand by the window, looking out. She could only see his silhouette against the sunshine and she felt there was no more to say.

She left the vicarage, not sure if she felt better or worse for having shown him the letter, but she had put it back in her handbag – she would never get rid of it, she would keep it to remind her never to take lightly things which other people found distressing. Yes, she had received a little comfort from the meeting with this sad man. It was something that after all Dorothy had not had to take her own life – it had been taken from her.

18

The village of Shelbourne began to rumble with gossip. Some, alas, came from Carmen. In spite of her resolution and in spite of the anonymous letter, she felt that some of the bits and pieces she had learnt here and there must be told.

Dorothy's death, her cremation, the engagement of Nigel Fisk and his young lady Amelia, the departure of Nigel Dawson for a flat in London after a pretty hectic row with his father the Brigadier, the – according to Carmen – budding romance between Michaela and the Brigadier – all of these were pleasant enough morsels, but hadn't greatly enlivened the coffee mornings. None was exciting enough to produce exclamations such as 'No, surely not' or 'Oh really, that can't be true' or 'You don't mean it'. Carmen lived alone and the gossip of the village, if it was truly scandalous, was the breath of life to her. 'Poor Dorothy' and 'Isn't it romantic' were not comments that stirred the blood. However, in the post office she heard a little exchange of remarks which was well worth storing up. It had passed between Mrs Thornton and Edith Jevons, the postmistress.

Mrs Thornton was cashing her pension and Carmen was standing behind her waiting to post some letters. She was considering whether to put first or second-class stamps on them when she heard Mrs Thornton saying, 'Well, I feel sorry for him. He looks so poorly and his daily is off sick. I think someone should offer to help. I would, but Ted says I mustn't. The treatment has made me feel a bit tired.'

Carmen could guess that she was talking about the vicar, so she had broken into the conversation.

'Well, his wife will be home soon. After all, he needs her to run things and her sister must be better by now.'

Edith Jevons had pushed Mrs Thornton's money and pension book under the glass window; Mrs Thornton was busy storing her notes and coins in her purse.

'That's what I was thinking was a bit funny, Carmen,' said Edith. 'That sister business, everyone's saying that, the vicar as well.' She bent forward to peer round into the small shop area to make sure no one was there – it was empty.

'Why funny, Edith?' Carmen asked, laying her letters on the piece of counter vacated by Mrs Thornton.

'Well, she hasn't got a sister – the vicar hasn't either. They were both talking about it in church one day – after the service. Philippa is an only child.'

Carmen forgot her letters and her stamps for a moment. Mrs Thornton, who was a little deaf, had not heard or was not interested in the almost whispered conversation; she gave a little smile and a nod to Carmen and Edith Jevons and left.

'Well, where is she then?' Carmen suddenly remembered the letter that Philippa had shown her. 'You don't think it's . . .'

Edith put her finger to her lips as another customer came in. 'I don't know, but there's something funny going on – that's my opinion.'

She switched on a smile for the new pensioner and Carmen left, full of what she had heard, longing for another coffee morning so that she could impart the news. She thought of the anonymous letter she had received accusing her of gossiping – well, that would have to be forgotten, just during the next coffee morning anyway. She had not long to wait for that coffee morning; Jane Fisk, whose invitations were always few and far between, telephoned and asked her to her house in a couple of days' time.

Carmen arrived at Jane Fisk's promptly at ten thirty. She was longing to break all the vows she had made to herself and have a good gossip – a gossip with some meat in it. She was longing to discuss the fact that the vicar was telling lies about his wife, but she did not want to reveal anything until the other guests had arrived and she was not sure who Jane had asked.

'Am I the first to get here?'

'Yes, I've only asked a few. I thought I'd ask Ida Hardy – she's such a nice woman and seems a bit lonely. You probably know she's working for the vicar, not because she had to but to give herself something to do.'

Jane Fisk took Carmen's jacket and hung it up. At that moment the door bell rang again; this time it was Mary Harris, a short fat little lady. Carmen was surprised to see her: Jane had once said she was terribly dull, wouldn't take part in any conversation but just sat there. Mrs Harris had no coat on so the three ladies went through to the sitting-room.

'Ida Hardy has not been well,' explained Jane, 'but she's better now and has gone back to help the vicar out.'

This stimulated Mrs Harris to say something. 'I understand his wife's still away.'

Before anyone could answer the door bell rang again.

'That'll be her, I expect.'

Jane left the room and in a few seconds Ida Hardy appeared. Jane ushered her in and went off to the kitchen to get the coffee. Mrs Thornton was the last to arrive.

When the coffee was served and the biscuits offered around, the conversation turned, as it often did, to health. Mabel Thornton was pleased to tell them that she had finished her radiotherapy treatment and that on her last visit to the hospital the doctor had said that everything was all right and she hadn't got to go back to see him for three months. She spoke loudly so that Mrs Harris, who was a shade deaf, could hear her and they all said how pleased they were. Mrs Harris then talked about her tinitus and what a funny sound it was in her ear, like a motor bike – not loud but sort of humming. 'It must be annoying,' Jane Fisk said. Then the conversation came round towards Ida Hardy's recent indisposition. 'Oh, it wasn't much. I had a throat infection. Dr Barnes gave me some antibiotics. I'm all right now.'

Carmen thought the moment had come for her revelation. The talk had been dull enough up till now. 'How's the dear vicar?' she asked.

'Don't ask.' Ida Hardy raised her eyes to heaven, but of course they all did ask and Ida didn't mind telling; like Carmen she lived alone and loved to talk. 'The state of the place when I got back – burnt saucepans, dirty crockery, laundry all over the place, in the bathroom, everywhere.' She paused, giving Carmen time to put in her bit.

'Well, I think there's something funny going on. I heard in the post office . . .' She left out the fact that Edith was the source of her information.

'What did you hear?' Mabel Thornton asked. She looked anxious as if she didn't want to hear any more.

'Well, she can't be – I mean, Philippa can't be with her sister. She hasn't got a sister; she's an only child and so's her husband. So I said to myself, how can she be with her sister? And if she isn't, who is she with?' Carmen leant back in her chair, sipped the remainder of her coffee.

'Do you think it could be some other relative who's ill?' Mrs Thornton suggested.

Ida Hardy broke in. 'No, I don't and I'll tell you why.' Ida's rather loud voice overcame Mabel Thornton's soft tones. 'All her clothes are still there; no suitcase has gone – even her handbag and her shoes, and all her make-up! And her credit card is still there!'

There was complete silence after she had finished speaking. Jane Fisk had her coffee cup half-way to her lips and held it there, her eyes wide. Carmen leant forward in her chair, her mouth slightly open.

'You don't think –'

Ida Hardy put her cup down with a bang. 'I'm not thinking anything, Carmen – I just work there. I'm just saying what I think – or rather what I saw when I came back.'

'Yes, but –'

'Yes, but nothing.' Ida's mouth clamped shut.

Jane Fisk got up. 'More coffee, anyone?' she asked.

Everyone said yes and she left the room. Mabel Thornton looked decidedly uncomfortable. Mary Harris had listened without much expression – indeed, the others thought that because of her deafness she hadn't taken it all in – but suddenly she spoke up: 'I think he's murdered her – like in that play the night before last on television. He said the very same thing – she was away at her sister's.' She took the others by surprise; they all looked at her. No one else had quite had the guts to say what they were all thinking.

Before anyone had recovered Jane Fisk came back with a refilled coffee jug. They all sat like statues, silent for the moment, unable to believe that little Mary Harris, quiet little Mary, had said such a thing.

Then Carmen spoke: 'Not the vicar, Mary – he wouldn't, surely he wouldn't?'

Ida sipped her coffee, looking at them all. 'Well, if she did leave why didn't she take all her things with her – that new suit, her handbag and shoes?' She paused and her eyes over the rim of the cup went from one woman to another. 'And another thing,' she went on, more determined now, 'I've just remembered, that credit card that was still in the handbag and her purse, with money – she always took them with her everywhere. Never went out without her purse.'

'How do you know that – I mean that her credit card and money were . . . ?' Jane Fisk's voice was crisp as she asked this question.

'I looked,' Ida said, with a shade of defiance in her voice. 'I looked.'

'Well, we can't do anything about it – it's only our . . .' Carmen suddenly felt frightened and it showed on her face. 'Well, we could tell the police,' she ventured.

'What?' Jane Fisk's voice was a shade contemptuous. 'Tell the police we think the vicar has killed his wife – and then she turns up as large as life? We should look fools!'

161

She started to pile up the coffee cups and saucers on a tray – a hint that the party was over. They all got up, thanked her and filed out. Jane watched them walking up the road together: Mabel Thornton, who had little to say, Mary Harris, who now had plenty, Carmen, who had started it all, and Ida Hardy, still talking.

Jane Fisk carried the loaded tray through to her kitchen, washed up, put the left-over biscuits back in the biscuit barrel, stacked the crockery neatly away, then with a very purposeful step, she left the kitchen and went and sat down at her son's typewriter.

Amelia stood just inside the door of Jane Fisk's dining-room. The polished dining-table was beautifully laid: a bottle of wine, un-corked, stood in the centre; the wineglasses (the best ones, Nigel noted) had been polished till they shone; and at each setting was a small plate containing a generous twist of smoked salmon, laid across a piece of the yellow heart of lettuce, and beside it a perfectly cut, flower-shaped, peeled tomato.

'Ma, my favourite, and Amelia's – smoked salmon!'

'The table looks lovely, Mrs Fisk.'

'Don't you think it had better be Ma now, like Nigel calls me – unless you . . . ?'

'I'd love that, Ma.' Amelia loosed Nigel's arm and came forward and kissed Jane's cheek.

They all sat down at the table. The starter was followed by a fillet steak each with asparagus and french fries; after that came ice cream caramel. When they had all finished eating Nigel leaned back in his chair. 'Ma, that was a super meal.'

'I'll second that. I've never eaten better,' said Amelia.

Jane smiled and, as Amelia made a move as if to collect the crockery, she interposed. 'No, dear, straight into the sitting-room. The clearing up's later – and not for you to do.'

In the sitting-room Jane brought in coffee and glasses of brandy.

'Ma, this is really . . . What are we . . . ? We've had our engagement dinner.' Nigel looked at Amelia, then put his arm round her shoulders. They were seated side by side on the settee, Jane in the armchair opposite them. Nigel squeezed Amelia's shoulder. 'Ma, it was a wonderful celebratory meal – and a surprise, too.'

'Yes. I've got to admit that I did it first because I love you both and you've made me so happy – but there is something else.'

From the coffee tray Jane handed them a folded piece of paper. 'I typed this this morning, just as a sample of what I would like you to write. It would make me even happier if after the registry office you would go to the church for a blessing – just one or two people. But if you don't want to I'll quite understand.'

Nigel and Amelia read it together; they grinned at each other and then at Jane. Nigel got up, came over and looked down at his mother.

'Ma – that lovely, gorgeous, expensive dinner was a softener up, wasn't it?' Jane nodded.' Well, thank goodness we didn't tell you last week. We've already talked about a blessing.'

'True.' Amelia laughed as well, then she came over and embraced Jane. 'Lovely dinner though, Ma.'

Nigel read the letter again. 'Right. I'll go and type this on our headed notepaper – something like it anyway.' He left the room.

'Now, can I help clear away, Ma, please?'

Jane shook her head. 'No, we'll just pile up the things on the draining board, dear – but another cup of coffee first. Right?'

'But there's loads of washing up,' protested Amelia.

'Mrs Hardy, the vicar's superior help, is coming in tomorrow morning to wash up and clear up – so relax.'

'Oh, I'm so glad,' said Amelia. 'I'd hate you to have all that washing up to do.'

Jane leant back in her chair. 'I'm glad, too – but I'm also glad about the blessing,' she said.

At that moment Nigel came back into the room carrying a letter he had just typed. 'Is this all right, do you think?'

Dear Mr Ainsworth,

On Thursday, July 4th, my fiancée, Amelia Wheeler, and I are to be married at the Newport Registry Office at 11 a.m. We should be most grateful if you would conduct a blessing in the church after the ceremony at Newport – say at midday. However if, owing to the fact that we are not members of your congregation, you feel you are not able to do this, we should quite understand. Expecting to hear from you whichever way you decide,
Sincerely,
Nigel Fisk.

'Nicely put, darling,' Amelia said and Jane nodded in approval. Their close and loving attitude to each other was so obvious.

Nigel looked across to his mother. He was delighted that she was so happy, and that Amelia seemed to find it easy to accept and understand her sometimes rather overbearing manner. They seemed to get on wonderfully – they had even been out house-hunting whilst he was at work and Amelia had found a cottage, rather remote and isolated but she had fallen in love with it. Tomorrow evening she and Nigel were going to see it together.

Nigel, satisfied with their opinion, folded the letter and put it in an envelope. 'We'll drop it into the vicarage letterbox as we pass, darling,' he said.

The night was clear and starry. 'Wasn't that sweet of her – and such lovely food. Everything thought out with such care. All my favourite things – smoked salmon, that lovely steak – and the table looked so pretty. She had taken so much trouble. It was certainly a celebration, even if she was, as she admitted, trying to soften us up.'

'It was, darling, and how much there is to celebrate – for me, anyway.'

'And me, love.'

Nigel stopped the car outside the vicarage and popped the letter through the letterbox. The place was in complete darkness, although it was only about ten thirty. 'Gone to bed, I expect. Ma was saying he didn't look very well.'

They drove off, quite unaware that eyes were peering through the curtains of the front room, there in the darkness, watching until their red tail lights disappeared into the night.

Michaela stood looking at the notice that had been put up by her front gate. They had come a few days ago in a white van, a man had got out, a little banging and there it was, nailed to the gate-post – a wooden structure, and at the top in red letters 'For Sale, Manson & Leigh, Estate Agents', followed by their telephone number. The notice gave her a little pang every time she passed it, a sadness. Dorothy and she had loved Hawthorne Cottage; the name, the cottage itself had immediately appealed to both of them. There had been a sign up then, put up by the same estate agents, but that had been taken down after the surveyor had examined the cottage and they had decided definitely that they must have it. Dorothy and she had had so many ideas for the garden, the decorating, the furniture – now it was all over and poor Dorothy was gone. Michaela sighed, then looked down at the ring on her engagement finger. So much change in what had seemed in some ways an age and in some ways no time at all.

She walked back up the path. The sign creaked a little as she did so. She was waiting for some prospective buyers to come. She was living at the Manor now; Frank had suggested her coming to stay there. His old-fashioned way of suggesting the idea had entranced her: 'Separate bedrooms until we're married, my dear. As to your living here, let people say what they like.' 'Whatever you say, darling,' she had answered, 'whatever you say.'

His proposal had in some ways been a surprise to her. They had been out together several times, but on this particular occasion he had insisted on taking her over to the other side of the Island. The night had been warm and moonlit. The hotel, new to Michaela, had been surrounded by trees, the drive lighted by fairy lights, like glow worms, partially hidden in the flowering shrubs. As they had got out of the car there had been a large lilac tree, its deep purple flowers hanging down, giving off a lovely perfume. The meal had been excellent, also the wine. Frank had suggested a kümmel with their coffee.

The night was warm enough for them to sit outside. Strange how some occasions in life can be so memorable, and she remembered now every detail – the small white-painted table at which they sat, the smell of kümmel rivalling the lilac and the aroma of the hot coffee, the rather uncomfortable white iron chairs they were sitting on . . . Frank had appeared slightly nervous, but at last had started the conversation after a rather long, but companionable silence.

'You never married then, Michaela?'

She had shaken her head. 'No. I tried living with someone, but it didn't work. Perhaps our interests weren't the same. He was quite a nice man, but . . .'

Frank had turned the kümmel glass round and round.

'And you? You never married again? You told me, I think, it was fifteen years since you lost your wife. Perhaps you couldn't find anyone to replace her?'

'Not until now.'

Michaela's eyes met his. 'Now?' she said.

He looked down at the table and went on moving the little glass in a circle. 'Well . . .' He looked up at her. 'Would you marry a crusty old set-in-his-ways fella, Michaela?'

Michaela shook her head. 'No, I wouldn't dream of marrying a crusty old set-in-his-ways fellow – but I would marry you, Frank.'

She felt her cheeks going pink, like a girl's. He took her hand, and with his other hand pushed across the table a small navy blue velvet box. Michaela opened it; the ring was beautiful, three large diamonds.

'Frank, it's beautiful. Would you put it on for me?'

He slipped it on to her engagement finger. The moonlight and the fairy lights made the diamonds sparkle. She had leaned across and kissed him on the lips.

Now as she remembered, the sunlight of the morning sparkled on the diamonds again. Michaela felt the warmth of his love, even as she stood outside the no longer inhabited cottage. Soon she would be starting a new life and starting it late in life – but starting it, too, with a man whom she trusted and loved, the man she was going to marry. She would no longer be lonely. She felt how lucky she was.

Two people opened the gate, the girl young and pretty, the man tall, handsome and serious. His glasses, like the diamonds, flashed in the sunlight.

'The estate agent said we might look at the cottage if you were in and would allow us.'

Michaela smiled at them. 'Certainly. I'll show you around.'

They looked such nice people that she wouldn't mind Hawthorne Cottage going to them – but it wasn't quite as she had thought.

'We're looking for a holiday cottage,' the man explained. 'We saw this the day before yesterday when we were passing. We wanted to buy a place on the Island, just to come down to when we . . . you know.'

Another pang went through Michaela – a holiday house. They must be well off. Perhaps they wouldn't love it after all, just use it as a place to come and visit when they wanted to be by the sea.

'Yes, of course. I'll show you around with pleasure.' She led them through the front door and they started the little tour.

'May we go upstairs again?' the young woman asked.

'Of course'.

As they mounted the stairs Michaela felt they wanted to have a private chat – to compare notes about their impressions of the cottage.

She stood in the sitting-room for a few minutes. The room

depressed her – so many of her friend's things remained there, though her relations had been and chosen all the items they had wanted to take away. She strolled out into the garden. The pink climbing rose was just coming out, it was late in blooming. A thick leafless dead branch stuck through the lower leaves – they should have cut that back sooner. Dead – lifeless – it reminded her of Dorothy.

The man and woman came downstairs. Michaela saw them to the front door. They left, saying nothing of their decision.

The coloured windows of the church shed a warm glow on the two people standing in front of the altar steps. Hugh Ainsworth, a little above them on the first step, was speaking.

'When two people fall in love it is like no other experience in the world. They are drawn and held together by a cord, which, if it is true gold and not just the tinsel of a passing infatuation, will last them all their lives. They may quarrel, disagree, but always if the love is a true love nothing will part them.' Hugh Ainsworth gazed round and paused. He stood in front of Amelia and Nigel Fisk. The few people in the pews behind them were held by his words. He had never been able to speak like this before; it was like a gift that had suddenly been given him.

Two Sundays ago it had come to him; he had preached then without notes, with no reference to the Gospel, no paragraphs picked from a dusty book of sermons on the shelves in his study. He had preached a sermon on the hideousness, the harm of malicious gossip. He had accused no one in particular in his small congregation, but the next Sunday a dozen more people had attended. That Sunday he had talked – he could hardly call it preached – about the importance of community support, help given one to another in illness, bereavement and trouble. This was the third time he had spoken with a strange feeling of rebirth; was it because he knew that Philippa was not sitting there, eyes contemptuous with hardly hidden boredom? And when they got home after the service, why had he always asked her, felt impelled to ask her, 'What did you think of my sermon?' And her inevitable reply, 'The same as usual.' How had he suffered it for so long? He could not imagine.

He continued his short address in much the same vein. Once he saw Carmen Delano put her handkerchief up to her eyes to wipe away a tear – one of the worst gossips in the village, he had thought wryly, followed closely by his wife . . . He knew he held the few people in front of him by the words he uttered; this is how it should always have been – why had it come now? He felt as if he had had a dead branch cut off, lightening the weight of his life, his very thoughts.

He finished: 'Love looks on tempest and is never shaken, but when there is no love then a tempest shakes and kills.' He stopped and for a moment looked so far away that Amelia thought he had forgotten them – then he smiled and motioned them to come through with him to the vestry.

Jane Fisk could hardly believe that it had been Hugh Ainsworth she had been listening to, giving that blessing. She had heard how his sermons had improved and was determined to attend church next Sunday.

Only a few people had been asked to the blessing – Michaela and the Brigadier, Carmen, Mabel Thornton, Mary Harris, Ida Hardy, the deputy headmaster and a form mistress from Nigel's school. After the little ceremony Amelia and Nigel got straight into their car, calling their goodbyes to everybody. They were to drive to the ferry and then on to Paris.

Jane felt curiously empty. As she watched them drive off she knew she had done it – protected her son through hazards. A tiny feeling of doubt at the back of her mind nagged her; was this right, had she put them both in a perilous relationship that might change? It dogged her thoughts. But they seemed so happy together, so relaxed. She was sure the marriage would be . . . Well, only time would tell. After the ceremony at the registry office she had felt drained; now as they stood outside the church, in the rather untidy graveyard which flanked three sides of the church, she felt her seventy years weighing heavily on her.

Mr Hewitt, the deputy head, and Miss Miles, one of Nigel's colleagues, were shaking hands with the vicar and saying goodbye . . . 'Sorry to dash away.' Mr Hewitt, young, long-haired, tieless, was, in Jane's eyes, a dreadful-looking young man, specially for a teacher, but Nigel had assured her he was very reliable. His companion, Pat Miles, young, also with straight hair, much longer than his, was a silent young woman, her long skirt and tight velvet bodice making the rest of them – Carmen, Jane, Ida, Mabel – look prim, old-fashioned and old.

As they drove away Jane said to Carmen, 'I suppose I should have done something in the way of drinks . . . but I just feel too tired!'

The vicar came over to her and shook her hand; it was obvious that he had heard what she had said. 'No, Mrs Fisk, you've had quite a morning already – a marriage, and now a blessing.' Carmen agreed. Hugh Ainsworth's face, still white, looked even more ashen in the sunlight.

Ida Hardy came up to him. 'Mr Ainsworth, I'm . . . Well, I hope I'm not being pushy, as my daughter says, but while your wife is still away wouldn't it be a good idea if I came in and prepared you a meal every day?'

'That would be nice. I would appreciate that, I'm not much of a cook, Mrs Hardy.'

'Right then, just until Mrs Ainsworth gets back.'

The women moved off. 'Did you see his smile when I said that?' Ida Hardy asked Jane.

'He's really got quite a nice smile.'

'I think Philippa has left him; he looks so sad – has gone off with someone else. I think he knows it and is trying to keep it from us – sort of ashamed, that's what I think.'

'Me, too.' Carmen stopped at the lychgate. 'Let's all go to my house and have a gin and tonic and some sandwiches. Somehow I feel I need it – and I've got a bottle of brandy, perhaps we'll open that.'

They trooped away together, feeling a unity and a new companionship that they couldn't really understand – but savouring it, realising it was there.

Meanwhile Hugh Ainsworth went back into his church; he liked it now. He turned his back on the altar and stood looking down the aisle to the door; the breeze was increasing a little and the long green grass at the foot of the graves blew and ruffled. He must talk to the verger – the place needed a gardener. His own garden, too, was a mess. The verger, who seemed to know everybody in the village, would probably have someone in mind to tidy up the place. Philippa had hated everything to do with his . . . vocation. Perhaps she was happier now, lying there quietly in the woods.

He walked down the aisle and out of the door. He thought again of Philippa – where she was. Should he go and look, go and see . . . ? No. If ever she was found he would be arrested, tried, no doubt found guilty . . . But if he never was . . . ? If anyone did find her . . . ? He felt so happy now, so contented. He remembered Mrs

169

Hardy's suggestion: 'I'll make a meal for you, every day until your wife comes back.' The remark made him smile wryly. He closed the door firmly behind him and locked it. A lot of meals that would be, Mrs Hardy, he thought, and for a moment felt no remorse. Regret but not remorse.

Jane got home from Carmen's not looking forward to letting herself into an empty house. Suddenly Nigel seemed so far away, divided from her not so much by distance as by his new commitment. She was pleased for Nigel, pleased for Amelia, but she felt that the years ahead would be bleak. She must find interests, new interests. As long as she kept healthy . . . Jane was not particularly superstitious, but she tapped the pine dresser in the kitchen – just tapped it with her knuckles – and it gave out a dull wooden sound.

19

Two and a half years went by and several small changes and events had happened in the village of Shelbourne. The Brigadier and Michaela had got married in the church, with a small reception at the Manor afterwards. This had been mildly exciting to the ladies and 'What shall I wear?' was on many lips. Nigel Dawson had come, with his wife and son – the first time many in the village had seen her or the boy. 'Leopard changing its spots, eh?' Ted had whispered to Mabel and had been told off for the remark.

Pat Beattie, the minister, had left the village. The little chapel was falling into greater disrepair. The churchgoers had drifted back to the village church; Hugh Ainsworth was a popular preacher, liked by everyone. His wife had never returned and, still attended by the faithful Mrs Hardy, he had put on a little weight and looked happier and healthier. The churchyard was cut and trimmed and the vicarage garden, too, all done by Ernie Biles. He was slightly backward in everything but gardening. He cut, weeded, planted, edged, trimmed back and pruned, but seldom had much to say.

Amelia and Nigel had a year-old baby girl. Sadly they had moved up north to a better job, so Jane saw less of them than she would have liked and had taken in a lodger, though she preferred to call her a 'paying guest' – a young policewoman, slim and self-sufficient, who was posted in Newport. Jane did not grow fond of her, but the fact of having a policewoman in the house gave her a feeling of safety and reassurance.

Mabel Thornton kept well and Ted had a hip replacement. The small superstore did not materialise, just as Edie Jevons had predicted, so she continued to dispense groceries as well as pensions and stamps, and had even installed a deep freeze cabinet. Ida Hardy continued to work for Jane, having started soon after Nigel had left. The two women got on fairly well, though Jane resented a little the fact that she was working for the vicar for three pounds fifty an hour and was charging her, Jane, four pounds an hour. Still, she made little of it, saying to herself that people like Mrs Hardy preferred working for men.

The people in Hawthorne Cottage came and went in the summer, at Christmas and Easter and some bank holidays. The village saw little of them; they neglected the garden and Michaela walked by, when she had to, with eyes averted. Dorothy was becoming a distant memory, but sometimes when she did notice the garden, in spite of her resolution not to look at it, she was saddened and the memory of her friend was for a moment brought sharply back.

Carmen Delano still gossiped, but this was not unexpected and a lot of the gossip was very dull. True, the Benson boy was caught smoking hash and his father was had up for growing the stuff – but that was not really village gossip and only promoted such remarks as 'Teenagers these days!' and 'We didn't need such stuff in our day'.

A pop festival was threatened and some, the young, were all for it. There were rows in the local council, but it hardly affected Shelbourne – if the festival did happen it was to be held miles away.

A sex shop opened in Newport and only Carmen had the temerity to visit it. That made for one lively coffee morning while she described, with highly artificial reluctance, the vibrators, plastic you-know-whats, inflatable you-know-whats, and even nipple you-know-whats. It had been a lively and enjoyable morning, but that was about all the entertainment anyone could conjure up.

Then something really nasty hit the village: an attacker in the woods struck again, with greater ferocity!

March had come in like a lamb, but was leaving like a restless lion. The trees in the small forest at Shelbourne waved their tops. There were fewer of them to wave: several trees had been cut down and the small wood could now more accurately be described as a copse. Out by the road through the village several sad stumps gleamed pale and bleeding in the wind. There had been some opposition to felling the trees, but it was argued that they were unsafe and would have to be uprooted anyway to make room for the road to be widened. There was some need for the curve in the road to be clear as this was a blind corner and would be decidedly less dangerous without the trees, so in the end the opposition had collapsed, allowing the council to take its course.

Young Chris Hansford, however, knew or cared little about such things. At twelve his main interest was centred around computer games and at the moment he was trying to sell some to buy more new ones. As he rode up towards Shelbourne the plastic Tesco bag rattled on his handlebars. He didn't particularly want to pass by Shelbourne's little police station as quite a few of the games and videos in the carrier had been nicked. The video shop in Newport was also a paper shop and if he went in early in the morning when the papers were being sorted he could steal a video, buy a paper for his dad – who didn't want it anyway – and split. He didn't do it often, that was a fool's trick, but just now and again. In Shelbourne at the far end of the village was a man who bought his stuff; computer games were easy sellers, but videos, particularly video nasties, brought in only small sums unless they were deemed really dirty, really nasty and hard to get. He usually had to argue with the man when he met him in his allotment shed.

He pedalled up the slope and into the wood. It was quite dark there, spooky he thought. The ground crackled and splashed under his tyres. He stood up, his young round buttocks leaving the saddle. He began to think of his bike, too, that was dead old, three years at least; he would like a new one, but his dad . . . His thoughts broke off abruptly as his front wheel hit a hidden root, slewed sideways, let out a depressing hiss of air and he landed face down among the dead leaves. He got up practically unhurt except for a cut on his knee and a tear in his already torn jeans. 'Jeez,' he said. He picked up the bike – puncture, the front tyre flat and horrible-looking. The handlebars were a bit bent, too. 'Shit!' he said loudly, leant the machine against the tree and sat down, searching in his pockets for a handkerchief with which to mop his bloody knee, or a tissue, but there was neither. He'd have to walk now and wheel the damned bike. Perhaps Peter Drake, his potential buyer, might have a puncture kit in his shed – he knew he had a bike.

He got up, turned round, put his foot on a tree stump to get a better look at how much damage he had done to his knee – then he saw it, a nice-looking BOAC bag, navy with white piping, the letters stark and white in the gloom. He looked up and down the path – no one! He took a step forward; a little blood ran down his leg, but it wasn't bad. The bag was some way into the brambly undergrowth. His trousers catching on the spiky strands of the plants, he got right up to the bag, but it looked empty. He bent down to pick it up, then about four or five feet away, he saw her . . .

The body lay slightly curved, the head bent forward away from him, one arm stretched backwards, the other under the body. She was dressed in a red, tartan sort of top. His mum had gear like that, but it wasn't his mum. The girl was young, her hair abundant, curled, frizzed – then he saw her face as he passed round the body a little. Her eyes were wide open, her face blue and swollen and her tongue sticking out of her mouth. There was something round her neck, tied tight – tight – tight. He felt frozen, as if he could not move. His eyes travelled down to her legs; they were sticking out, one brown shoe was off and lying a little way from her foot, the other leg, just slightly bent, was covered in blood. The stocking gone, that shoe was . . . he saw, further away from the body.

Chris couldn't look any more, he felt slightly sick. He scrambled through the brambles, nearly falling over the bag as he did so. It tipped over on its side and the contents, or some of the contents, spilled out: a small black purse, a lipstick, something else, a packet of some kind, but Chris had seen enough. He drew his breath in sharply and the small sound it made broke the spell for him. He could run – his legs were working now, he could run. He made for the path, left his bike where it was and started to run to the village. Half-way there he remembered he had left his bike . . . His father had told him never to leave his bike anywhere, it would get stolen. He hesitated in his run, his small chest heaving – then decided he couldn't go back. The bike must take its chance. He drew a deep breath and started running again. Out into the road he felt better, up the small gradient to the house marked 'Police'. There was a small blue lamp over the door

173

and it was with relief that Chris ran up the path and bashed on the door.

The news spread through the village like a bush fire, not only from the papers but by word of mouth. Probably the most affected was Hugh Ainsworth. Mrs Hardy was early coming to prepare his lunch and did not hold back on the gory details. 'Covered with blood she was, and her own stocking tied round her neck.'

'A local girl?' he had asked, having to clear his throat before he could get the words out.

'Yes, she lives at the corner of the lane – you know, in that old cottage up that little lane by the Manor.'

Hugh felt faint, ill, as if he was going to collapse. He fought against the feeling. He wished Mrs Hardy would stop, yet he wanted more information. His *Times* had not mentioned the murder, or at least he had not seen it.

'You would recognise her, I think, vicar – hair all frizzed up, tall and thin, thought she was somebody, too. A bit of a madam, if you get my meaning.'

'Don't speak ill of the dead, Mrs Hardy.' This had surprised her.

Hugh felt very strange, as if he was responsible for the death – responsible himself for the girl lying . . .

Mrs Hardy put some potatoes in the washing-up bowl and turned the tap on. 'That wood's not safe; remember there was another girl – was it night-time? She was attacked . . . oh, some time ago now – about three years, wasn't it?'

'Yes, I remember that, she screamed and got away.' Hugh's stomach gave a small lurch. Philippa . . . Would they search all of the wood? Probably not, but the hand that took Mrs Hardy's cup of coffee shook, she noticed.

'Don't worry, vicar,' she said. 'I know you'll have to go and see the family, and that must be terrible, but you're so good at that kind of thing. I think she lived with her mother – not much of a churchgoer, though, neither of them, I'd take a bet on that.'

She began to peel the potatoes and the vicar took the coffee through to his study.

His reaction to the killing was, he realised, peculiar. The feeling that he was responsible persisted – responsible for the girl's death . . . but that feeling was ridiculous. He thought of his walk through the wood with the Brigadier and the dogs; he had told him, Frank Dawson, that his wife had gone off with another man – that was the only person he had told. He remembered the Brigadier's kindness and the brandy. Well, if they searched the wood and came upon Philippa, what then . . . what then? He drank his coffee; he was so happy now he didn't want it spoiled . . . so happy. He would fight hard to hide what had happened. The anonymous letter was still in his desk drawer; he had never thrown it away, thinking one day he might need it – it might be useful . . . Well, maybe that day had come.

He got up: he ought to be out talking to people – comforting them. They would need him now, the relations and friends of the dead girl. The members of the parish who probably hadn't known her well, but knew her a little, they too would be affected and frightened. He went out through the kitchen.

'I'd better go and see if I'm needed, Mrs Hardy.'

Mrs Hardy nodded. 'I'm sure you will be, vicar.'

The whole village was talking about the crime, exaggerating it, and it gradually emerged, perhaps through the Hansfords (the parents of the boy who had found her), that the girl had been strangled with her own stocking, sexually assaulted . . . Little tremors of excitement – almost pleasurable excitement in some cases – swept through Shelbourne. No one came into the post office without mentioning it. People gathered in groups of three or four in the street reacting in their own ways, but all of them remembered the attacker of three years ago – was it the same man back again?

The police, too, were wondering. They had also been told in their briefing about the potential murder of three years ago. The body had at last been taken away to the mortuary and the area cordoned off, the blue and white tape fluttering in the wind. Two policemen were posted near the road, keeping away the dwindling number of sightseers. A row of policemen, side by side, some seconded from the mainland, paced slowly through the brambles, thrusting them aside with sticks, seeking for anything that might have been dropped or disturbed when the killer had taken off. The row of men proceeded slowly in a straight line. 'Damn!' One man exploded as a bramble scratched his hand. He changed his stick over to his left hand and sucked the small bleeding scratch below his thumb. They went on, swish, swish with their sticks as

175

they came to a less overgrown part of the wood and stepped through rank, long grass – a relief from the entanglement of the grasping brambles – then back to the thick undergrowth again.

The man at the end nearest to the path, rather fatter than his colleagues, suddenly let out a yell and half sank to his knee on the grass, his arms flailing in the air to try and keep his balance.

'I've got me foot in a bloody rabbit hole – give us a hand.'

'OK – don't make such a song and dance about it. You haven't broken your leg, have you? If you wave your arms about like that the DI will think you've found something.'

The next policeman took his colleague's hand. 'Hup,' he said then looked down at where the left leg of his colleague had been. 'Oh God, reckon you have found something,' he said, as the deep hollows where Philippa Ainsworth's eyes had been stared up at him.

He stood, turned round and put up his hand holding the stick. 'Sir!' he called to the detective inspector, who had turned back as if making for his car.

'What is it?'

'It's another one, sir.'

The line of men stopped. The wood became quiet for the moment. A grey squirrel, disturbed by all the commotion, ran down a branch and leapt to another as if it was flying. Right at the other end of the column another officer watched it. 'Look at that. Tree rats they call them.' Then they stopped talking, waiting for orders.

Gently, after the photographs had been taken and a pathologist called, the corpse, or what was left of it, was uncovered. More photographs, then the second body was taken to the mortuary. The row of police walked on, even more slowly now.

'That'll make the national front pages,' said one, his eyes watching the rank grass and brambles for anything that might lead them to the killer.

'Overtime here anyway,' said another.

'Yes, but bloody house-to-house. Let's hope we don't come on another the bastard's topped.'

They reached the end of the wood, came out on a small lane that ran up beside a house, turned and began to search back again the way they had come.

Jane Fisk was nearly the last to be questioned by the police. She had been horrified, almost knocked off balance, when she learned that Philippa Ainsworth's body had been found. Jane's house was almost opposite the smaller entrance to the wood. The road there widened a little. That was where Nigel and Amelia and sometimes Jane's friends used to park their cars – still did.

Had Hugh Ainsworth killed his wife? Had they had a quarrel about Jane's letter accusing her of having an affair? Jane felt acutely guilty, but nothing could alter the fact that Philippa had said that terrible thing about Nigel, for which Jane would never, never forgive her, alive or dead. She felt that whatever questions she was asked she would do her best to protect Hugh Ainsworth.

She answered the door when her turn came and the policeman arrived. He was a small man – Jane had always thought of policemen as being tall.

'Mrs Fisk?'

'Yes?'

'I'm Detective Inspector Cole and I would like to ask you a few questions, if I may.'

'Of course.'

Jane ushered the man into her sitting-room. 'You look tired,' Jane said, and indeed the man did look pretty exhausted. 'Can I get you something, tea or coffee?'

'I'd love a cup of tea, Mrs Fisk.' He consulted the book in his hand as if to remind himself again of her name.

'Any clues yet, detective inspector, as to who did these terrible things?'

'It's early days yet,' he replied evasively.

Jane nodded. 'Sit down, I won't be a moment.'

When she came back with the tea he sipped it gratefully.

'Now, what do you want to ask me? I'll help you in any way I can.'

He finished the tea and put the cup down on the table beside him. 'What I will ask first is: Did you see or hear anything unusual on the night the girl was killed? Did you know her from her pictures in the newspaper?'

Jane answered carefully. 'Yes, I did recognise her. I have seen her in the village, but have never spoken to her – at least not as far as I can remember.'

That statement was true, but from then on Jane began to lie, inspired by hatred for the dead Philippa and a new liking and admiration for Hugh Ainsworth. She felt as she lied much the same as when she had written the anonymous letters and she was extremely anxious that no one should ever lay the responsibility for those letters at her door.

After a few more questions she began her carefully thought out untruths. 'There's just one thing I feel I must tell you, inspector. It may be completely irrelevant and involve a person who is perfectly innocent of any crime, but . . .' She paused.

Cole shook his head. 'No, please, Mrs Fisk, don't hesitate to tell me any detail, no matter how small.'

'It's the fact that this happened so long ago. I am not a young woman and I have hesitated to tell anyone in case my recall is impaired.' She was inwardly amused by how sincere she sounded.

'Never mind, please tell me.' The detective leant forward in his chair.

Jane got up. 'Well, first I must show you the location.'

She led the detective through the hall and over to the hall window. 'Three years ago a local girl was attacked – not badly. She screamed and the man took off – but you probably know all about that.' She looked at him. He nodded. 'You see that slightly wider stretch of the road opposite? My son or friends have used it in the past when they visited me, still do. It's wide enough to park without obstructing passing cars.'

Having shown him, Jane led Cole back into the sitting-room and they sat down again. 'Inspector, three years or more ago, when that young girl was attacked, there was a blue van parked there.'

'Did you report this to the police?'

Jane shook her head. 'No, inspector, I didn't; the girl got away and I couldn't be sure . . .'

'I see. So, what else?'

'Well, that same blue van came back about three or four weeks later. The time was earlier in the evening, but it was getting dark, so I think it must have been early in the spring.'

Cole listened attentively, his eyes fixed on her face. Jane realised she was enjoying herself. She went on, 'I don't sleep very well, inspector, and at about one or two o'clock, I can't be sure, I got up to go to the kitchen to get myself a cup of tea. The van was still there. The last street lamp just lighted it up a little. As I watched, a man got out from the back of the van – scrambled out, really – and went into the wood. He was carrying a spade!' She stopped for a second and drew a deep breath. 'I was curious, but it was cold; I made my tea and went back to bed. In the morning the van had gone.'

Cole was writing in his notebook. 'Did you see the man plainly? Could you describe him?'

Jane hesitated again, looking at him earnestly. 'Not really, inspector. He was medium height, I suppose, slim. His hair was long – well, to his shoulders, I think. He had a jacket on, or it could have been an anorak, but I couldn't tell you the colour or anything.'

'Why didn't you report this, Mrs Fisk?'

Jane looked surprised. 'Why should I have, inspector? As far as I knew he was doing nothing with the spade that was very criminal. I thought he was going to collect some plants – primroses or ferns. I know that's against the law, but nothing else happened as far as I know so I didn't want to get involved.' She sighed again. 'Now, of course, the vicar's wife has been found and I . . .' She stopped.

'Did they get on well, the vicar and his wife?' the inspector asked.

'Never got on well, inspector. The vicar and Philippa, his wife, well . . .' She paused. 'There had been talk of another man before that.'

He nodded. Now she felt she could deliver her *coup de grâce*. 'Inspector, I'm sorry I have taken so long to get to the point.'

'What point is that, Mrs Fisk?'

'Well, the night, two nights ago, when that poor girl was killed, the van was there again.' She waved her hand towards the hall window. 'Parked there, where we have just looked, pointing towards the Newport road.'

The inspector sat upright. 'And you didn't report that?'

'No, I knew you were coming to all the village people and I waited for you to reach me – and you have.'

The inspector sighed. 'It would have been better, Mrs Fisk . . . anyway, did you see the man this time?'

Jane shook her head.

'Can you give me a description of the van?'

'Well, it was blue, not royal blue but sky blue. The front door slid open. There were doors at the back.'

'Make of van? Registration number?'

Again Jane shook her head. 'There may have been an X in it, but I – I can't be sure.'

'Mrs Fisk, would you be willing to come to the station at Newport and make a statement again?'

Jane felt her heart skip a beat. Perjury, she thought – but so what? Philippa had been a bitch. And supposing she hadn't been killed and supposing Nigel's marriage had not been a success and he'd come back – that woman, she would have said anything about him, anything about why his marriage had failed! Well, she *was* dead and Hugh now must be protected. Perjury was a small price to pay.

'Yes, of course, inspector. If you think that what I have told you is important, then I will make a statement about it.'

'Will you come now?' he asked.

'Yes, if you want me to.'

As they reached the front door he paused. 'Tell me, Mrs Fisk, have other cars parked there since the van?' he asked.

'I'm afraid so. There was a builder's lorry there and another car, I think – I can't remember.'

'Never mind, Mrs Fisk.' He pointed to the little path behind the wider part of the road. 'That path goes straight up into the wood, almost to where the girl was found.'

Jane Fisk got into his car and they sped off to Newport. Jane was silent, trying to keep what she had told the inspector straight and tidy in her mind. It was nice to feel that she was helping to get justice done . . . They, the police, were obviously no nearer to catching the real criminal and the man in the blue van, well . . . as he didn't even exist, they would never catch him.

At the police station she was treated with the greatest courtesy. She repeated what she had told the inspector. A policewoman drove her home, which was very enjoyable as she was a friend of Jane's paying guest.

Mrs Hardy arrived at the vicarage front door, opened it and turned round as she heard footsteps coming up the path behind her.

'Good morning, Mrs Hardy.'

'Oh, Inspector Cole. Are you coming to worry the vicar this early? Not again, surely.'

The inspector put on his rather nice smile. He glanced at his wrist-watch. 'Yes. I'm sorry, it *is* rather early, but I hoped to catch him . . .'

Mrs Hardy sniffed. 'He may have gone out.'

She led the way into the house, then opened the door of the vicar's study. The desk light was on, but the room was empty.

'Not there?' Inspector Cole stood in the hall.

'I'll just go upstairs.'

Mrs Hardy knocked on the bedroom door – no answer. She opened it cautiously and peered inside . . . no one.

Downstairs again she shook her head almost accusingly at the policeman. 'Sorry, he's out.'

'Already?' Inspector Cole said mildly.

'Sometimes he goes over to the church; he gets his own breakfast.' Mrs Hardy obviously wanted to get rid of him; she rather noisily opened a cupboard door and got out the vacuum cleaner. 'All these questions after his wife's body has been found – it's not right, inspector, he's had enough.'

'Yes, I know, but we do want to find the man who did these terrible killings, don't we?'

'Well, you'll do no good asking Mr Ainsworth – his wife . . .'

'Yes, I know, but I won't trouble you any further, I'll just go over to the church and see if he's there.'

Mrs Hardy switched on the vacuum cleaner, then kept it going until the inspector had gone down the path and closed the garden gate behind him. She switched it off and put the kettle on. She was worried about the vicar. Everything had been going so well but now the poor man, since they had found his wife 'all rotted away', as Mrs Hardy put it, had not been the same. She would cook him a really nice lunch today, roast beef which she had bought yesterday; she did all his shopping now . . . Roast beef, Yorkshire pudding, roast potatoes and some nice spring greens and carrots. She put the vacuum cleaner away in the cupboard and made herself a cup of Bovril. She sat down at the kitchen table – just for a minute, she told herself. She picked up *The Times*. Too high-falutin, she called it – couldn't understand what they were talking about half the time.

Some time went by and still no sign of the vicar. It looked as if she was right, he had gone to the church – he'd done that one or two mornings lately, probably to quieten his nerves. His new-found happiness seemed to be melting away since Mrs Ainsworth's body had been found. Well, it had been a shock. Jane Fisk had told Mrs Hardy about seeing a blue van all that time ago, just when Mrs Ainsworth had disappeared, and she told her how, when that poor girl was murdered, she had seen it again.

She thought it over whilst she was preparing and cooking the vicar's lunch. Since talking to Jane Fisk she could distinctly remember seeing that blue van in the village – well, she thought she could. Carmen, too, thought she had seen it. They had both told the police, but it was evident to Ida Hardy that Jane was a very reliable witness and that the man or person in that van had killed poor Philippa Ainsworth and now the girl – that poor dead, mutilated girl – and probably he had attacked the other girl who had got away three years ago. She realised they would want to catch the killer, but why keep troubling the poor vicar – pestering was her word for it.

Hugh Ainsworth arrived home early for lunch. Ida Hardy greeted him. 'I've got such a nice lunch for you, vicar, roast beef.'

He looked preoccupied. 'Thank you, Mrs Hardy.' He went towards his study, where she knew he usually had a glass of sherry before his lunch.

She called after him, 'I'm sorry I had to tell the inspector where you were.'

He turned; he looked tired and pale. 'That's all right, Mrs Hardy, he only wanted to ask one or two questions – he just . . .'

'He's a nuisance, that's what he is, vicar.'

Hugh sighed. 'Just doing his job, Mrs Hardy – just doing his job.'

That's what he would say, Mrs Hardy thought, he's too nice, too tolerant, that's his trouble. 'Shall I dish up?' she asked.

He didn't turn round again, but answered, 'Yes, do,' and disappeared into his study.

He hardly touched his lunch. She was so disappointed – the beef was tender and just as rare as he liked it, the Yorkshire pudding she had taken special care with and it was perfect, roast potatoes and the spring greens, so good for him, but he couldn't seem to get it down. He ate a little bit of the meat and a tiny piece of pudding and one potato – that was it.

'Treacle tart, vicar?'

He shook his head. She took away his nearly full plate. 'Oh, it's your favourite.'

He looked at her almost pleadingly. 'I couldn't, Mrs Hardy, I'm so sorry, when you've taken so much trouble.'

'It's that detective; those stupid questions,' she told him. He appeared to be hardly listening. She gave up. 'Some coffee?'

'Yes, thank you, I'd like that.' He got up. 'I'll have it in my study.'

He left her. Ida was really upset. 'Poor man, it's a shame,' she muttered to herself as she prepared the coffee.

She could not hear Hugh's mutterings in his study. He was sitting at his desk, his head in his hands; he couldn't work out what the inspector's questions meant. Did they think he had killed that young girl? And what was this about a blue van? Did he or had he ever driven one – what did they mean?

'Thank you,' he said as his housekeeper put the coffee in front of him on his desk.

'Don't worry about all this questioning, vicar – everybody's being questioned.'

He nodded. 'I know, but . . .' He left the sentence unfinished; he looked so strange. Ida Hardy didn't like to say any more.

Just as she got to the door she turned. 'I'll do a casserole for tomorrow. I've got a coffee morning with Carmen Delano.' He might have heard, she wasn't sure. She shut the door behind her.

Something, she thought, was happening to the village – something was making it fall apart. He, the vicar, sitting now so isolated, so withdrawn, in the room she had just left . . . He'd done such a lot to draw it together, stopping the gossip, making people help each other more, now she was sure he needed help – but with what? How could people help when they didn't know what was the matter? Anonymous letters, gossip, attacks on people, murder. Ida thought suddenly of a teenage girl who had said to her once in the post office, she couldn't remember who she was or when it was, but the girl had said, 'Nothing goes on here, does it – it's so dull and boring!' Ida wished it was like that now – just dull and boring, comfortable and quiet.

She finished the casserole and left the house. The study door remained shut. Well, there was nothing she could do. She had put the meat and vegetables in the slow-cooker and switched it on. She didn't like leaving Hugh Ainsworth, but tomorrow she wanted to go to Carmen's coffee morning; there were not so many of those lately. Anyway, she wanted to go to Newport this afternoon, too, so she would not be looking in on the vicarage in the evening – she did that frequently now just to see that the poor man, as she called him in her mind, was all right, or to see if he wanted anything from the shop. Hugh was very absent-minded as to his own welfare and, she felt, more so in the last few days.

As she walked home she noticed a uniformed policeman going into the post office; they seemed to be all over the village still – but not as many as there had been a few days ago. This one looked a mere boy, slim. 'When the policemen look younger you are getting old.' She had heard that saying many times. Now as she walked home her back ached a little, and she felt older because of the thought.

The whole village was beginning to get tired of the activity that a gory murder in your vicinity causes. Policemen came and went – certainly as time went on they became fewer; some went back to the mainland, but Inspector Cole in his black car was often seen and the little police house in the High Street was like a beehive. Their local policeman looked slightly harassed and was not his usual talkative, matey self. If you asked him a straight question – Have they caught anyone, is anyone suspected, has the blue van been found, is there going to be a funeral for the two victims? – he would evade it. The newspapers told the people of the village most – or at least the tabloids did. The local paper, too, was informative – it gave the name of the local girl, her address, news of her grieving relatives and, a new talking point, the fact that she had been pregnant at the time of her death. Her past behaviour was talked about, her reputation veering from not being a bad girl to being no better than she should be. 'Bit of a goer, put it about a bit,' one young man said, then looked rather shamefaced after saying it. It did show, however, that in spite of the would-be attacker of three years ago, the wood had been used as a secret meeting place for secret couplings. Rumour had it that the police had found a number of condoms scattered in the wood as they searched through the long grass.

Jane Fisk was quiet. She had said her say, done her bit to protect Hugh Ainsworth, but it struck her that she was perhaps always a protector. She was happy to have protected Nigel through thick and thin, and now letters and an intended visit from him and Amelia made her happier still. He had been worth protecting, and she felt that their vicar was too. Amelia and Nigel would stay at a hotel in the village when they came.

She still thought of the man in the blue van who didn't really exist. He became real to her and she knew that when she talked about him he became real to others also. Her only worry was the vicar; he seemed, after doing so well, to be going downhill again. She couldn't speak to him and reassure him that the story she had told Inspector Cole was believed and that consequently he had nothing to worry about.

Carmen was giving a coffee morning and she, Jane, was going. She was determined that if she could mention the blue van and bring it very casually into the conversation, she would. In spite of the boredom that was creeping in about the two bodies in the wood, there was usually a new detail to be talked about and as there hadn't been a coffee morning for ages she was quite looking forward to it.

20

Carmen put the cups out in the kitchen. She put the saucers and the plate of biscuits on the trolley and the cups on the work surface for the coffee. She turned the heat down low for the milk. She, too, was looking forward to her guests coming. Of course, there was bound to be some talk about the old subject, the wood – but there was something else now, another topic had arisen, the village fête; that was next week and everyone was expected to do something towards it. Stalls would stretch all the way down the High Street and all kinds of charities would be represented. Carmen and her friend, Mary Harris, were doing a cake and bric-à-brac stall for the Save the Children Fund. Mrs Thornton and Ted – Ted probably sitting in a chair because of his hip – were having a plant stall in aid of the Friends of the Hospital. The Turners had offered to have a stall, too, in aid of the Canine Defence League, and Mr and Mrs Chalmers, who rarely took part in any of the village activities, were having a stall in aid of something or other – Carmen couldn't remember what was for sale on it, but thought it was something to do with antiques. Ida Hardy was having another cake stall in aid of Cancer Research, and there were lots more. It had always been a jolly affair and Carmen hoped it would take people's minds off the murders and make them talk about something else for a change.

Everybody came on time except Ida – Jane Fisk, Mabel, Mary Harris, Michaela Dawson, Margaret Eales (pleased to be asked as she really wasn't one of the set), Agnes Turner (Carmen considered her coming a bit of an honour – after all, she was married to a quite famous author and she herself was so rich – that lovely car and her perfume). They waited for Ida Hardy until eleven o'clock, then decided that the coffee had better be drunk. 'I'll make some more when she gets here,' Carmen said, so they sipped and chatted and, except for Jane just once mentioning the blue van, the talk skittered around the village fête. However, everyone could feel the unspoken words in the background.

No one in the village ventured out much after dusk, particularly the women and more particularly if they lived alone. Of course the men went out to the pub, but even they didn't go alone, but walked there and back with a mate or two. There was no doubt about it, there was a slight feeling of apprehension in the air.

'Well, I wonder what's happened to Ida – she rang me yesterday and said she would be coming,' Jane Fisk said at about eleven thirty. 'I wonder what's the matter? I hope she's not ill.'

They were soon to learn . . .

Ida had decided she would call at the vicarage, 'just to see', as she put it. Her charge's lack of appetite, his pale drawn face, it was so disappointing. She realised, of course, that the finding of Philippa's body had been a terrible shock. She wished they'd never found her, even if that man that Jane had seen had buried her. Perhaps it would have been better if she had stayed buried, then things would have gone on as they had been doing – the dear vicar preaching his wonderful sermons, looking so well and happy, eating her food with such relish. Anything, she decided, would be better than this. She'd just call in, simply to say good morning and pretend she was checking on the casserole in the slow cooker. Plenty of time – ten o'clock – just to pop in and then go on to Carmen's coffee morning. She didn't want to miss that.

She was surprised to find the vicarage front door was wide open and the light in the hall was on, too, although it was light enough in spite of the fact that it was overcast and stormy and a dark cloud, almost a black cloud, was drifting over the village from the west. As she reached the door a large drop of rain fell on her forehead. Well, she'd just have a look.

'Vicar,' she called. No reply. She ventured further into the hall, switching the light off as she did so. His study was empty – again, like the other morning, his desk light was on, its green shade making the room look a little eerie in the gathering storminess of the morning. She hesitated, then tapped on the bedroom door. Nothing. She went in, the bed was made – he never did that now, she had taken on the task. The bed, she felt, had not been slept in.

Everything was neat and tidy. She went into the kitchen and put a hand on the kettle – stone cold. The tray which she always left made ready for morning tea had not been used; cup, saucer, milk jug, sugar basin, all just as she had left it.

She went into the garden. Ernie Biles was right at the bottom digging over the compost.

'Ernie,' she said when she got near him. His broad stooped back was towards her. He turned round quickly, surprised, guilty-looking, as if he was doing something that he shouldn't and had been caught misbehaving.

'The vicar said to do it, missus,' he said. There was sweat on his forehead and a little trickle of saliva ran from one side of his full mouth. His lips were surprisingly red and like those of a girl. On his head was perched the usual tweed cap, too small for his large skull.

'Of course, that's all right, Ernie. Where's Mr Ainsworth?'

He looked puzzled at the remark, but after a pause said, 'Oh, the vicar! Don't know. Haven't seen him, but he told me to do this.'

'When did he tell you to do this?' she asked.

He straightened up, his brows drawn together in concentration. 'Yesterday,' he said at last.

'And you're sure you haven't seen him this morning?'

He shook his head, wiped his mouth with his hand, then turned away from her and continued forking over the heap in front of him. Ida knew him well enough; he always looked and sounded the same – she had never known him to lie. The police had even spoken to him about his movements, asked him questions. The vicar had told her that Ernie had giggled when the young police-man asked him if he could drive and talked about the blue van and asked whether he had seen it. Ernie had been very positive. 'No blue van – never. A red one with gold on it, not a blue one,' he had said.

Ida glanced at her watch – plenty of time, she'd just go over to the church, he was probably there. He wasn't. The verger was, though, collecting the money from the offertory box. He gave the same answer. 'No, I haven't seen him this morning. Wanted a word with him anyway, about Sunday, but he hasn't been to the church this morning.' He paused in his collecting. 'Is he all right, Mrs H?' he asked.

'Why?' Mrs Hardy didn't like being called Mrs H.

187

'Well, I saw him yesterday and he looked pretty rough, I thought – I know he's had a shock, them finding his wife, but even so he looked right distracted.'

Mrs Hardy walked away, back to the vicarage. The wood! she thought. In his present mood he might go there. The two areas were still cordoned off, but perhaps the police . . . He might have gone to where they had found her. It was half-past ten now, but she felt she must go, just to make sure, even though it looked as if it was about to pour down. Black clouds darkened the sky, and Ida was not too keen on going into the wood – but where they had found Philippa Ainsworth was not too far in.

She was right. The Vicar of Shelbourne was there – but not standing grieving by what had been his wife's grave. No, he was in that grave.

He lay neatly, fully dressed, his head where his wife's skull had been, his clerical collar gleaming white, legs straight out, arms by his side. For a moment Ida could not take in the scene; then a flash of lightning lit up the trees – the face was like wax, the eyes closed, the lips bloodless. The next flash and her eyes travelled down from the vicar's face – his hands so neatly by his side were drenched in blood. The earth round his hands was wet with it. His clerical grey suit was untouched by earth or mud, but near his chest on the buttoned jacket was a spray of tiny dots of still-glistening blood. Something flashed in the next sheet lightening – Ida Hardy could see, half closed and clenched in his blood-soaked fingers, a cut-throat razor, like the one her grandfather had used and treasured. It was the bloodstained blade that had reflected the flash of lightning.

One more look at the white marble-like face and Mrs Hardy fled, running and tripping over roots and brambles. She ran and ran. The nearest house was Carmen's. She ran all the way, not stopping for breath, not letting the feeling of sickness overcome her. She banged on Carmen's door. The running, the running . . . She had difficulty in drawing air into her lungs.

Carmen opened the door – the smile, the welcoming smile, froze on her face. 'Ida! Whatever's the matter?' she asked and drew the shaking woman into her house.

The stone angel looked down at Ernie Biles. He had left the vicarage garden now and was trimming the grass round the angel grave. Now and again he looked up at it – the stone eyes seemed to look back at him. He always did the angel grave very carefully because someone, some nasty man, had broken off one of its wings and he was sorry. He talked to it. 'I was naughty in the wood, Angel. She was laughing at me and putting her clothes back on. The rude man had gone – I watched them. I felt funny in the stomach and my legs shook and when she saw me she laughed.' He clipped a little more of the grass. He looked up again. 'And the birds had heard her, they had flown away. I hated it.' He stood up and began to cry, 'I tied her stocking round her neck, tight, I knocked her down – I'm strong – and I kicked her where she had been rude with that man. I kicked her again and again so there was blood – she didn't laugh any more. That was better, wasn't it, Angel – better.'

The tears dried on his cheeks. He went down on his knee, still snipping the grass away, neat, and close to the grey of the base. 'That was better, wasn't it?' he said and the birds sang in the churchyard and the black cloud blew away and the sun came out.